I0657779

RISING FROM ASHES

THE ACTS OF VALOR SERIES
BOOK FOUR

REBECCA HARTT

ALSO BY REBECCA HARTT

The Acts of Valor Series

Returning to Eden

Every Secret Thing

Cry in the Wilderness

Rising From Ashes

Braving the Valley

Without limiting the rights under copyright(s) reserved below, no part of this publication may be reproduced, stored in or introduced into a retrieval system, or transmitted, in any form, or by any means (electronic, mechanical, photocopying, recording, or otherwise) without the prior permission of the publisher and the copyright owner.

This is a work of fiction. Names, characters, places, and incidents either are the product of the author's imagination or are used fictitiously, and any resemblance to actual persons, living or dead, business establishments, events or locales is entirely coincidental.

The scanning, uploading, and distributing of this book via the internet or via any other means without the permission of the publisher and copyright owner is illegal and punishable by law. Please purchase only authorized copies, and do not participate in or encourage piracy of copyrighted materials. Your support of the author's rights is appreciated.

Copyright © 2022 by Marliss Melton. All rights reserved.

Book design by eBook Prep
www.ebookprep.com

September 2022
ISBN: 978-1-64457-294-8

Rise UP Publications
644 Shrewsbury Commons Ave
Ste 249
Shrewsbury PA 17361
United States of America

www.riseUPpublications.com
Phone: 866-846-5123

ACKNOWLEDGMENTS

My profound thanks to my talented editor, Jeanne Olynick, and to my incredible beta readers. Deborah Whaley has been a loyal reader from time immemorial. Julee Schwarzburg is a freelance editor who has taught me how to be a better writer. Andrea Perez is an author of young adult Christian stories. Lastly, there's my amazing mom, who never lets me get away with anything, least of all a mistake!

FOREWORD

In 2007, under a different name, I published a bestselling novel that had just scratched the surface of its potential. For years, I have longed to explore that story's spiritual aspects and to plumb the depths of my characters. Breathing new life into the bones of that novel, I have created *Rising from Ashes*. I hope you enjoy the contemporary setting, the realism, and, most of all, the richness of the characters. It has been a pleasure giving this tale a new life.

PROLOGUE

AFGHANISTAN

I can't believe I'm back in the "Sandbox," Lieutenant Commander James Monteague, aka Monty, marveled as he led his squad up the steep mountain pass. Viewed through his night-vision goggles, the rugged terrain was all rock and sand. No human in sight—just what the heat-seeking drone had assured the SEALs right before they parachuted in. Monty could relax and enjoy himself.

Way back as a mere lieutenant still new to the Teams, Monty had spent a total of four years in the Middle East—sarcastically referred to as the "Sandbox." He never thought he would miss this part of the world or that it would smell like home. At eight thousand feet above sea level, the air was dry and crisp. A light breeze carried the essence of cypress up from the valley where the hardy evergreens grew.

The adrenaline streaking through Monty's veins really wasn't called for. The war was over, but his body didn't get that. Both his energy and senses were in overdrive. He felt like he could climb forever. The air smelled impossibly sweet, and the stars twinkled like diamonds.

Monty set a brisk pace for the younger SEALs to follow. Taking Ben Harmony's place earlier that night had been a good idea. The chief couldn't have made this grueling hike to the top of a mountain, not with a fever.

Besides, this op wasn't crucial to national security. The SEAL squad was here to rescue five Americans who'd refused to leave Afghanistan when the US withdrew. No doubt the stubborn Americans had discovered their host country wasn't such a friendly place with the Taliban in charge. In fear of their lives, they'd fled toward Kandahar, found refuge in a shepherd's hut, then pleaded via sat phone for the US to get them out. Since sending in troops was out of the question, US Navy SEALs, who performed secret operations all the time, were given the task.

As recovery missions went, this one would be simple. Parachute in, close to the Americans' location. Make a beeline to the recovery targets. Convey them down the mountain, through a wooded valley, and up the opposite hill where a helicopter would land to transport all of them to Al Udeid Air Base in Qatar.

Monty paused to check his tactical watch. A press of his thumb made the face of it glow. They were practically on top of the hut where the Americans were waiting. As he lifted his head to search for it, a dozen neon green figures emerged from behind the very building Monty was looking for. Were the Americans coming toward them? Wait, why were there so many of them?

"Tangos, look out!"

Smiley's cry of warning coincided with flashing lights and a clatter of gunfire directed straight at them. Monty and his men flattened themselves against the ground, then scuttled backward, downhill. The onslaught didn't let up.

"Go!" Smiley yelled, rolling behind his M60. Belting out a barrage of bullets, he gave three of them the chance to retreat. Monty slipped and slid down the near-vertical terrain. Coming across a sizeable rock, he took cover, firing so Smiley could pull back. Through his NVGs, he watched Smiley run with the agility of a cat, straight downhill, toting a twenty-three-pound weapon like it was nothing. What Monty saw beyond Smiley filled him with dismay. At least a hundred Taliban were swarming after them.

A mortar round exploded so close to Monty that he went momentarily deaf. He checked on Smiley, saw that he had found cover behind a ledge and was ready to fire again. Monty retreated, pivoting and firing occasionally. He could tell Kelso and Mikos were caught up in their own dance of fire and retreat.

The moments that followed were a blur of constant evasion and tactical shooting. Monty came to realize his squad was going to spend all their ammunition just to stay alive. For the sake of speed, they had dropped their packs. They had each killed dozens of combatants, but the Taliban kept coming. Monty and his men only had about six rounds of ammo left apiece. Their rescue targets, he was sure, had been tortured and killed, as this was plainly a trap. The SEALs themselves would be lucky to get out of Afghanistan alive. He took a claymore mine from his cargo pocket, prepared to set the fuse, then tabbed his mike.

"Break contact." He knew his decision was the right one when his men all stopped shooting right away. As they melted out of view, Monty armed the mine to deter the enemy, then hustled away from it.

They'd been driven nearly to the valley. Here the branches of stunted cypress trees glowed green in Monty's NVGs as he scurried through them, counting the seconds until the claymore exploded.

"...nineteen, twenty."

Bang! The loud crack was accompanied by the screams of the Taliban giving chase.

Monty hoped they would give up and not follow them clear to the LZ. He could see the Landing Zone now, a plateau at the height of the hill in front of them. Within the valley, they could hide for a while, biding their time until the Taliban grew bored or tired and went away. In the wake of the claymore's destruction, the enemy gunfire had abated. Wind whistled eerily through the boughs of the evergreens shielding them.

At the bottom of the wooded valley, Monty checked his watch. They'd been swapping bullets for hours, not minutes. At least the window was still open, and the satellite was still in position to contact their commander and let him know what was happening. But first, he needed to check on his men. He tabbed his mike for a situational report. "Sit rep."

"Kelso here. I can see you."

"Smiley. Same."

"Mikos. Oh, crap. That's not good."

Monty stiffened. "What wrong?"

"I'm hit. It's not good."

"Rally up," Monty instructed.

Three men drifted toward him, one of them limping heavily. Breathing hard, Mikos collapsed next to Kelso, the corpsman, who dropped to one knee to assess the wound. Monty bent over the pair, taking in the severity of Mikos's situation in the glow of Kelso's penlight. "Not good" didn't come close to describing how bad it was. Mikos's entire pant leg was soaked in blood.

They needed to call for extraction immediately, or Mikos was a goner, even with Kelso working fast to strap on a tourniquet. So much for waiting for the Taliban to go away. Monty took the radio, walked into a clearing, and put in a call to their task unit commander, Captain Michaels.

"There you are, Monty. What the devil's taken you so long?"

"Sir, the Ts found the hatchlings before we did," he said, encoding his words. "They were waiting for us. We're heavily outnumbered, and Mikos has been hit. We need a hot extract, now."

Michaels swore. "Roger that, Monty," he added grimly. "Chinook's already on its way."

Monty gulped. The thunderous arrival of the Chinook helicopter would not be overlooked by the enemy who, given the way this op was going, most surely had rocket-propelled grenades.

"We need a Spectre gunship to clear the area first. We have dozens on our tail."

"Hold one." Michaels muffled the mike on his end. "Sorry, Monty. I can't scramble a Spectre anytime soon. The Chinook will have to cover your retreat. She's only fifteen minutes out. Get to the LZ quickly."

With a sinking in his gut, Monty dismantled the SATCOM and rejoined his men. "Let's get to the LZ." He tried to sound upbeat.

The men scrambled to obey him. Kelso pulled Mikos to his feet and propped a shoulder under his armpit. Smiley hefted his M60 and took point. Lean and agile, the twenty-year-old darted out from behind cover to tackle the sixty-degree rise like it was nothing. Ascending fifty meters or so, he set his weapon on a boulder, prepared to cover Kelso and Mikos, who hobbled painstakingly after him. Monty watched anxiously as they leapfrogged Smiley's position, moving farther up the hill.

Then it was Monty's turn. He was as physically fit as the younger men, but the soil slipped beneath his boots, and his rawboned, thirty-six-year-old body strained for speed as he dug his toes in. Over the pounding of his heart, he heard the *whop-whop-whop* of the approaching Chinook.

No doubt the enemy could hear it, too. *Come on,* he urged both the helicopter and his men. It wouldn't take the enemy long to spot the four SEALs clambering up the adjacent mountain, not with a twenty-five-ton helicopter landing at its summit. To make matters worse, the first hint of dawn was silvering the sky.

It was Smiley's turn to take off. He pushed to his feet and bounded uphill like a mountain goat. At the same time, the Chinook surged closer, its blades chopping the air like the wings of a thousand angels. Any minute now, its shape would materialize out of the charcoal sky.

Mikos and Kelso struggled now to make their ascent. Monty was about to abandon his position to give Kelso a hand when both men slipped and took a tumble that had Monty scrambling after them. *Dang it!*

The Chinook thundered into view, and they were nowhere near the LZ yet.

"Kelso, Mikos!" Monty finally reached them.

"I couldn't hold him, sir." Kelso sat cradling an unconscious Mikos.

"Get his feet," Monty instructed as he lifted Mikos under his armpits. Kelso got up and grabbed Mikos's ankles. Together they schlepped him uphill.

They were maybe a hundred yards from the top when half-a-dozen missiles streaked toward them from the other side of the ravine. "Incoming!" Monty and Kelso threw themselves on top of Mikos. Grenades pounded the earth around them, sending up spumes of rock that peppered their backsides as they fell back to earth.

Finding himself intact, Monty peeked up at the helo. It was still waiting for them, rotors spooling impatiently. He heard the loading ramp hit the ground. Reinforcements would be pouring out to fire back at the Taliban. "Let's go!" he yelled, preparing to haul Mikos all the way to the ridge without stopping.

When neither man answered, Monty pushed up his NVGs. "Kelso!" He stared in disbelief. The young SEAL's skull had been crushed, presumably by falling rock.

Monty thumbed his mike. "Smiley, I need your help. Both men are down."

He glanced up again. What was taking the reinforcements so long to open fire? Just then, four more missiles sizzled across the ravine at them.

Monty gritted his teeth and curled into a ball. *Boom, boom, boom, boom!* The mountainside trembled. It regurgitated rock and dirt, all of which rained down in a merciless beating on Monty's back. When he looked up, Smiley was gone. Monty groped for his NVGs, but they were gone, too.

His last hope was the Chinook. Peering up, he saw reinforcements standing on the ridge, bearing grenade launchers. Monty pushed to his knees and waved them down. He needed hands to pull his men up, get them into the belly of the Chinook, and bear them home again, dead or alive.

But it wasn't to be. Another missile shot across the ravine like a falling star. And there wasn't even time to make a wish.

In the next instant, the helicopter exploded into a giant fireball that mushroomed outward, blasting Monty with heat and flaming shrapnel. The force of the explosion thrust him backward, tearing him away from Mikos and Kelso.

He felt himself falling. Rock and flaming bits of debris fell with him.

With bone-jarring force, he hit the ground and rolled. The earth beneath him was vertical. He grappled to slow his descent, but he was moving too quickly, glancing over rock and shrub. He tucked and rolled, protecting his head and extremities. He crashed through the boughs of an evergreen, struck the base of a tree, bounced off it, and rolled again.

At last, he skidded to a stop on a carpet of cypress needles.

Cracking open an eye, he could see beyond the boughs of a cypress tree the Chinook in flames. Spumes of smoke darkened the brightening sky. Monty sucked a ragged and painful breath into his lungs.

Jubilant cheers floated over the ravine, followed by volleys of gunfire as the Taliban sounded their victory.

Not a soul aboard or near the Chinook could have survived that explosion. His men were either dead or dying. *God help me,* Monty thought, losing consciousness.

It was the first time since childhood that he had asked God for anything.

CHAPTER 1

he chiming of Opal Bonheur's doorbell elicited a groan. She had just kicked off her shoes and sunk onto her overstuffed couch to watch the six o'clock news and to indulge in a slice of cheesecake. She'd certainly earned her dessert, having tended not only to her own patients at the Portsmouth Naval Medical Center but those of the physical therapist on maternity leave.

Leaving the cheesecake on the coffee table, Opal rolled to her aching feet to answer the summons. As she approached her front door, she tightened the sash on her flannel bathrobe. Perhaps it was her neighbor, the Navy SEAL, back from his assignment and looking for his cat.

But the face peering through the door's glass oval wasn't that of the awe-inspiring Lieutenant Commander James Monteague. It was Opal's twenty-four-year-old drama queen of a little sister, Ruby.

"Hi." Cracking the door, Opal braced herself for trouble. "What's up?" Crisp October air surged inside, bearing the scent of wet leaves.

"Um, I need to stay here awhile." Ruby cast a frightened glance over her shoulder. "Can I park my car in your garage?"

Opal tucked a strand of copper hair behind one ear. "You can't keep running to me every time you break up with a boyfriend, Ruby."

"It's not a boyfriend this time. Please, I need to put my car in your garage now."

Ruby's obvious fear convinced Opal to agree. She glanced toward her driveway at her sister's rust-bucket of a ride. "Hold on a sec. I'll need to move some stuff first."

Moments later, the '01 Oldsmobile was parked snuggly in the single-car garage, and Ruby was stepping out of it, dragging a suitcase behind her.

Opal's stomach sank. The suitcase was a sure sign that Ruby had failed to pay her rent—again. "How long are you planning to stay this time?" The garage door rumbled shut behind them, leaving the sisters in darkness.

The whites of Ruby's eyes were still visible. "I don't know. Let me tell you what happened, and you can decide for yourself."

Oh, dear, this didn't sound like a simple situation. With her concern rising, Opal led the way through the laundry room into her hard-earned, three-bedroom, single-family home. It was supposed to be the house that she lived in with her husband and babies, but, at thirty, she still wasn't married, and if her sister kept landing on her doorstep, Opal might never lead a normal life.

Ruby dropped her suitcase in the foyer and headed toward the kitchen, which flowed into the family room, wringing her hands as she went.

"I have leftovers if you're hungry." Opal took note of Ruby's longer hair. Its copper hue was just like hers, only Ruby's hair fell in long ringlets, whereas Opal's hung smooth and straight to her shoulders. While Opal dressed comfortably and sensibly, Ruby liked to test the limits of fashion using sequins, tie-dye, lace, and beads.

"That's okay; I'm not hungry." But spying the opened box of cheesecake, Ruby pounced on it, serving herself a giant slice.

Opal folded her arms across her chest. "So, what happened?"

Ruby ignored the question. "Hey, I didn't know you had a cat." She pointed the fork she was using toward the family room.

Commander Monteague's huge orange-and-white tabby cat was crouched over Opal's dessert. "Sunny!" She rushed over to scoop him up. "He's not mine. He belongs to my next-door neighbor."

"The Navy SEAL?" Ruby's tawny eyebrows shot up as she stuffed her mouth with another forkful. "He asked you to babysit his cat?"

"No, one of his girlfriends is supposed to be pet-sitting, but Sunny likes to eat on a regular basis—don't you, big boy?" She scratched the cat under his chin. "Now, can we get to the point of your visit?"

Ruby's shoulders drooped. She put her plate and fork abruptly on the counter. "Well, first of all, the tourists have gone home, and I'm not making much money waitressing."

"Right." Opal had advised Ruby to get a real job when this same thing happened last year.

"But that's not the only thing." Ruby heaved a troubled sigh.

Opal thought of the worst possible scenario. "I hope this has nothing to do with Daddy's journal."

Ruby dragged her lower lip between her teeth. "I'm afraid it does."

The news made Opal's heart drop. "What did you do?"

"I called Eric." With her pretty turquoise eyes, Ruby begged Opal to understand. "I was angry. I wanted him to explain himself."

Opal clasped the cat more firmly, furious that her sister might have blown their chance to seek justice. "What did you say to him?"

"I asked him how he slept at night, okay? I didn't accuse him of stealing the ricin or murdering Dad."

"And what did he say?"

"Nothing. He couldn't say anything. You know how he talks. He started stuttering and stammering and—believe me—his stutter is even worse when he's nervous, and he wouldn't be that nervous if he wasn't guilty!"

Opal regarded her sister over Sunny's twitching ears. "Did he threaten you?" She didn't know whether to scold Ruby or to comfort her. "Is that why you just hid your car in my garage?"

"I told you. He can't even talk. He just breathes into the phone."

"Breathes? You make it sound like you've talked more than once."

Ruby swallowed visibly. "He's called me a few times since," she admitted. "But, like I said, he doesn't say anything."

Opal shivered as she caught a whiff of Ruby's apprehension. "Oh, boy." Ruby had taken their discovery to a whole new level, and now she was paying for it.

"I'm sorry," her little sister added with uncharacteristic sincerity. "I don't know what made me call him. I just couldn't let it go."

"I understand, honey, but we need to let the FBI take over from here."

"Have you shown them Daddy's journal?

Opal put the cat down. "Not yet. I have an appointment on Thursday."

"Good." Ruby rubbed her arms as if chilled.

"I'm glad you're moving in with me for a while." Closing the distance between them, Opal offered her sister a hug. "We're better off forming a united front."

As Ruby hugged her back, the words of the newscaster on her television caught Opal's notice. At the mention of U.S. Navy SEALs, she released Ruby, hushing her to better hear.

"...Operation Mother Eagle," the female anchor was saying, "a failed attempt in Afghanistan to rescue five Americans citizens fleeing persecution by the Taliban. It is believed the Taliban reached the Americans first, killing all, then ambushing the SEALs when they showed up. Outnumbered, the SEALs engaged in a running gunfight while awaiting support and extraction. A Chinook helicopter with twelve more SEALs aboard had just landed when it was struck by an RPG fired by the Taliban. All twelve SEALs aboard were killed. Three of the four SEALs on the ground were found dead nearby. The Taliban claims to have beheaded the fourth SEAL in reprisal for what they are calling an act of aggression on the part of the United States. But with no actual proof of the SEAL's death, an unprecedented search using drones continues in the hopes that he is still alive and can be brought home."

As the anchor moved to the military coup in the Sudan, Opal directed her gaze out of her window to her neighbor's dark, empty home. Her heart flooded with compassion. *I wonder if Monty knew those men.* The Teams were a tight-knit community.

Ruby followed her gaze. "You think your neighbor was involved?"

"Oh no." Opal looked back at her and shook her head. "He's a lieutenant commander. He'd never be out in the field. But I bet he knew some of the victims." And the tragedy would trouble him deeply. Having watched him build a ramp for a young veteran in their neighborhood, she knew he took care of people.

If it wasn't enough that he was six-feet-three inches of sculpted muscles, with sun-streaked hair and golden-brown eyes, Commander Monteague's act of kindness had left Opal with a serious crush on him. She couldn't compete, however, with the gorgeous women jumping in and out of his hot tub. Thus, she'd never even tried to catch his eye. They'd lived side by side for the last three years, yet he'd never said more to her than a polite greeting. Certainly, he had no idea she cared for his cat and kept his yard tidy while he was off playing commando.

With a sigh of worry, Opal carried her plate of half-eaten cheesecake to the kitchen. "I'd better get to bed," she said to Ruby as she rinsed it and stuck it in the dishwasher. "I have to get up early for work. You'll find everything you need upstairs."

"Thanks." Ruby, who'd flopped onto the recliner, was already flipping through channels.

With a shake of her head, Opal checked the locks on both the front and back doors, then plodded upstairs. How long would Ruby stick around this time? Slipping into bed minutes later, she remembered the victims of the rescue-op-gone-wrong. As a lieutenant in the Navy and a proud patriot herself, Opal grieved the loss of so many young, highly skilled commandos.

Comfort their loved ones, Father. She considered the fourth missing SEAL. *Let him be alive. Protect him until he is safely found.*

Her thoughts then turned to her neighbor who was most certainly impacted by the awful news. His first name was James, but having overheard his friends call him Monty, that was how she thought of him. *Give Monty solace, Father. And bring him safely home, wherever he might be.*

∾

Monty collapsed in the meager shade afforded by a rock overhang. *I'm going to die here.*

He panted, his lungs hungry for the oxygen needed to feed his fast-beating heart. The mountainous terrain where the U.S. citizens had taken refuge stood as high as fourteen thousand feet above sea level. Here, the air was incredibly thin. Temperatures soared by day, then plummeted at nightfall, leaving Monty shivering in his dust-covered uniform.

The relentless wind chapped his lips and stung the burn on his cheek. His mouth was so parched that his tongue had swelled. If he didn't find water soon, he would have to steal it from the Taliban hounding him. And wouldn't that be fun?

All operations had an escape-and-evasion plan. The plan for this op called for him to walk clear to the Pakistan border and turn himself into border officials. Being pursued as he was, he couldn't walk in a straight line, however, so he'd made minimal progress toward the border. Moreover, all he'd eaten in the last three days was a lizard, caught basking on a rock.

He'd come so close to being caught. But the fear of death by beheading kept him moving. How could one small rescue op have gone so wrong?

The sound of something buzzing drew his gaze toward the blinding sky. A drone zipped overhead before diving down into a valley. *It's searching for me.*

But there was no way to signal his location. Along with his floppy hat, he'd lost the glint tape he kept Velcroed to the underside of the brim. He'd ditched his infrared strobe when he'd ordered his squad to drop their rucksacks. His Escape & Evasion kit, with its signal mirror, was lost when he fell four days ago. Frustration made his eyes sting with tears that wouldn't come. He was too dehydrated.

If he held still for too long, he risked capture, but he'd driven himself to exhaustion. Lying in the scant shade afforded by the large rock, Monty panted what might be his final breaths of life.

He couldn't believe it. He had been alive on Earth for three-and-a-half decades, and all that time, he had never tasted defeat. His every accomplishment up to that point had come with accolades. He'd received the leadership award in ROTC at University of Nevada Las Vegas. He'd graduated from Basic Underwater Demolition and SEAL training on his *first* attempt. He was the youngest lieutenant commander in the Teams. Women lined up in droves vying to become his wife. He had thought himself practically immortal.

Hubris. The word jumped into the center of his thoughts. *Excessive pride inevitably leading to ruin.*

Voices, carried on the breeze, floated toward him. *I'm getting delirious. It's just the howl of the wind.* He tried to rouse himself, but he could scarcely move his limbs. As he pulled his knife free, it clattered from his clumsy fingers and rolled away.

Great, he'd just given away his location.

The voices stopped talking. Cautious footsteps came closer.

Be merciful, he prayed, struggling to his elbows.

A vision of two men swathed in cream-colored robes and wearing turbans greeted him. *Angels?* He blinked them into focus. But then he heard the bleating of sheep. *No, they're herdsmen.*

They approached him cautiously, conferring between themselves, casting glances all around. The only word Monty recognized was *Amerki*—American.

One of them produced a blade, and Monty flinched, then realized they were returning his knife to him. The elder of the two reached under his robe, produced a goatskin canteen, and offered it, his eyes watchful and concerned.

"Thank you." Monty bore the canteen to his lips, but his trembling caused some of the precious water to spill.

The stranger helped him. As Monty sipped life back into his veins, the older man said something to the younger. Then he spoke to Monty, urging him to sit up.

Monty resisted. Who was to say these men wouldn't turn him over to the Taliban?

"Amerki," the man repeated.

Hope made Monty nod in agreement. Maybe, just maybe, they were going to help.

Eric Novak's persistence paid off. On his third visit to Ruby Bonheur's apartment, a woman, with her hair in rollers, stuck her head out of the opposite apartment and demanded, "Vhy do you knock every day on Ruby's door vhen you can see she isn't home?"

Crossing the breezeway to speak with her, Eric summoned a smile. "Do you know...w-w-w-where she is?"

The Frau ran a jaundiced eye over his gaunt frame. "Vhy shoult I tell you?"

"I have to...t-t-talk to her." His body twitched with the effort needed to get the sentence out.

"Like I said, I don't vant to tell you." She stepped back into her building, intending to shut her door.

"Wait!" Eric threw his shoulder against it before she got it fully shut. "Please. You m-m-must!"

"Go away! She vent to stay vith her sister, okay? Dat's all I know!"

He stepped back suddenly, and the door slammed shut. Her sister? Ah, yes, Danny Bonheur's older daughter. Eric had preferred her over the impious Ruby. But Sonja, his wife, had liked the younger daughter.

"Isn't she beautiful?" she used to say, marveling at her red-gold hair and striking eyes.

"She's lovely," he would agree, *"but the older girl is kind, like Danny."*

Eric's heart grew heavy. Danny had been his best friend. He had guessed Eric's awful secret. And because of that, Danny had been killed, taking Eric's secret to the grave. Or so Eric had hoped. But the younger Bonheur sister seemed to know the truth. *How do you sleep at night?* she'd demanded of him.

He hadn't slept a wink since her call.

How could she have guessed the truth, unless Danny left a note, a clue, a message from the grave? It wouldn't take long for the elder sister to get the feds involved.

Eric would have to silence both sisters, or they'd all be sorry.

CHAPTER 2

The hospital facility at Al Udeid Air Base in Qatar was made of prefabricated materials and powered by generators. There was no hot water. Monty stood under a tepid trickle in the communal shower house, intent on scrubbing a week's worth of filth from his body, mindful of the burn on his left cheek, treated and patched. He'd been told to keep it dry.

Soap stung the cuts and blisters on his hands. As he lathered his torso, he realized how lean he was. His body gave testament to how desperate his plight had been.

The men who rescued him turned out to be a tribal elder and his son. Monty still didn't know how they'd sent word of their discovery to SOCOM. But a stealth helo had landed in their remote mountain village and whisked Monty out of Afghanistan to Qatar, where he was fussed over and denied even a moment's isolation in which to mull over his role in the disaster.

His commander, Captain Michaels had blamed the Taliban for the tragedy. He'd greeted Monty with tears in his eyes and a tremor in his voice. *It's good to get one of you back, son. Who would have thought they'd score a hit like that with a decades-old RPG? It sure did the job for them, though.*

He was sending Monty home to Virginia to recuperate. *"You'll need time to deal with this, Monty."*

How could it have happened? Monty watched the water swill down the drain. He'd done everything he'd been trained to do. Those men should not have died.

He put a hand against the shower wall, fighting to inhale. The weight crushing his chest made him want to double over. He had never known defeat could hurt so much.

Sure, he'd known a sliver of doubt at BUD/SEAL training, when for the first time he'd encountered men as fit and focused as he was. But, even then, it hadn't taken long to prove himself, to rise above.

The sound of a door closing snatched Monty from his misery. He turned off the water, then reached for the towel. Hips girded, he pulled aside the shower curtain, only to freeze at the sight of Chief Harmony planted in the center of the locker room.

Ben Harmony wasn't a tall man. Not only did Monty tower over him, but he significantly outranked him. Not that rank meant much in Spec Ops. Wearing a crisp desert-patterned Naval Working Uniform over his athletic frame, his head shaved as smooth as a baby's bottom, with piercing eyes and a hard jaw, Harmony cut an intimidating figure. His expression could go from warmly accepting to coldly unimpressed in the blink of an eye.

Right now, Harmony's face betrayed his shock as he took in Monty's lean, bruised body. "I'm glad you made it, sir," he said in a gruff voice.

An invisible noose squeezed Monty's throat. All he could do was nod.

"I want to know what happened." Harmony's voice thickened. Moisture glittered in his blue eyes. "Those were *my* men." His hands curled into fists. "I should have been with them."

A cold sweat bathed Monty's pores. It sounded like Harmony blamed him. "Everything went wrong at once." He sought to convey their helplessness. "We had no idea the Taliban had gotten to the targets first. We had a running gunfight with them. We started getting low on ammo. Mikos got hit and was bleeding out. We had to get him out of there, but the enemy had RPGs." He couldn't begin to summarize the odds they'd faced.

Harmony shook his head. He'd heard Monty's version, and it wasn't enough. "I should've been with them."

"You were sick." Not for the first time, Monty asked himself if sending Harmony in with a fever would have resulted in fewer casualties.

"I told you not to take my place."

Harmony's reminder compounded Monty's doubts.

"I could have gone in, sir, fever or no fever."

Monty widened his stance as the room seemed to spin. "The same thing would've happened if you'd been there," he insisted.

"Maybe so." Harmony clenched his jaw as his chin began to quiver. "But my men needed me."

Monty relaxed slightly. Maybe Ben wasn't blaming him. Maybe he was just coping, like Monty was, with the overwhelming knowledge that the operators they had trained with, eaten with, swapped stories and tender moments with were gone.

"They were my men, too." Monty held the chief's burning gaze with difficulty. "And I'm sorry, Ben. I'm so *incredibly* sorry that it ended this way."

Silence fell between them, as deep and hopeless as a mortal wound. Finally, Ben broke it, clearing his throat and nodding at the gauze on Monty's cheek. "I hope that burn heals for you, sir."

"Thank you."

Drawing himself upright, Harmony snapped off a tight salute, totally unnecessary under the circumstances.

With a leaden arm, Monty managed to return Ben's gesture of respect.

The chief performed an about-face and marched quietly out of the bathing area. Monty waited five seconds before he wilted on one of the benches that lined a wall of lockers. *Was it my fault?* He dropped his face into his hands and sobbed without making a sound.

~

It took three days of debriefing, processing paperwork, packing, and traveling to finally arrive at home. Monty nosed his black, soft-top Jeep into the driveway of his suburban, four-bedroom family home in Virginia Beach, cut the engine and stared.

In the past, he viewed R&R as a necessary but annoying lull between missions. This time, there was no future mission to anticipate. He would not be returning to his work as operations officer with SEAL Team 2. Every journalist in America was trying to determine who the sole survivor of the Mother Eagle disaster was. The best way to hide from them was to transfer to another Team.

"*Go home and wait for SOCOM to find you a billet,*" his commander had advised.

Yet home struck Monty as unfamiliar. When he'd left Virginia back in May, the dogwoods were still blooming. It was late October now, and the ten-year-old maple in his front yard had turned crimson. Its brilliance enhanced the curb appeal of his large, white house, as did the landscaped flowerbeds. He'd paid some kid to cut his grass over the summer. Someone must have raked his leaves because the yard looked pristine.

Too apathetic to be grateful, Monty pushed out of his vehicle, grunting at the pain it caused him. It'd become apparent that his strained back wasn't going to heal on its own. He would need to see a physical therapist. Yet he'd refused the muscle relaxers and painkillers prescribed to him at Al Udeid. Pain kept his thoughts on his discomfort and not on the tragedy.

He had just shut his door when a flurry of grass-muffled footsteps had him turning his head. His next-door neighbor—what was her name?—was hurrying across her lawn to see him, cradling his orange-and-white tabby cat in her arms.

"Sir!" she called as she neared him. Her shy smile wavered as she beheld the nasty burn on his face, no longer bandaged. "You're home." Pinning her smile back in place, she came to a halt in front of him.

"Yes." His tone was curt. While he was pleased to see his cat again, he was not in the mood for small talk.

"Opal," she reminded him. Her unoffended gaze broke over him like a warm Caribbean wave. "I was worried," she admitted, causing him to drown in her next words. "I heard about the tragedy on the news, and I'm *so* sorry. You must have lost some very good friends."

Her sincerity was just too much. "Thank you." Monty had to look down at his cat. "Sunny, you big mooch. What are you doing taking up Opal's time?" He reached out to greet his cat with a head scratch.

"Oh, it's not a problem." Opal's smile became rueful. "Sunny just realized he could get a steadier diet by coming to my door. Your—uh —cat sitter isn't terribly punctual."

Her cool reference to Jenny had Monty glancing up. He caught the neighbor taking in the scratches on his hand, and he snatched it back, turning away to reach into the Jeep's rear seat for his duffel bag. As he dragged it out, the weight of the bag made him groan. He turned back, freeing one hand to take the cat. "Thanks for watching him."

Looking concerned, Opal relinquished the feline. "If there's anything I can do to help..."

"Thanks," he said, more remotely. His true feelings were anything but remote. Emotion clawed at him.

"I'm glad you're home." She backed away. Then with a forced smile and a flutter of fingers, she spun around to cross her lawn. She didn't sway her hips when she walked—not intentionally, anyway.

Bemused by her friendliness, Monty gave a mental shrug. He hefted his cat so he could look him in the eye. "You've been playing the field, haven't you?"

Sunny butted Monty's chin with the top of his head. "N-n-reow."

"Liar," Monty muttered, heading toward his front door. Every step shot pain up his spine.

Opal closed her front door, then sank back against it. Good gracious! Her neighbor hadn't looked like that when he'd left. He was now gaunt and sunburned, with more cuts and scrapes on him than on an active three-year-old. And that wound beneath his eye! What, besides an intentional branding or an awful accident, could have caused such a terrible burn?

Poor man! Having overheard his groan when he'd pulled his bag from the Jeep, she'd known at once that he was in pain. And she would guess back pain, having treated many a sailor or marine who moved in that same stiff manner. Given how gaunt and banged up he looked, he must have undergone some serious hardship.

But how and why? Lieutenant commanders sat in their offices, delegating while junior officers and enlisted did the dangerous work. He must have been in an accident of some kind. Nothing else explained his condition.

She pushed away from the door, dismayed by her conclusions and wishing she knew more.

"Hey, it looks like your SEAL's home." At ten o'clock that night, Ruby blew in from her waitressing job. "Every light in the house is on."

"I know." Opal sat on her couch, eying her neighbor's house through a window while her favorite TV sitcom went unwatched. It was out of character for Monty to run up his electricity bill. She tore her gaze from the window to ask Ruby, "How was work?"

"Slow." Ruby flopped onto the couch, still wearing the tight top and short shorts she was forced to waitress in. "All the tourists have gone home."

Opal focused on the word *Showstoppers* emblazoned across Ruby's cropped T-shirt. "So, why not get a real job?"

Ruby, pretending to be engrossed in the sit-com, kept silent.

Opal heaved an inward sigh. "I need to ask you a favor," she said instead of lecturing Ruby for not living up to her potential.

Her firm tone wrested Ruby's attention from the television. "What?"

"I found out today that I have to work tomorrow. The other PT is on maternity leave, and we're short-handed until she comes back. I can't make that two o'clock appointment with the FBI."

Ruby's turquoise eyes rounded with worry. "Can't you reschedule it?"

"Sure, I can if we wait two more weeks, but I don't think that's smart, considering Eric knows of our suspicions, do you?"

Ruby visibly braced herself. "What do you need me to do, exactly?"

"I need you to go in my place. Take the evidence and explain our suspicions to FBI Special Agent Casey Fitzpatrick."

Ruby dropped the back of her head against the couch. "I was afraid you'd say that. Why are we meeting with a special agent? Why can't it be someone who's not special?"

"You can do this, Ruby," Opal stated with confidence she didn't feel. "The FBI Field Office is right off 264 and Military Highway, so you won't get lost. I'll give you money to fill up your gas tank." She hoped a little bribery would do the trick.

Ruby kept silent for a moment. "Fine, I'll go."

"Great." Opal rolled to her feet. "The journal and gas money are right here on the kitchen counter." She crossed to the counter and patted the items. "Don't forget to show the agent the printout of that email we found. It's folded right here inside the back cover." She cracked the cover for Ruby to see.

Just then, Ruby's cell phone shrilled. With a worried expression, Ruby took it off the coffee table and looked at it.

Opal thought immediately of the prank calls her sister had been getting. "Do you recognize the number?"

"No." Ruby answered anyway. "Hello?"

Opal strained her ears to hear who was on the other end.

"Hello?" Ruby said again. As she met Opal's worried gaze, her pallor made it clear Eric was harassing her.

"Leave me alone!" Ruby thumbed the call closed.

Concern cramped Opal's stomach. "Just block his number."

"I have. He calls from a different one every time."

"Well, show that number to the FBI tomorrow. Maybe they can trace the call somehow."

Ruby nodded. "Okay."

"Listen, call my cell phone as soon as your meeting is over, and leave me a message letting me know what Fitzpatrick has to say and whether the FBI can help us."

Ruby managed a wan smile for her. "Got it. Good night, Opal."

"Good night." Opal checked the doors before going upstairs.

Minutes later, she slipped between the cool sheets of her queen-sized bed and closed her eyes. As was her custom, she cleared her thoughts and clasped her hands in prayer, but Eric's recent call had left her with a nagging sense of danger; she couldn't find the centeredness she needed.

Then, too, the lights shining out of Monty's windows filtered through the cracks of Opal's blinds, keeping her room unnaturally bright. Was it the recent tragedy keeping him awake? Her own worries faded as she pondered his physical and mental states.

Would he tell her what troubled him if she just came out and asked? Or would her concern betray the fact that she was smitten with him? What woman with a view of his hot tub wouldn't be? From the top of his golden-brown head to his tan calves, he was captivating. The scar on his face didn't detract from that. But it wasn't solely his appearance that drew her to him. It was also the way he carried himself and his compassion for the veterans in their neighborhood. A man as self-assured as Monty was wouldn't appreciate her gushing concern.

Yet, something deeper than a polite "hello" had passed between them today. Or was that just wishful thinking? He'd looked at her with intelligent, golden-brown eyes, and she'd sensed that for the first time ever, he'd taken note of who she was.

It wasn't exactly the start of a beautiful friendship, but it was something. With a sigh, Opal closed her eyes, dreaming of getting to know her neighbor better.

CHAPTER 3

*R*uby entered the Norfolk FBI Field Office with a gulp of intimidation. The ponderous three-story building surrounded by an eight-foot, wrought-iron fence, exemplified the rules and regulations she regularly flouted. When she'd stopped at the gate, the scowling guard had subjected her trunk to a search before admitting her into the parking lot. Now she was facing two more guards, a metal detector, and an X-ray machine.

"Put your purse on the belt and step through here." One of the guards waved her through a metal detector while giving her ripped jeans and mesh, coral-colored sweater a disapproving once-over.

The other guard snatched her purse as it came out of the X-ray machine. He started pawing through it. "You'll need to leave your cell phone and this can of pepper spray with us. Where are you headed?"

Miraculously, the instant she mentioned Special Agent Fitzpatrick's name, the guards turned polite. They gave clear directions to Fitzpatrick's office—straight ahead, last door on the right—then promised to keep Ruby's confiscated objects safe.

As she coursed a long hallway, her salmon-pink flats scuffed the marble floor. She spotted the agent's name on the door that was right where the guards had described it. His title, special agent, made Ruby's mouth turn dry. The door was cracked. She gave it a hesitant knock.

"Come in, Miss Bonheur," rasped an unnaturally gruff voice.

Inching into an office space far less intimidating than what she'd imagined, Ruby blinked at the man inside. From his wavy auburn hair to his sky-blue jacket and Kelly-green tie, Fitzpatrick resembled a leprechaun. He stood up, extended a freckled hand, and said in his ravaged voice, "You're not what I was expecting."

Glimpsing the scar on his neck, Ruby assumed he'd been wounded. "That's because I'm not Opal. I'm her sister Ruby. We were named after some ancestors," she added, preventing the inevitable comment.

"I see. Nice to meet you, Ruby. You can call me Fitz." He dropped his hand and gestured to a chair. "Have a seat and tell me why you're here."

"Okay." Feeling more relaxed by the minute, Ruby occupied one of the two chairs facing Fitzpatrick's desk and took her father's journal from her purse. "This was my father's diary. He used to work at BioTech; that's a biochemical lab outside of Langley Air Force Base."

The special agent nodded, indicating that he'd heard of it.

"Two years ago this December, a toxic byproduct of castor beans went missing from the lab. There was a big stink about it in the news."

"Ricin." The leprechaun nodded again, telling Ruby he'd heard as much from Opal's original query.

"Everyone in the company was scrutinized, my father included. Then, a couple of weeks later, Daddy died in a car accident in West Virginia. He was hit from behind and knocked off the edge of a mountain. Whoever did it, fled the scene.

The man's green gaze rose to meet hers. "I'm so sorry. You believe that was intentional?"

"Well, at first, we thought maybe a drunk driver hit him. But then Opal found this diary." Ruby handed it across the desk. "If you read the last few entries, you'll see why we think he was murdered."

Silence filled the little room, broken only by the ticking of a tiny metal sculpture of a golfer teeing off, over and over again. Ruby studied it a moment then looked back at Fitz. His burnished eyebrows had pulled together as he skimmed the final entries. When he reached the end, he unfolded the page tucked inside the back cover. "Is this the email your father mentioned?"

"Yes, we found it inside the diary. My dad saw it on Eric's laptop and printed it out."

The agent read the short bit of text aloud, "Sixty-four thousand dollars was wired this morning to the account specified.'"

"My sister thinks that when our father saw the email, he realized Eric had stolen the ricin. He wouldn't have called the police, though, not without giving his friend a chance to do the right thing." Ruby pushed her suspicion through a tightening throat. "Apparently, Eric wasn't interested in that. He killed my father instead."

"Where in West Virginia did the accident take place?"

"Morgantown. There's another BioTech lab there."

Looking thoughtful, the agent folded the email and stuck it back inside the journal. Ruby started to worry. "There isn't, like, a statute of limitations, is there? I mean, it's been two years."

Fitz met her gaze. "If we're talking murder with malice aforethought, then no. We can still press charges. The problem here is whether the trail has gone cold."

"Right." Ruby's hopes for justice floundered.

"Do you have a copy of your father's death certificate?"

"Um...no, not on me. But Opal would have it." For the first time, Ruby realized Opal must have dealt with all the legal aspects of their father's death. All Ruby had done was try to numb her pain with pills.

"I'd like you to send me a picture of that certificate." Fitzpatrick slid a business card across the table with both his office and cell numbers on it. "I'm assuming the car was totaled and hauled to a junk yard?"

Ruby had no idea. "I think so."

The agent thought for a moment. "To connect Eric Novak with your father's death, we'd have to prove he sold the ricin, which means we'd have to prove he was paid for it, as this email suggests. We can try tracing his deposits, but chances are good it was sent from a bogus account."

Ruby blurted her confession. "Um, I might have made your job a little harder."

"Oh? How so?"

The man's raspy voice didn't seem so threatening anymore. "I, uh, I confronted Eric over the phone." Ruby sucked her bottom lip between her teeth.

Fitz's eyebrows rose. "You made contact with the suspect?"

"Yes. When Opal showed me the journal, I kind of flipped out." Ruby shrugged by way of apology. Flipping out was an understatement. She'd been enraged to think that the father she'd adored with all her heart had been murdered by his friend, of all people. Daddy's death had ruined what ought to have been the best years of her life.

Fitz reached for a notepad. "What exactly did you say to Eric Novak?"

"I identified myself."

"Yes?"

"He made a sound of surprise. Then I asked him how he slept at night, considering what he'd done. He asked me what I was talking about, and I told him what Opal found inside my father's journal."

"Did you mention the ricin specifically?"

"No, but he knew what I was talking about."

Fitz scribbled a note. "And what did he say to you then?"

Ruby thought back. "Honestly, I'm not sure. It's hard to understand him because he stutters. But he did say something that sounded like 'You're gonna regret this.'" She hadn't told that part to Opal.

"When did this happen?"

"Two weeks ago. He's called me back several times since, always from a different number. I was going to show you the numbers, but the guards took my phone at the door."

"You can text them to me later."

"Okay. I was afraid he would show up at my apartment," she added, "so I sublet it, and I moved in with my sister." Of course, that wasn't her only reason. She couldn't afford another month's rent.

"What is your sister's address?"

Ruby told him where they lived. "Do you need her phone number?"

"I have that already."

Ruby licked her lips and dared to ask, "I don't suppose you offer any protection services, like bodyguards?"

Fitz lifted a dry look at her. "Sorry, no. If a witness in a major case is being intimidated, we would ask armed surveillance specialists to protect them. That's not exactly the case here."

Ruby's face heated and she nodded.

"But if you feel threatened, by all means, call the police. They'll deal with Novak's harassment. In the meantime, I am going to review the original investigation to see what, if anything, was overlooked. I'm sure Novak's financial situation would have been scrutinized. So, while this email suggests he was paid for something, it doesn't prove he sold the missing ricin."

"Right." But Ruby was certain he had. Why else would he be threatening her? "Do you want to keep the journal?"

"With your permission, I'm going to take pictures of these last few pages."

"Sure."

He produced a tiny camera from his drawer and snapped three pictures. He then slid the diary back to her. "Keep this in a safe spot."

"This means you're taking this case, right?"

The agent grimaced. "That depends. Given that ricin is considered a bioweapon for terrorists, the Bureau has every reason to investigate. As I said, I'll need to look at the original investigation first before I can pursue a new one."

"Oh." With a clenching in her stomach. Ruby realized the FBI wasn't going to rush out and arrest Eric anytime soon.

"But don't let that stop you from reaching out to me, especially if something important occurs." Fitz pushed his chair back. Nice meeting you, Ruby. Let me do some research and get back to your sister."

Disappointed by the agent's lack of commitment, Ruby left his office and returned to the lobby to collect her phone and pepper spray. A vulnerable feeling assailed her as she crossed the blustery parking lot and slipped into her car. Using the cell number on Fitz's business card, Ruby texted him all the phone numbers Eric had called her from. Next, she placed her father's diary under the seat so it wouldn't get lost. Then, she left the compound, eager to return home.

Minutes later, she found herself quagmired in traffic. Cars were backed up on the highway as far as the eye could see, no thanks to cars still pouring out of the Naval Station Norfolk.

"What is it with sailors getting off at three in the afternoon?" Ruby wrung her hands around her steering wheel. Carrying around her father's journal, their only proof of Eric's duplicity, kept her stomach churning.

Sunlight slipped behind the clouds. To ward off her chill, Ruby cranked up the heat in her Oldsmobile. She glanced in her rearview mirror, scanning the drivers behind her. For days, she'd had the feeling Eric was following her. Would she even recognize him after all these years? She had only met him on a few prior occasions, like at a Christmas party or for a Fourth of July barbeque.

If he *was* following her, what would he do—run her off the road like he'd done to her father? And how would she protect herself? She'd owned the same canister of pepper spray for three years now and never used it. Wait, didn't it expire after a while?

As she felt inside her purse, the traffic inched forward. Leery of being cut off by a lane-switcher, Ruby accelerated abruptly, only to brake again. With one hand in her purse, she sifted through the sea of makeup.

Mascara, lipstick, lip gloss, eyeliner. Aha, pepper spray.

She withdrew the can and turned it over. Where was the expiration date on this thing?

Bam!

Ruby lurched, barely catching herself from striking her head on her steering wheel. With horror, she realized she had plowed into the back end of the Honda Civic she'd been tailing. Her pepper spray was on the floor. She gripped the steering wheel. Oh, crap, not another accident!

A tan forearm emerged from the window of the car she'd hit. It pointed firmly at the breakdown lane, instructing Ruby to get off the road—probably a good idea since cars behind them were already beeping.

She was braking next to a Jersey wall when the door on the smaller car opened. Out stepped a frowning young man in battle dress uniform. Ruby had to blink because for a second she thought she was looking at a star from a TV show both of her grandmothers used to watch when she was little—Joey from *Friends*. She gulped as he headed toward her, prompting her to lunge for her pepper spray and snatch it off the car floor.

"What did you think was gonna happen with you tailgating me like that?" he asked through her closed window.

The first thing Ruby noticed was the young man's Philadelphia accent. She cracked the window just enough to retort, "I barely tapped you."

"Tapped me?" His dark eyebrows winged upward. He gestured at the back of his car. "Obviously, you haven't seen the damage any more than you were looking where you were going."

"I was looking!"

"Baloney. You were too busy looking at yourself in the mirror and texting on your cell phone."

Baloney? Who talked like that anymore? "I was not texting! I was reaching for this!" She pointed her pepper spray through the crack in her window.

"Whoa." He stepped back, throwing both his hands up. "Put that away. Are you crazy?"

"Yes, I'm crazy. Better get back in your car and drive away."

He eyed the damage done to his vehicle, then examined her larger car in disgust. "I don't think so."

Pulling his cell phone from his pocket, he met her widening eyes with a challenging glare, while he punched three numbers.

He was calling 911. "Stop!" Ruby unlocked her door as fast as she could, breaking a fingernail as she pushed her way out. "Ouch! Dang it! Stop. You don't need to do that."

His dark eyes seemed to take a snapshot of her body as she rose from the car. He thumbed his call to a close. "Oh, so you have insurance?"

His tone was suddenly more reasonable.

"Er, not exactly." She'd tried to pay her car insurance two months ago, but it was just too much.

His mouth curled with renewed contempt. If not for his battle dress uniform, he would look like a college kid.

"But I'll pay you whatever you need to get your back end fixed."

He flinched from her can of pepper spray. "Stop waving that thing in the air."

"Oh. Sorry. I think it's expired anyway." She tossed the canister back into her car while casting an eye at the traffic inching past them. "Look." She changed tactics abruptly, going for the damsel-in-distress routine. "Let's start again." She sent him a rueful smile. "I'm really sorry I tapped your car. I'm a little distracted this morning. Can't you just forgive me and let me go?"

"Hah. I don't think so." His response had her snatching her wind-blown hair out of her eyes.

She glared at him, frustrated by his heartlessness which contrasted with his ridiculous good looks. The eyelashes fringing his dark-as-coffee eyes made him look like he was wearing makeup.

"You're going to CashApp me two hundred dollars, and then I'll let you go."

"I can't." She gave the first excuse to pop into her head. "I don't have a cell phone"

Skepticism raised one of his eyebrows over the other. "Everyone has a cell phone."

She persisted in her lie. "Well, not me, and I don't carry cash on me, so I guess you're out of luck."

He assessed the traffic briefly, sent her a tight smile, thumbed his phone, and put it to his ear a second time.

"Wait, stop!" Ruby put a hand on his rock-hard upper arm. "We can work something out."

He lowered his phone just a tad. "I have an idea. How's about you take me out to dinner? Then we'll call it even."

"Dinner," she repeated, thinking fast. "Like where?" She couldn't afford to pay for an expensive meal.

"Rockafeller's Restaurant on Rudee Inlet. I'm partial to seafood. Meet you there this Friday at seven."

Rockafeller's sounded expensive. "How do I know that you're not a serial killer?"

He shrugged. "You don't."

"Oh, great. Very reassuring. What are you, like eighteen years old?"

He just stared at her.

With her childish words hanging in the air between them, Ruby's face grew hot. "Fine." She spread her hands, pretending to agree. "I'll meet you at Rockafeller's this Friday at seven."

He leaned closer. "Just so you know, I've got your agreement on video, so you'd better show up."

He'd been filming her? Ruby gasped as he put away his cell phone. "Give me that necklace you're wearing," he added unexpectedly.

"What?" Ruby clapped a hand over the cameo pendant once belonging to her namesake.

"If you want it back, you'll show up on Friday."

"I am not giving you my great-great-grandma's necklace!" She looked down at herself. "Here, you can have my ring." She twisted the cheap pinkie ring off her left hand. It'd been a gift from her last boyfriend, the jackass. She would never miss it.

"Thanks. Off you go before we get sideswiped." Soldier Boy reached past her to open her car door. "I'll see you Friday."

Suspicious of his gallant gesture, Ruby eased back into her car. He shut her door for her. "Seat belt," he added, tapping on the glass.

Annoyed by his suggestion, she whipped the seat belt across her chest and locked it into place, looking up just in time to see Soldier Boy slipping into his car. He skewered one last look at her through his rearview mirror, then he zipped into a space between two moving cars, his motor roaring loudly.

"Annoying brat." Ruby pulled at her gear shifter, put her signal on, and waited for the opportunity to squeeze her big car into traffic. The incident had left her shaken, but it served to take her mind off greater worries, like whether Eric knew that she had gone to the FBI and whether he was plotting his reprisal.

At seven-thirty in the morning, Opal stepped out of her house in her uniform, relieved that it was Friday. On her front stoop, she paused to savor the crisp air drawn in by last night's rain. The sun edging over the house across the street had turned the sky a buttery yellow. She savored the view, relieved she would have the coming weekend off.

The thud of a closing door drew her gaze to Monty's house. She blinked at the sight of him wearing his dress blues. Golden tassels, gleaming brass buttons, and a daunting array of service pins all topped off by a smart combination cap made him a sight to behold. What function was he headed to, dressed like that?

His head turned and his stride faltered as he caught her staring at him. Even with the brim of his cap casting a shadow, Opal could see lines of pain bracketing his mouth.

"Good morning," she called across the lawns separating them. Had he slept at all since his return? He'd left the lights on in his house all night.

"Morning." The greeting was scarcely more than a growl. Avoiding her gaze, he continued doggedly toward his Jeep.

She watched with concern as he shut himself inside and backed the vehicle slowly out of his driveway.

He used to drive like a NASCAR racer. Now he drove like an old man.

With a shake of her head, Opal told herself not to fret over him. There were plenty of patients at Portsmouth Naval Medical Center who welcomed her attention.

Monty wanted to die. The pain in his chest took up so much room, there wasn't space for oxygen. His eyes burned. His knees quaked as he stood in formation with the other SEALs in attendance at Smiley's funeral.

Arlington National Cemetery was a palette of autumn hues. Clumps of mums girded the many headstones. Vermillion maples and golden oaks flanked the perimeter of the graveyard. Was Nature mocking him? How could she seem so vibrant in the presence of such loss?

The air was saturated with the scent of lilies. In the center of their dripping blossoms lay Smiley's coffin, draped with the stars and stripes of the American flag.

The bugler lifted the horn to his lips to emit the purest notes Monty had ever heard. They cut straight through his heart. *"Day is done. Gone the sun. From the lakes. From the hills. From the sky. All is well. Safely rest. God is nigh."*

Boom. The first volley of the seven M14s cracked into the silence. Monty locked his knees to keep them from buckling. In his mind's eye, Mikos passed out, dragging Kelso down with him.

Boom. Mortar rounds punched into the earth and made the mountain tremble.

Boom. The fireball within the helo mushroomed outward, thrusting Monty away on a wave of incinerating heat.

He swayed. The men standing at attention on either side of him shifted closer.

"Sir?" one of them inquired beneath his breath.

"I'm fine," he rasped, but he wasn't.

If the men around him knew that he'd been Smiley's OIC, they were circumspect enough not to mention it. If they didn't know, they would never guess. Lieutenant commanders didn't take the place of savvy, experienced chiefs. It was unheard of, a put-down to the enlisted man's integrity.

So, why had he done it? Was it just to feed his ego?

Beyond Smiley's mourning family, there stood the press, momentarily subdued, oblivious to the fact that he was the sole survivor of that hideous disaster.

He hoped to God it would stay that way.

I have to get through this. Monty scrounged for his composure. It was nearly over. The funeral detailer stepped forward to fold the flag into a shape reminiscent of the tri-corned hats of the Revolutionary War. Vice Admiral Holland presented it to Smiley's mother who cradled it in her arms like a baby, the way she'd once cradled her son.

Monty squeezed his eyes shut. He couldn't watch.

The honor guard withdrew. It was the SEALs' cue to merge and form a line. Monty fumbled to remove his Trident pin. His fingers were still swollen, tender. He couldn't see through his tear-blurred eyes. He trailed the man in front of him. And then it was his turn to hammer his pin into the lid of the coffin.

Boom. Half-blinded by tears, it was a wonder he managed to align his pin with the others. His teammates went to shake hands with family members. Monty broke rank and limped toward his car.

Once inside his vehicle, he clung to the steering wheel and let his chest heave. The salt of his tears stung the wound still healing on his cheek.

Help me, God. The pain in his heart was getting worse, not better.

Why would God help him, anyway? It wasn't like he deserved an ounce of solace.

Twenty minutes later, Monty drew his first full breath without his lungs convulsing.

With a sharp sniff, he lifted his gaze to the coffin, awaiting burial at the height of the hill. Smiley's family still hovered around it, loath to leave their beloved Richard.

I'm so sorry. Monty looked up at them. *If my arrogance and ambition got him killed, please forgive me. I will never forgive myself.*

Twenty-eight Trident pins winked in the sunlight.

Her neighbor was finally back. Opal rolled over in bed as the headlights of his Jeep strafed her ceiling. He cut his engine and slammed his door shut. *Now I can sleep.* She snuggled deeper into her pillow.

But then strange noises started flowing through the window she'd cracked so she could enjoy the cool autumn air. Faint thuds and shouts snatched her from sleep. She cracked an eye and realized that, in contrast to the previous nights, her neighbor was keeping the lights off. What on earth was going on with him?

It was out of character for the SEAL to make any noise. Certainly, he'd thrown a few parties that had dragged on past midnight. But the commander by himself was so stealthy Opal never noticed his comings and goings.

Until tonight. Strange sounds continued to emanate from the house next door, intruding on her sleep. Opal had dealt with wounded soldiers too long not to sense that something was wrong. Another thud reached her ears, followed by a sound like a roar.

"That's it." Throwing back the covers, Opal vaulted out of bed. What if he was hurt and shouting for help? The professional in her could not turn a blind eye.

She snatched up her flannel bathrobe, wriggled her feet into slippers, and left her room.

A peek into the guestroom showed Ruby sleeping with her head buried under pillows. Opal went downstairs, fetched her house keys, and locked her sister inside.

The keys jingled in her pocket as she crossed her and Monty's connecting lawns. A heavy dew dampened her slippers. The air was so moist her breath formed a vapor. She arrived at Monty's door, chilly in her night attire, and knocked.

What am I doing here? Nothing but silence now emanated from within. All the same, she felt compelled to check on him. If he rebuffed her, she would at least tell him to tone it down.

She raised a hand and knocked again.

Nothing. Perhaps he'd finally gone to sleep.

Lovely. She could go back to her own bed. But as she turned to go, the sound of shattering glass reached her ears, and a lurid curse followed.

Not only was her neighbor still awake, but it sounded like he'd just hurt himself. Opal swiveled toward the door and knocked more loudly, calling, "Commander? Are you okay?"

She put her ear to the cold door and overheard an unmistakable moan. Reaching for the doorknob, she found it locked, of course.

Okay, she had a choice: help herself to the key she'd seen the cat sitter use or walk away. She started to walk away. Three steps from the door, she sighed and doubled back. Retrieving the key from under the third flowerpot, she let herself in, slipping his key into her pocket next to her own.

"Commander?" she called with a shiver of uncertainty. "It's your next-door neighbor, sir. I'm coming in."

CHAPTER 4

Opal slipped into Commander Monteague's house, shutting the door quietly behind her. Not only was the interior steeped in darkness, but it was bigger than hers with a different layout. She waded into shadow, arms out in front of her to keep from running into something.

A light, shining from deep within the recesses of the home, was her only source of illumination. As she felt her way past a flight of stairs, something silky rubbed against her calf, emitting a yowl.

"Sunny!" Her heart hammered.

The hardwood under her slippers transitioned into two carpeted steps that descended to a sunken family room, silvered by the light she now could tell was coming from over his stove in the adjacent kitchen. What looked like broken glass glinted on the countertops amidst a dark-red stain that looked like blood. The potent scent of whisky reached her nostrils.

"Commander?"

A shackle seemed to close around her right ankle, startling a screech from her as it yanked her off her feet. She threw her arms out to break her fall and landed across the hard body of a man lying concealed in shadow.

He wasn't content to bring her down, either. He grappled and rolled her to the floor. In the next instant, she was lying on her stomach with her right cheek embedded in the carpet and her left arm locked behind her back. A heavy weight pressured her spine. Her legs were immobilized.

"Who're you?" he growled in her ear, his words slurring together.

Something warm and wet plopped upon her cheek. The scent of blood identified it.

"Lieutenant Opal Bonheur, sir," she said breathlessly, "from next door." He was bleeding on her.

"Opal Bonheur." Some of the pressure eased from her spine. "Never knew your eyes were so pretty."

There was no way he could see her eyes in the dark, which meant he'd noticed them the other day. "Sir, I believe you're hurt. I'm in the medical profession. I can help you," she added in a no-nonsense voice.

"Cut my hand on glass," he affirmed. He grew abruptly heavier, and she feared he was passing out on top of her, in which case, she might never get out from under him.

"Commander!"

He lurched to attention. "Hmmm?"

"You're hurting me. Do you mind getting off me, sir?"

"Sorry." He withdrew his weight, and she rolled to one side where she watched him struggle to sit back on his heels. A dark stain streaked down his right cheek, coming from a cut above his right eye. He had cut more than his hand, apparently.

"Let me help you." Coming to her feet, she grabbed his muscular arm and tugged. "Up you go, sir, before you bleed all over your carpet."

He went up easily enough, but then he nearly pitched over again, and she had to muscle him upright, then prop herself against him. "Which way to a bathroom, sir?" The kitchen, with all that broken glass, wouldn't do.

"'hind you."

Turning, she made out a short hallway and an open door. "Okay, let's get you cleaned up."

She half-dragged, half-carried him toward the opening. It was impossible not to notice how warm, big, and solid his body felt, draped over hers. "Watch your eyes," she warned, fumbling inside the door for a light switch.

As he flinched, she took in the room beyond her with second thoughts. Oh, dear, this was his bedroom. And what a bed he had, she marveled, her gaze momentarily glued to the California king. It was covered with a thick charcoal comforter that reflected the rest of the room's décor—mahogany furniture with uncluttered surfaces, black-and-white photos with burgundy accents. Tasteful. Utterly masculine.

He started toward the wide, inviting bed, dragging her with him.

"Oh no, in here." Opal urged him to change direction toward what had to be a bathroom.

As she wrestled him into the room and flicked on the light, she noticed the blood dripping from his right hand. Had he cut his hand first or his brow ridge?

She positioned him in front of the vanity, noting through her peripheral vision the gray-and-cream wallpaper, the handsome quartz countertop, and matching tiles. "Let's have a look at you."

She craned her neck to assess the cut beneath his eyebrow. Blood still pulsed in a sluggish trickle. Meanwhile, two fingers on his right hand were bleeding all over the textured tiles.

"We're going to treat your hand first," she decided, cranking on the water.

"What happened?" He squinted at his reflection, touching the cut. "Ow!"

"Help me out here, Commander." The crisp order resulted in his immediate cooperation. As she lathered his hand with the liquid soap found in the dispenser, she noted the sheer number of scabs and calluses on his fingers. How could he have damaged his hands like this in an accident? Pulling someone from the wreckage?

"Do you feel any residual glass in your fingers?" She reached for a clean gray towel rolled up neatly and stored beneath the sink.

"No. Feel stupid."

His eyes closed as she dabbed his hand dry. All at once, he started to sway. Opal threw her arms around his waist. "Don't fall again, sir. Here, do you want to sit down?"

"Yes."

She helped him settle onto the closed toilet seat. "Keep pressure on your fingers while I take a look at your eye."

His whisky-laced breath could have lit a fire if she'd had a match. Oddly the scent of it was not unpleasant as it rose into her nostrils. She wet a clean washcloth and gently dabbed the blood from his face while he sat in a silent stupor, his breath fanning her. "You really ought to get a stitch or two," she said, stifling her awareness.

"No medic."

Well, he was apparently coherent enough to make his wishes known. She pursed her lips in disapproval but didn't argue. The cut would leave a scar if it went unattended, but compared to the nasty burn on his cheek, who was going to notice?

"I don't suppose you have a first-aid kit—"

Her request was cut short by the sudden weight of his head against her chest. He'd nodded off with his ear plastered to her heart.

For several seconds, Opal caved into the urge to stroke his thick, honey-colored hair. It ran silky and springy through her fingers. No one would ever know. But then she cupped his head and pushed his torso upright, rousing him with the firm question, "Do you have a first-aid kit?"

His golden-brown eyes focused on her mouth. "Under the sink."

She eyed him firmly. "Sit still. Don't move." She took her hands off him long enough to locate the box beneath his sink, marked with a red cross. "This is good," she praised, finding it well stocked. From the corner of her eye, she noticed Monty assessing her figure in the frumpy, flannel robe.

"How'd you get in here?" He suddenly sounded more sober.

"Let's not worry about that right now." She used her best bedside voice. "Hold still while I put this bandage on you." As she affixed a butterfly bandage across his handsome eyebrow, she examined the wound on his cheek. "How did you burn your face?" she asked casually.

He blinked. Then surprised her by answering, "Shrapnel."

"Not a car accident?" It wasn't any of her business, she knew. But the only way to really comfort him was to know what he'd been through.

"No." His eyes grew glassy.

Sensing dark memories rising inside of him, Opal wondered what, if anything, she could do to dispel them. Maybe if he talked about it. "Let me see your fingers." As she taped bandages over his cuts, she added, "You had a rough day, huh?"

Moisture pooled in his bloodshot eyes. "Yeah."

"Where'd you go this morning?" She kept her tone light.

He was quiet for so long that she thought he wouldn't answer.

"Funeral," he said at last.

Her breath caught at his pain-laced admission. "I'm so sorry. Who died?"

"One of my men." His voice sounded hollow.

She resisted the impulse to smooth his hair again. "That must have been awful for you."

His Adam's apple bobbed. To her dismay, tears overflowed his eyes, only he was too drunk to care or notice. But the sight of them tore at her heartstrings. She'd always suspected Monty was the sort of leader to take the loss of a junior SEAL seriously. "How old was he?" she asked, encouraging him to unburden himself.

"Like...twenty."

Opal found herself tucking a curl behind his ear. "He was just a baby," she commiserated.

"Yeah." With a start, Monty realized that his face was wet. He swiped impatient hands over his cheeks and swore, appalled to have been caught crying.

"Why don't you get some sleep?" Opal recommended. "Maybe you'll feel better in the morning. Where do you keep your pajamas?" She eyed his bloodstained, button-up shirt.

The question seemed to confuse him. "My what?"

"Pajamas," she repeated, checking the hook on the back of the door.

"I don't wear any." He started pushing to his feet.

Opal put her hands on his shoulders, keeping him seated. "Well, you can't sleep in that shirt, or you'll ruin your sheets." She tackled the buttons with efficiency, steeling herself against the thrill of baring his shoulders. He wore a sleeveless T-shirt that highlighted the breadth of his torso, making him look like a superhero. The scent of soap and fabric softener tantalized her as she drew his sleeves down his arms.

"Wait right there." She draped the shirt in the sink, stoppered the drain, and filled it with cold water, all the while keeping an eye on her patient.

"Would you like some privacy?" she asked him.

He squinted at her. "What for?"

Her face grew hot. "Never mind. Let's get you into bed."

She helped him to his feet. Then, with her arm encircling his waist, she escorted him toward his mammoth-sized bed. He'd lapsed into silence—embarrassed, no doubt. She pulled back the covers and moved him closer. "In you go."

She thought he would act like a docile child and fall into bed. Instead, he pulled her down with him. For a second time that night, Opal ended up falling on top of him. Only he didn't wrestle her down this time. Instead, he groaned, his grip on her arm almost painful.

"Are you okay?" she asked in consternation.

"Don't move," he begged with his eyes squeezed shut.

Loath to cause him any more discomfort, she held perfectly still. She couldn't help noticing his thigh was thrown across hers like they belonged together.

Bit by bit, the grip on her arm eased, and then he gave a sigh, as if a spasm had passed.

"Go to sleep, sir," she whispered, thinking he'd just passed out.

He pulled her closer without warning. She scarcely had time to gasp before his lips covered hers. Opal's eyes flew wide. She could have resisted, but, instead, she stole a purely selfish moment in which to gauge whether her fascination with her neighbor was warranted. His kiss was gentle, persuasive. The feel of his palm sliding up her back jolted her.

Opal squirmed away and, to her relief, he let her go. At the door, she snapped off the light. "Good night, Commander."

He didn't say a word back. Perhaps he'd passed out already.

Opal tottered into his family room. Mercy! No wonder women flocked to his door in droves. Still under the spell of his kiss, her knees felt spongy. Too bad she would never know another like it. Monty hadn't known whom he was kissing.

As she crossed his still-dark family room, she made out the silhouette of a table lamp lying on the floor. Curious to see what other damage he'd done, she flicked the switch and caught her breath.

The room was a disaster. Honestly, it looked like a bomb had detonated, especially with all that blood smeared across the carpet—the cream-colored carpet.

"You've got to be kidding me." It would be ruined by morning unless someone took the stain out tonight.

Envisioning Monty's dismay the next day at the destruction he'd wrought out of grief, she groaned. He was already heartsick over the death of one of his men. He didn't need to deal with this and what promised to be a monstrous hangover. That left only one thing to do.

With a sigh and a squaring of her shoulders, Opal headed for the kitchen in search of hydrogen peroxide.

Monty felt like he was being stabbed in the eye with a needle. It turned out to be a ray of sunlight piercing his blinds. He groaned and rolled toward the wall. That prompted a pounding in his head and a wave of nausea.

What have I done to myself?

At least he was at home and safe in his bed, although he still wore the slacks he'd changed into after the funeral, but not the shirt. He couldn't remember undressing.

What time was it? He blinked at the clock. It took several seconds to process that it was afternoon already—three o'clock in the afternoon, to be precise. What on earth? How late had he stayed up? He tried to remember and drew a blank.

Careful not to jar his pounding head, he scooted off the bed and plodded into the bathroom to relieve himself. There he found his shirt soaking in bloodstained water and dried blood marring his tiled floor.

As he went to unzip his pants, he discovered bandages on his right hand. A glance in the mirror revealed a butterfly bandage crossing his eyebrow. He inspected the bandage more closely when he went to wash his hands. What the heck? He'd given himself quite a shiner.

A vision flickered and he seized it, recapturing a memory, followed by another, and then another. No, that could not have happened.

The lieutenant next door. She'd been in his house. She'd washed the cuts on his hand and patched up his brow, her tone both efficient and firm.

She'd asked him questions. Lots of questions.

He put a hand to his forehead, trying desperately to remember. What had she gotten out of him last night? His jaw tightened. The last thing Monty needed was for others to know who he was. The press was on a quest to find him, to publicize his story. Other SEALs knew better than to say anything. They would fiercely guard his identity. But what if his nosy neighbor was eager for money or fame? Exactly how much had he told her?

With his thoughts in a tailspin, Monty splashed water onto his face. The cut on his brow got wet and stung. He removed the bandage to assess the wound, decided it would heal without stitches, and covered it with a fresh bandage. Then he brushed his teeth and helped himself to headache medicine.

Resentment simmered. It was hard enough living with the thought that taking Harmony's place had cost fifteen men their lives. He didn't need the media to ruin his anonymity—or worse, ask him if he blamed himself for the disaster. He shut the medicine cabinet with more force than necessary. Obviously, he was going to have to face his ministering angel and find out how much she knew.

Dressed in clean clothes and searching for his tennis shoes, Monty stalked across his family room. The realization that his socks were turning damp had him looking down. His carpet had been freshly scrubbed. His gaze flew to the kitchen. He knew he hadn't left it like that, with every surface wiped down, no broken glass in sight.

Unbelievable. His neighbor had some gall, cleaning up his house like she was his wife or something!

He'd planned on eating breakfast first—make that lunch. But with his temper at a boil, he couldn't stomach the thought of food.

He wanted an explanation, and he wanted it now.

Opal backed down her porch steps to admire the life-sized scarecrow that she'd just stuffed. Seated on her porch in a rocking chair, it guarded her door, a festive reminder that Halloween was less than a week away. All she needed now was a cornucopia of gourds and several pumpkins to complement the chrysanthemums that graced each step.

"We need to talk."

With a gasp, Opal whirled to find her neighbor standing less than a yard away. Heavens, where had he come from? She put a hand to her pounding heart, aware that its beat was not subsiding beneath his glare. Sober and in the light of day, he looked ten times more danger-ous, more forceful, and more appealing than ever.

The memory of his kiss warmed her like a ray of sunlight.

"Of course." She forced a smile. Questions whirled, like just how much of last night did he remember and what, exactly, did he have an issue with? "Why don't you come in?"

With several neighbors working in their yards, Monty nodded in favor of the suggestion.

Opal led the way inside, guiding him through her foyer to the kitchen. "Would you like a cup of cider?" She hoped desperately to put their talk on a friendlier level.

"This isn't a social call." He crossed his arms and planted his feet.

Opal drew a breath and met his gaze. Monty stood a foot taller than she. His frown put a crease between his eyebrows. It was all she could do not to appear as intimidated as she felt. "Okay, then. How can I help you?"

"You broke into my house last night," he accused, his expression grim and watchful. "How'd you get in?"

"You keep a key under one of your flowerpots." And when she'd left, she'd put it right back where she found it. "I could tell by listening at your door that you were hurt, sir. I'm sorry for entering without permission." Since he didn't want to be neighborly, she fell back on military-speak.

His eyes narrowed at the intentional formality. "Did it even occur to you that I would rather have been left alone?"

Opal considered whether that was true. "With all due respect, sir, you weren't in any state to know what you wanted."

Anger flashed in his golden-brown eyes. "Whatever state I was in, in my own home, is none of your business, *Lieutenant.*"

Really? Did he have to emphasize her inferior rank like that? "Correct, Commander." She swallowed her intimidation. "But your physical well-being is my business, as is the well-being of any serviceman or woman," she added, impersonalizing the incident.

His hot glare should have incinerated her. "If you tell a soul about last night," he warned, on a low growl, "then you can kiss your career goodbye. Is that clear enough?"

What on earth was he afraid of? Opal wondered. Did he think she would accuse him of indecent behavior? Did he even remember kissing her? "Crystal, sir." Indignation that he would think her so indiscreet emboldened her to add, "Perhaps you'll tone it down next time so that I'm less privy to your business."

A dull blush highlighted his cheekbones, and she felt a little better for it.

"I don't know what kind of game you're playing." Both his words and his scowl conveyed confusion. "But whatever it is, you're wasting your time."

"I don't play games."

Her answer made him hesitate. She could see him struggling to understand her.

"You cleaned my rug," he said, his tone still accusing.

"Yes, I did."

"Why?"

Did he really want an honest answer? "Because the blood would have stained it otherwise, and I thought you'd been through enough already."

His frown became ferocious. He took a step forward, and Opal took a cautionary step back. "Leave me alone," he said through gritted teeth. "I don't need a nosy neighbor prying into my business."

The words *nosy* and *prying* stung too much for her to make a reply. Uncertainty chased across his face in the wake of his anger, before he pivoted, stalking toward her front door. It closed quietly behind him.

Five seconds elapsed before the silence was broken by the crescendo of running feet. Ruby burst into the kitchen, her face a reflection of outrage. "Was that our neighbor?" She seized Opal's arms. "Who does he think he is, talking to you like that?"

Opal blinked away her numbness. Consternation rose in its place as she realized Ruby had just overheard every word Commander Monteague had said to her. "Don't worry about it." She held up a finger. "He wasn't threatening me; he was protecting his privacy."

"What do you mean he wasn't threatening you?" Ruby propped her hands on her jean-clad hips. "I heard what he said. He implied that he was going to ruin your career. And for what? All you did was patch up his cuts and clean his carpet."

Opal had explained why she'd slept until ten that morning. "I said, forget it," she repeated. "He's been through enough, okay? He didn't mean to threaten me. If he really knew me, he wouldn't have bothered."

"Oh, come on!" Ruby stared at her in disbelief. "There's no excuse for him talking to you that way! He's the one who got drunk last night."

Opal copied her sister's stance. "You need to forget about that, too."

"What?"

"Stories like that can damage a man's career. He's hurting inside. Try to be sensitive to that, and forget the rest, okay?"

Ruby slapped a hand to her forehead. "I can't believe you're just going to let that pass."

"Yes, I am." Opal nodded emphatically. "He's grieving." Perhaps he'd watched his colleague die and even tried to save him. He'd been hit by shrapnel, he'd said, implying that there'd been an explosion.

Ruby's eyes widened. "You're crazy about him. You have to be. Otherwise, you would never have let him talk to you that way."

Opal wanted to deny the truth, but she wasn't good at lying. "I admire him for his commitment to this country." She crossed her arms over her chest. "Now, leave it alone, Ruby. I don't want to talk about this anymore."

Thoughts glimmered in Ruby's jewel-like eyes. "Whatever," she said, airily.

That wasn't the reassurance Opal was looking for. "I mean it, Sis. Don't even look at him if you see him again."

"Okay. Gosh." Ruby pushed past her to raid the kitchen cabinets.

With a sigh of mistrust, Opal headed for her purse. "I'm going to the store to pick up pumpkins," she said, expecting her sister to tag along. Ruby had developed a habit of shadowing her lately. "Are you coming?"

"No, I want to watch an episode of *Euphoria*," came the unexpected reply.

Opal sighed and headed for the door. "That show is awful. Why don't you work on your résumé?" she tossed over her shoulder.

"I'll think about it."

Thinking about it was all Ruby had ever done with her degree in journalism. "I'll be back in an hour." Opal shut the door behind her, scanned the street, as was her habit, to make sure that Eric wasn't stalking them, and hurried toward her powder-blue Toyota Matrix.

Backing out of her driveway, Opal snuck a peek at her neighbor's house. He'd closed the blinds in all his windows. Now he was blocking the world out, hiding in his lair.

What secret was he harboring? She couldn't dismiss the question any more than she could stop Monty from hijacking her thoughts.

CHAPTER 5

*R*uby waited for Opal's car to disappear before she stalked out of the house and across the adjoining lawns to their neighbor's front door. Undeterred by all the closed blinds, she pounded on the heavy oak door, tugged her yellow sweater over her belly-button ring, and waited, her heart beating fast.

It took forever for the neighbor to answer. When the door yawned open, Ruby wavered at the unfriendly look on his suntanned face. "I'm Opal's sister," she announced. Her training in journalism kept her voice strong and steady. "And I'm here to give you a reality check."

His cut eyebrow quirked, but he didn't try to stop her.

"Number one, Opal is the most selfless, hardworking, nurturing person you will ever have the privilege of knowing in your entire life."

His eyes narrowed, but she was just warming up.

"That you should speak to her the way you did after what she did for you, staying up half the night to scrub your carpet, makes you the most selfish, self-righteous jerk I have ever laid eyes on. If you knew what Opal gave up for me when our father died, you would be licking the soles of her feet."

She could feel the incredulity building in him but raised a finger to keep him quiet. "Don't even think about saying another word to her that is less than humbly apologetic." She gestured at the yard behind him. "Who do you think has been raking your leaves and feeding your cat all this time? You need to wake up and get a life!"

With her courage running dry, Ruby whirled away, chin angled into the air as she cut through his mulch bed to hike it back to Opal's.

Her pricked ears caught nothing but the sound of silence.

She was dying to look back but worried the smirk on her face might push him over the edge. He'd looked a little unpredictable there toward the end, and it wasn't her intent to incite him to violence, just to open his eyes to Opal's virtues.

As for herself, Ruby felt better for having defended her sister. After all, the last man Opal had been crazy about was her fiancé, Brad, who'd dumped her—because of Ruby, who'd developed a habit after their father's death. If Opal hadn't thrown her heart and soul into Ruby's rehabilitation, she would be happily married by now, maybe expecting her firstborn. Ruby could never make up for robbing her of that, but she sure felt better for setting the neighbor straight.

Dazed, Monty shut his door against the autumn chill. He stood in his quiet foyer, processing the awful fact that a third person had witnessed the exchange between Florence Nightingale and him. He cringed to realize the sister had overheard every nasty word he'd said.

Her scolding words returned to him. *"If you knew what Opal gave up for me when our father died, you'd be licking the soles of her feet. Who do you think has been raking your leaves and feeding your cat all this time?"*

So, it was Opal Bonheur who had tended his yard and cared for his cat, not Jenny, who had happily taken the credit. Go figure. Apparently, in addition to being nosy, Opal was quite the do-gooder. He applauded her selflessness, but he'd never asked for her help.

Monty limped into his sunken living room and eased onto one end of his leather couch. Directing his gaze at the television, he checked the score to see what he'd missed. On the widescreen TV, his alma mater, UNLV, was getting the snot beat out of them.

His gaze flickered to the carpet. If Opal Bonheur hadn't scrubbed it last night, he'd have had to hire a cleaning crew, who might or might not have gotten the bloodstains out of his carpet.

With a mutter of annoyance, Monty snatched up his bottle of hard lemonade. "So that makes me a selfish, self-righteous jerk?" he asked his cat.

Sunny sat at his feet with his tail twitching, and Monty realized he'd forgotten to feed him that morning. With a groan, he pushed to his feet.

Okay, so maybe he was a little self-absorbed, enough to keep him from seeing what his neighbor was up to. Honestly, he'd never given her much thought except to notice she was in the Navy, just like him.

She wasn't the type of woman he tended to notice. She had a trim but unremarkable figure, did nothing with her copper-colored hair but put it in a bun, and wore very little makeup.

He dumped the contents of a can into Sunny's bowl and straightened. Opal's face was pleasant but not striking. In fact, only her Caribbean-blue eyes could truly be called beautiful. They seemed to see right through him, which left him feeling terribly exposed.

She had looked at him like that last night when he'd been sitting ignominiously atop the toilet seat. His breath caught as snatches of their conversation returned to him.

"Where'd you go this morning?"

"Funeral."

"I'm so sorry. Who died?"

"One of my men."

"That must have been awful for you."

Monty shook his head in disgust. He'd always prided himself on being circumspect about SEAL business. The Spanish Inquisition could not have gotten him to confess the tiniest detail of any given mission. But with two short questions, Opal Bonheur had him telling all and blubbering like a baby. He'd actually cried in front of her!

Monty washed down the bad taste in his mouth with a long swig on the bottle.

His memory fast-forwarded, and he stilled at the recollection of her lying next to him in his bed, eyes glimmering like aquamarines in the semi-darkness. Oh, no. His heart stopped beating. Surely, he hadn't done anything inappropriate. Yet, the memory of her soft, sweet lips returned to him with sudden clarity.

Apparently, he had. How far had it gone? He searched his memory and drew a blank.

Swiveling on the balls of his feet, he hurried to his bedroom. He thrust open his door and approached the rumpled, unmade bed while trying to dredge up memories. When he still drew a blank, he released a shuddering breath. Good. He'd never pegged himself as the type to take advantage of a woman, but, then again, he'd never thought he would get his own men, plus the rest of their platoon, killed on an op.

The sudden urge to shave his bristly jaw and to dress in something a little less slovenly had him turning toward his bathroom. *What does she want from me?* he brooded as he spread shaving cream on his jaw, careful to avoid the burn on his left cheek.

In his experience with women, they always wanted something. The women he'd known were beautiful, but they were also ambitious, conniving, and calculating. They wanted Monty for what he could give them. Some were after his money. As an 0-4, he brought home a nice salary. Others just enjoyed his prestige. Some wanted to be with him so they could play the field when he was out of the country. For all he knew, Opal Bonheur could be like any one of them.

She would bear watching. If she turned out to be as selfless as her little sister insisted, he would apologize. Why not? He was man enough to admit when he was wrong. On the other hand, if she became a thorn in his side, she would soon regret it. He valued his privacy and his integrity above all things.

~

Tony Caruso pounded on the apartment door in a tidy but aging complex two blocks from the oceanfront. A peek through the window revealed an eclectically furnished apartment. It looked exactly like the kind of place where the flame-haired beauty who'd crashed into his car would live. He nearly had her now.

"Can I help you?" demanded a voice from across the breezeway.

Tony turned and found a middle-aged woman leaning out of her door, glaring at him. She wore curlers in her faded blond hair, a housecoat over her lumpy figure, and pink slippers on her feet.

"Yes, ma'am. I'm looking for the young lady who lives here, Ruby Bonheur?" He had passed her license plate number to a friend in law enforcement, who, in turn, had given him Ruby's name and mailing address. "Do you know when she'll be back?"

The woman took quick inventory of his naval working uniform. "*Nein*, she von't be back," she replied in a thick German accent. "She mooft out last veek."

Tony pointed at the window. "But her furniture's still inside."

"She rents the place to friends of hers." The Frau tightened her robe against the cold.

"Well, do you know where she went?" Would the self-appointed watchdog even tell him?

The woman rolled her eyes. "How many more men vill come around askin' me that question?"

Tony didn't like the way that sounded.

"She don't vant no strange men comin' after her," she insisted, hunching her shoulders.

"I'm not a stranger, ma'am. I'm a friend," Tony exaggerated. "I just want to give her this ring back." He pulled it from his pocket and crossed the breezeway to show it to the woman. "I found it in my car."

The Frau obviously recognized the ring, which told him she and Ruby were tight.

"Vell, you don't seem like a bat man," she allowed. "Vat do you do?" She gestured at his uniform.

"I'm a Navy SEAL." He was also a student taking classes at the local

61

community college and this was his first night off since Friday, when Ruby had failed to show up at Rockafeller's.

"Oh, *ja*? My son is in the Navy." The watchdog's face grew friendly. "Ruby vent to stay vith her sister," she divulged suddenly.

Her sister! Tony hid his disappointment. "Where does she live?" Not far away, he hoped.

The Frau made a thoughtful sound. "Just a minute." She shut the door, disappearing into her apartment.

Tony waited, his blood thrumming with excitement. Thoughts of the beauty who'd smashed in his taillight had obsessed him all week. Her feisty tongue and slippery tactics had amused him. She was about to find out that Navy SEALs were as tenacious as pit bulls, and they didn't like being stood up.

The woman's door popped open. "I forward her mail to her," the Frau explained, stepping out again. She handed Tony an index card with an address scribbled onto it.

Noting the Virginia Beach address, Tony nearly let loose with a "hooyah." Instead, he bestowed on the woman his best Boy Scout smile —though he'd never been one. "Thank you so much, ma'am." He slipped the card into his pocket as he turned away. "She'll be so happy to get her ring back."

"I hope so." The Frau called after him. "You're not like the other man."

Tony turned slowly back around. "Yeah? What was he like?"

"Older." She squinched up her face to convey displeasure. "Quiet and creepy."

Tony wasn't surprised. Having discovered Ruby's driving history, he'd already suspected she had serious skeletons in her closet. But that didn't scare him. "You have a good day, ma'am." Swiveling on his buffed boots, he walked off, wondering how well Ruby Bonheur handled surprises.

~

"The therapist will be in shortly." The corpsman who'd taken Monty's pulse and blood pressure smiled at him, then left so he could change into his patient's gown.

Once changed, Monty went to sit on the hip-high examination table, grimacing at the pain that simple act engendered. The room was chilly, and the gown barely reached to his thighs. A draft blew down the back where the two sides of his gown gapped.

He hadn't wanted to seek medical help, but in Qatar, he'd been subjected to an MRI and informed that he'd strained the serratus posterior inferior, right in the middle of his back. The American medical doctor had recommended physical therapy. Monty didn't know what the future held for him beyond his R&R, but if he wanted to continue as a SEAL—and there wasn't any question about that—he needed to recover fully.

Light footfalls approached the closed door. He could tell by her footsteps Lieutenant Sparks was a woman. She paused to pull his chart from the holder on the wall in the hall. Announcing herself with a brisk knock, she stepped into the room. Only total mastery of his facial muscles prevented Monty from revealing his dismay upon recognizing his neighbor.

"Commander." She greeted him with poise, having had the advantage of seeing his name on the chart first. "Lieutenant Sparks is away on maternity leave, and I'm standing in for her."

Her tone was so impersonal, so professional, that it threw Monty even more off-kilter. "I'd like to be seen by another therapist." His words came out sounding like a growl.

Her soft mouth firmed a little. "I'm the only therapist available until Lieutenant Sparks comes back. She'll be working part-time in about three weeks." Opal shrugged to convey that was his choice.

Monty considered his options. He could go to a civilian PT and pay out of pocket, or he could suck up his pride and keep their exchange impersonal.

He cut a critical glance at Opal's uniform. She wore the standard work attire for officers: a tan-colored blouse and skirt that hugged her trim figure. Her hair was in a tidy bun, as usual. Navy-issue pumps made her look a little taller than she really was. Aside from those eyes and that soft mouth, she was unremarkable. So why did she rattle him so much? "I'll stay," he muttered.

"Let's talk about your back." She blinked down at his physician's diagnosis. "It says here you've strained an intermediary muscle, the serratus posterior inferior. How'd you do that?"

"I hurt it in a fall," he bit out.

She laid the chart down and walked around the table. Stepping onto a stool, she unlaced the ties at the back of his gown and slipped a cool hand through the opening to prod the muscles along his spine. "How far was this fall?"

Her touch made him jumpy. "I don't know. A long way."

"You don't remember?"

He ground his molars together. "No."

She pressed her thumb into muscle, making him flinch. "I'd say you've got an accurate diagnosis. Here's what we're going to do." She stepped off her stool and rounded the table to face him. "We'll start with moist heat packs on the affected area for twenty minutes, followed by a brief cold-laser treatment, then a fifteen-minute massage to enhance blood flow."

She was going to massage him? Monty's mouth went dry. His heart started thudding.

She picked up the chart again, perusing it. "Have you been taking the meds you were prescribed in Qatar?"

"No."

"Good," she glanced at him quickly, "because you're not supposed to mix that stuff with alcohol."

There wasn't an ounce of judgment in her voice, but Monty felt his face grow hot.

"I'll send in a corpsman to set you up with those heat packs. See you in twenty minutes." Lieutenant Bonheur snapped his file shut and headed for the door. It closed quietly behind her.

Monty scowled, cursing his luck. Of all the physical therapists in the Navy, his had to be his next-door neighbor?

Minutes later, Monty lay in solitude, weighted down by lovely warm packs that had put him instantly to sleep. He was jarred awake by Opal's entrance. She wordlessly removed the heat packs and wheeled a machine closer to him. Then, extending a mechanical arm from the machine, she applied a light weight on his strained muscle, moving it in slow circles. At first, it just felt like pressure, but then it began to sting like a hot lightbulb.

"This is cold laser?" he asked incredulously.

"Yes, it's the latest technology, combining wavelengths and outputs of low-level light to the strained muscle. The body tissue absorbs the light, and cells respond with regeneration."

"Feels hot."

"I know. But the results are remarkable. Hang in there. It doesn't take long."

For the next five minutes or so, she didn't speak but moved the wand over the affected muscles. For some reason, the threats he'd hurled at her the previous day returned to Monty, causing guilt to burn like the wand. He wrestled with his conscience. Maybe everything she had done the other night was selfless. Maybe it was her nature to be helpful. In that case, he'd stepped over the line by threatening her. But he had to be sure first.

"Lieutenant?"

"Yes, sir?"

"How much did I tell you the other night?"

She moved the wand slightly higher. "You said you were hit with shrapnel." Her tone was sympathetic. "One of your men died, presumably in the same incident. At first, I thought it was a car accident that wounded you, but given the fall you don't remember, I would also have to consider a helicopter crash?" She fell silent, waiting for him to deny or confirm her guess.

Monty did neither. Her assumptions were amazingly astute. He needed to tread with caution, or she'd come up with the truth on her own, if she hadn't already.

"What I do is classified," he reminded her.

He thought that would be the end of it, but then she added, "The only recent crash I know about was the Mother Eagle disaster. So many lives lost."

Monty tried not to tense, but every muscle in his body flinched.

"You knew those men," she guessed with sympathy in her voice.

He stayed quiet. To his relief, she didn't press him for an answer. Instead, she turned off the machine, mounted a stool for some much-needed height, and commenced with the soft-tissue massage, her hands warm and effective.

He didn't want to enjoy her touch, but he did. The pressure she placed on his tender muscles was exquisite. *Aw, man.* He'd gladly put up with her nosy questions if he got a massage like this every time. *Oh, yes. Right there.*

At the same time, her touch stirred memories he wanted to forget.

He remembered plummeting backward, falling slow-motion through space while the fireball of the helicopter chased him. The torso of one of his comrades issued from the explosion—no legs, head, or arms, just the trunk.

Monty swallowed a curse and willed the vision to disappear.

But Opal had brought up the crash. She'd brought it right into this room. He fought to keep his lungs from seizing, to keep the pain from overwhelming him.

To his mixed relief and disappointment, she removed her hands and wiped his back with warmed wet wipes.

Then she dusted his back with powder, whisking it quickly and lightly over his skin with a soft brush. "How do you feel?"

He shivered at the pleasant, almost hypnotizing caress. "Much better."

"I'm glad to hear it. I want you to put ice on your back at least twice a day, when you're watching television, reading, or resting."

Monty put his hands on the table to push himself up.

"Do you need help turning over?"

"No, I got it."

Protecting his modesty with the gown, he rolled over and swung his feet over the edge. Not a twinge, he marveled. "Wow." The word escaped him, revealing the depth of his relief. He had to admit that his neighbor was talented.

"I'd like to see you again on Thursday." She scribbled something in his file. "We'll run through the same treatment then."

He found himself looking forward to it. Maybe then he'd even be able to look into her eyes and not feel like the jerk her sister believed him to be.

"Check with the desk on your way out." She sent him a small, professional smile. Her skirt swished, her heels tapped, and she was gone.

Monty heaved a sigh of self-recrimination. Maybe little sister was right. Opal Bonheur didn't seem like the type to expose him. She had integrity. And given the magic in her fingers, he was probably lucky to have her as his neighbor, not to mention his physical therapist.

At eleven o'clock that night, Opal was still thinking of her session with Monty. Portions of their conversation looped again and again through her mind as she tried to fit the bits of information she'd squeezed out of him into a coherent picture. He hadn't denied involvement in a helicopter crash, but what crashes had there been apart from the Mother Eagle disaster?

Realizing the only way to fall asleep was to find answers, Opal scooted out of bed and left her room. She crossed the landing to the guestroom where Ruby was sleeping and closed her sister's door. Then she headed to the adjacent room, which was going to be a nursery one day but which she'd been using as an office. After flipping on the light, she eased onto the ergonomic chair at the desk and powered up her laptop.

Minutes later, after an extensive search, Opal confirmed there hadn't been a single recent helicopter crash apart from the Mother Eagle incident. The possibility that Monty had been involved in the attempted rescue of American civilians had her skimming through several websites for proof. Her gaze jumped back to the line she'd just read. There it was, under her nose the whole time. One SEAL had apparently survived the fiasco. He'd been chased for days by the Taliban, only to be later found and rescued.

The blood drained from Opal's face. How could that have been Monty? Lieutenant commanders didn't operate in the field. That was for younger men.

She continued reading, and her certainty congealed. *Military officials said the survivor was knocked off his feet by the explosion of the Chinook and slid down the steep terrain far from the landing site.*

Opal's heart started pounding. She read the rest of the article carefully, her certainty growing with each printed word. Every detail dovetailed with his circumstances: his sudden arrival home, his physical condition, his refusal to talk about what had happened.

"Dear God," she breathed, understanding why he was so vehement about protecting his privacy. The last thing he would want was publicity. "Oh, Monty."

She sat back in her chair, envisioning the hell he'd been through and reeling at the heartache she knew he was left with. No wonder he had trouble sleeping at night! No doubt the memories haunted him. Currently, he was drowning them in liquor, but that wouldn't work. She pictured him in his dress blues limping toward his car, headed for a funeral.

The urge to comfort him had her clasping her hands together. She could do more than ease his physical discomfort as his therapist. She could pray for him.

"Heavenly Father," she whispered, as tears of compassion rushed into her eyes, "help me be a comfort to him. He's suffered so much already. Please, let me help somehow."

A thud at the door caused her to start with surprise. There stood

Ruby in a diaphanous nightgown, her hair disheveled, her eyes widening as she beheld Opal's moist gaze. "What's wrong?"

Opal forced a smile while blinking her tears away. "Nothing."

Ruby's attention slid toward the open laptop. "Obviously, it's not nothing." She stepped closer and, under the pretext of comforting Opal with a hug, scanned the article Opal had been looking at. "You're reading about the recent Navy SEAL disaster."

"Yes, it's just so sad." The last thing Opal wanted Ruby to know was Monty's terrible secret.

Ruby pulled back to look at her. "You didn't cry when it was on the news."

Opal, who couldn't lie convincingly, kept quiet.

Ruby looked back at the article. Like a hound dog on a scent, she scanned the text more carefully. "One of the SEALs survived. Wow, he tumbled down the mountain and was missing for days." She cut herself off and turned her head with a searching look. "It was our neighbor."

Opal, astonished by Ruby's instincts, tried to hide the truth. "Of course it wasn't. Only junior SEALs go into the field."

Ruby's lips firmed. "I can tell when you lie, Opal. Besides, you wouldn't be so invested if it weren't him. It's okay. You can tell me. I won't say a word."

Opal closed her eyes in defeat. "Nobody can find out." She grabbed Ruby's hand and squeezed it. "I'm serious. If the press finds out our neighbor was the sole survivor, they will flock to his doorstep and dog him endlessly for interviews. If that happens, his face will be all over the news, and he will have to quit the Teams or else become a huge target for terrorists. Do you get how serious this is?"

Ruby wrested herself free. "Yes, I get it. Chill. Have some confidence in me, will you?"

Opal held back a sigh. "I don't have much choice now, do I?"

"My lips are sealed." Ruby mimed locking her lips and tossing away the key.

Worry sat in Opal's stomach like a stone.

"Now, if you don't mind keeping it down," Ruby added, "you know

I'm a light sleeper, and I didn't bring my white noise machine with me."

"Sorry." Opal closed the web browsers and put her laptop to sleep. Having answers to her questions, she hoped she could do the same, but she doubted she would sleep well.

Poor Monty had suffered something horrendous, something worse than just the death of his subordinates. Not only was he carrying around some truly awful memories, but he likely had survivor's guilt— who wouldn't? All she could hope was for God to work His Grace through her, to bring him relief for his suffering.

CHAPTER 6

"*Y*ou must be Monty."

Monty lifted a startled gaze from the magazine he was reading in the clinic's waiting area. He'd been well aware of the older man standing in front of him, clutching a cane and watching everything he did. He'd offered the man his seat about five minutes earlier, only to be rebuffed. Since then, Monty had assumed the man was lost in his thoughts, not pondering his identity.

"Yes, sir." Monty set the magazine aside, wondering, *Do I know this guy?*

Pale blue eyes stared back at him. "I'm Admiral Jenkins."

An admiral. Monty rocketed to his feet. "Sir, nice to meet you, sir." The old man wore civilian clothing and sported sparse silver hair atop his egg-shaped head.

"At ease there, Commander. You don't have to stand for me."

"You sure you wouldn't prefer to sit?" Monty gestured at his chair a second time, though there were empty seats not far from them.

"No, no. Sitting hurts my knees. They were shattered when the Vietcong first shot down my plane and then my parachute. It's not the long fall that hurts, by the way. It's the sudden stop at the end."

Monty joined the man in a chuckle. He could not have agreed more. "You fought in 'Nam, sir?" This seemed to be what the admiral wanted to talk about.

"More than that. Spent 103 days in a North Vietnamese prison camp."

"You're a hero, sir." Monty marveled that such an old and seemingly frail individual had survived what had to have been hell on earth. "You have my fullest respect." He glanced around to make sure no one could overhear them. "If you don't mind me asking, sir, how is it that you know me?"

Jenkins's rheumy blue eyes rested on Monty's face. "Let's just say, when something happens to my boys, I take it personally."

My boys? Who was Admiral Jenkins, exactly? Monty nodded and kept quiet.

The old man's eyes narrowed. "You ever ask yourself if someone's to blame for the hell you've been through?"

Monty's heart clutched. "No, sir." He knew exactly where the blame lay—right at his own two feet.

"If we'd stayed in Afghanistan, Mother Eagle wouldn't have been necessary. We were just making headway with our nation-building. That kind of stuff takes time, more than twenty years. We should never have made promises to those people if we didn't intend to keep them."

The words relieved Monty from a portion of his guilt. "Yes, sir." He fully sympathized with those in Afghanistan, especially the women, who'd embraced a democratic way of life only to have it wrested away from them by the fanatical factions within their own country.

"My only son was a Marine in Operation Enduring Freedom. Hmph." Jenkins scoffed. "Enduring my foot! Where's their freedom now that the Taliban are in charge?" With a sneer and wetness in his eyes, he looked away. "Norman gave his life for the Afghan people."

Ah. Suddenly, Monty could see why the admiral was so bitter. He had lost his son to a worthy cause, only to have that cause lose significance when the U.S. threw in the towel.

"I'm so sorry, sir." Monty was about to lay a comforting hand on the admiral's shoulder when the corpsman called him from the door.

"Admiral Jenkins, sir."

With a nod of acknowledgment for Monty, the admiral went in for treatment.

$$\sim$$

Admiral Jenkins's phone shrilled. Opal, who was about to remind him cell phones weren't permitted in the hospital, kept her mouth shut. Who was she to tell an admiral what to do, even if he was lying flat on his back on the table in front of her?

"Jenkins," he growled, then winced as Opal put her weight into bending his knee, trying to increase his mobility.

As the caller identified himself, Opal felt the admiral stiffen. "What the devil do you want?"

Mercy, Opal thought, releasing pressure to extend the leg fully. She'd never seen this gruff side to the admiral, who was always sweetly affable during his biweekly appointments. She moved to flex his left knee.

"I thought this matter was settled."

The old man was visibly upset. "Bend your leg, sir," Opal reminded him.

He did so, distracted by whatever the caller was telling him. The news was bad enough to make him put a death grip on the phone. "Are you certain?"

Opal glanced up to see Jenkin's jaw quiver.

"Fine, then. Do whatever it takes." With a shake of his head, he severed the call and clapped a hand to his heart.

Opal eyed him with concern. "Everything all right, sir?" She pressed on his shin, forcing his knee to bend farther.

"Oh, as all right as it can be, I suppose." With his eyes closed, he looked and sounded about a million years old.

Pity rolled through her. He had suffered so much in his life—from his torment in Vietnam to the death of his son ten years earlier. Opal couldn't fathom losing a child to war. She let up on his shin and slowly straightened his leg. "That's it for today, sir. I'll see you next week at the same time. Keep up the exercises." She laid a hand over his and squeezed it for encouragement. His skin felt like ice!

Leaving the room, she dropped off the admiral's chart and hurried down the hall to grab up the chart belonging to her next patient. Monty's name leaped out at her, filling her with anticipation. She'd been looking forward to this moment since their last session.

With a warning knock, she peeked inside. "Good morning."

She drew up short at the sight of him leaning shirtless against the edge of the table. Her gaze dropped toward his washboard abs before she jerked it back to his crooked smile.

"Morning. There aren't any gowns left. Davis just left to get more."

"Oh?" She averted her warm face as she crossed toward the cabinet to double-check. "Sure enough. How's your back feeling?" It took all of her willpower not to look over at him. The night she'd patched him up and put him to bed, he'd kept his T-shirt on. It had concealed how terribly lean he was. Every muscle, every sinew, every rib was visible. He needed to gain at least ten pounds.

"I was good for a day. Then the spasms came back."

"That's why you need to come here twice a week."

A knock at the door signaled the corpsman's return with more gowns.

Opal backed toward the door. "I'll let Davis get you started, and I'll see you in twenty minutes." She allowed herself another quick peek at his torso as she let herself out.

Returning twenty minutes later, she found Monty facedown on the table, his back covered with packs and a gown tied at his neck while hanging down on either side of him. Dove-gray boxer briefs were all that protected his modesty. She removed the packs, one by one, exposing the back she couldn't wait to work on. The packs had left her playing field ruddy and warm.

"How are you feeling?"

"Sleepy."

The drowsy timber of his voice made her want to lean over and hug him. She wheeled the cold-laser machine closer and turned it on. Extending the wand, she lightly touched it to the aggrieved area. "This will wake you up."

Sending the light waves deep into his muscle tissue, Opal prayed for Monty's healing—and not just his physical healing. He might look indomitable, sprawled with such masculine grace upon the table, but the depression that had driven him to drink the other night hung over him like a dark cloud. And his body still bore evidence of his suffering.

With the cold laser treatment done, Opal cut off the machine, eager to begin the portion of his treatment she enjoyed the most. She mounted her stool, applied warm oil to her hands, then dove in.

The words *soft* tissues were a misnomer on Monty. There wasn't anything soft about him. She thought of some baked goods she might make him to help him regain the weight he'd lost. The knots in his lean muscles left her fingers aching. Still, she didn't want to stop, not even when her hands cramped up.

"You think you could work on my shoulders some?" His request seemed to mirror her reluctance for their session to end. "They've been kind of tight lately."

Her impulse was to say, "I'd love to." Instead, she focused on the fact that Monty hadn't apologized for his behavior the other day. From her perspective, he owed her something. "Well, that kind of depends," she hedged. "You might have to do something for me first."

"Like what?"

His suspicious tone made her roll her eyes. What did he think she was going to ask for? "Like carve those two pumpkins I put on your porch."

"Oh." He went silent for several seconds. "I figured you put them there."

"Halloween is a week from today. You carved four jack-o-lanterns last year. The neighborhood kids will miss it if you don't make at least two."

"I'll think about it."

She didn't hear the commitment she was looking for. "Not good enough." She smoothed her thumb along the edge of his shoulder blade, encountering a thick knot.

"Uh!" He groaned, half in pleasure, half in pain.

"You could also keep an eye on my sister, Ruby, while I'm at work." It wasn't so hard to make demands in this position, she realized. Plus, Monty needed something to do besides mope around his house, reliving the accident.

"Her?" he asked in a horrified tone.

Did Ruby's flamboyance not meet with his approval? "She's been getting prank phone calls," Opal explained, "from the man who killed our father."

Startled silence followed her remark. "When did that happen?"

"Two years ago, this December. My father worked in a biological warfare lab where they tested ricin, among other things. That's a toxic biowaste—"

"I know what it is."

Since it seemed like he would agree to her bargain, she continued to work on his upper back. "Some of the ricin went missing, and not long afterward, my father was killed in a hit-and-run. We think his partner sold the ricin to terrorists, then killed my father, who had confronted him."

Monty craned his neck, sending her a look of consternation. "Have you gone to the cops with this?"

"The FBI is looking into it."

"Well, that's something." He laid his head back down.

"So..." She stilled her movements. "Can you keep an eye on my sister, or should I stop now?"

"I'll keep an eye out," he promised grudgingly.

"Thank you." With a satisfied smile, Opal worked her thumbs into his trapezoids. His entire back was a work of art—broad, smooth, and tan. But under his skin, his muscles were fibrous and knotted, suggesting incredible tension in his life. When her hands began to ache, she switched to using her right elbow. Monty made sounds of mixed pleasure and pain. Listening to him, she could tell what made him feel better.

A glance at her watch later told her that their time was up. She performed one last sweeping motion, then took her hands from his back and gave her weary arms a shake.

"You're really good at that."

She warmed at the longing in his voice. "Thank you," she said as she dusted his back with powder. "You could use more attention, but I have other patients waiting for me. Sitting in your hot tub wouldn't hurt, either, as long as you're still icing."

"I am." He pushed himself slowly to a sitting position while keeping the gown from slipping off the front of him. "When do you want to see me next?"

This evening? said her smitten heart. "Let's say Monday."

"I won't be back till Monday night."

"Oh, you're going out of town?"

He frowned and looked away. "Quick trip to Florida."

"Are you driving or flying?"

"Why so many questions?"

His brusque query conveyed suspicion. "Because your back will get worse if you sit for more than two hours straight," she said, steadily.

Chagrined silence followed her explanation.

"I'm flying to Orlando, then driving to Daytona in a rental."

"I see." His destination touched on a memory. One of the SEALs in the Mother Eagle disaster had hailed from Daytona. Monty was going to pay his respects, she realized. She nodded. "That'll be good for you."

He glanced at her sharply. "What will?"

"Paying your respects."

His tawny eyebrows drew together. "Did Admiral Jenkins tell you something?"

The challenging question confused her. "Admiral Jenkins? No, do you know him?"

"No, I don't. But he knows me and, apparently, you do, too."

His hard look demanded honesty. Opal sighed and clutched his chart to her chest. "That shouldn't be a threat to you," she pointed out. "I have no reason to tell anyone that you're the sole survivor of the Mother Eagle disaster."

There, she'd said it, half praying she was wrong. But the look that crossed his face nearly broke her heart. "I'm so sorry for what happened." She caught herself from laying a hand of comfort on his arm. "I know this has got to be a nightmare for you."

He averted his pained expression.

"Be careful in your travels," she said, wanting to spare him the indignity of losing his composure—again. "I'll see you Tuesday."

She left him alone to grapple with his demons.

Monty put his weight back into his leather couch and sought oblivion. If he could turn off his thoughts and let Jenny's soft touch distract him from the memory of his conversation with Opal, maybe he could actually enjoy his girlfriend's company. Honestly, though, if her itty-bitty red dress couldn't wrest him out of his dark thoughts, nothing could.

Jenny sat practically in his lap, nibbling on the column of his throat while telling him what she'd been up to these past months. He hadn't taken in a word of it.

"Oh, Monty." She cupped his jaw, turning his head so he would meet her gaze. "I hope you don't think that scar makes you any less attractive. If anything, it makes you more appealing than ever."

Her words brought it all back in an instant: the explosion, the fireball, dismembered torso flying at him as he fell backward. Monty felt suddenly sick to his stomach. "Please, get off me."

Jenny's eyes flew wide. She clambered away from him. "I'm so sorry, Monty—"

He couldn't even look at her. "It's not your fault." He tried to say more, couldn't find the words, and clapped a hand to his face to rub his aching eyes.

"Is there anything I can do for you?"

Her sincerity brought his head up. He met her anxious expression. "No. Thank you, Jen. You should probably go home."

She couldn't quite hide her gasp of hurt as she turned away, slipping her feet back into her heels. Monty got up and headed wordlessly to the door. Holding it open for her, he avoided looking at her face, but he could feel the emotion rolling off her as she stepped past him, out onto his porch. He didn't walk her to her car, as he normally would have. Instead, he shut the door quietly, then stood staring at the floor. Why had he ever been with Jenny in the first place?

They used to have fun together. That was all he could come up with.

As the sound of her car faded, he crossed to the half-bath under his stairs to splash water on his face. How could any woman find his scar attractive? He stared at his reflection. For the rest of his life, he would look at his face and think of the men he'd watched die, men who'd been like brothers and sons to him. He detested the scar. At the same time, he vowed never to surgically fix it. It was part of him, as much as those men had been part of his life.

Jenny would never understand that. But, for some reason, Opal did, most likely because she was in the medical field. He could also trust Opal in a way he had never trusted Jenny.

Thoughts of his neighbor had him glancing out of the bathroom's little window at the house next door. Opal's home was lit up with lights that told him she was home. Her story about the disappearance of ricin and her father's subsequent murder roused his protective instincts. Before he realized his intentions, he was donning a denim jacket and jamming his feet into the sneakers he kept in the front hall closet.

Crisp night air sharpened Monty's senses. A harvest moon put an icy luster on the lawn as he crossed it toward her home. While the FBI was looking into Opal and Ruby's situation, Monty hadn't gotten the impression they were deeply involved yet. The sisters were still very much on their own with a prank caller evidently harassing them.

Having promised Opal he would keep an eye on Ruby, Monty figured he had her permission to reconnoiter her yard in order to gauge any vulnerabilities.

Neither he nor Opal had fenced in their backyards. As he rounded the rear of her home, he noted the thick garden beds with approval. The roses blooming on her rosebushes had withstood the colder weather, so far. The bushes' thorns, along with the prickly hedge of holly, would deter anyone from wanting to crawl through a window.

He came to a neat brick patio, complete with an outdoor fireplace, wrought-iron table and chairs. The cozy setup tempted him to take a seat and listen to the crickets chirping in the dark corners of the yard. As a light blinked on above him, he looked up and realized he was seeing into Opal's master bathroom. One of the plantation shutters stood ajar, giving him a glimpse of her bare back as she stepped into her shower.

Stunned, Monty stood a minute, appreciating the view and realizing it pleased him the same way her magical touch did. Chagrined to catch himself peeping, he looked away. Annoyance followed on the heels of his chagrin. He didn't want to find his neighbor attractive. She had intruded on his solitude and placed demands on his time with her request to keep an eye on Ruby.

Speaking of Ruby, he could see the terror plain as day through the French doors of the family room. Curled up on the sofa, biting a fingernail as she watched television, she was open season to anyone with a thought of causing harm.

He wanted a closer look at the lock on the French doors. Monty mounted the back deck without Ruby even noticing. He walked right up to the door and peered through one of the many little panes of glass. Could someone simply break a pane, reach inside, and turn the dead bolt? Yes, they could. Ruby would scream if she glanced over her shoulder and caught sight of him. Backing away, Monty continued to circle the house, looking for more vulnerabilities.

The remainder of the windows and the front door were all tightly secured. Opal got points for that. He stood on her front steps a minute later, admiring Opal's scarecrow and wondering if she was out of the shower yet. He had no desire to talk to Ruby, who was scarier than a swarm of Taliban soldiers. Calling himself a coward, he stepped toward the door, knocking loud enough for Ruby to hear him.

His hope that Opal would answer evaporated as Ruby eyed him through the door's beveled glass, then pulled the door open, revealing her slender but curvy figure in a lovely silk bathrobe.

"It's you," she said.

Clearly, she was expecting the bad guy. "Hello, yourself. I have a message for your sister. Tell her she needs a different lock for the French doors at the back of the house, one that requires a key on the inside."

Ruby's puzzled gaze drifted over him. "Okay."

"And tell her to close the shutters in her bathroom."

Ruby's mouth twitched toward a smile. "Anything else?"

The aroma of baked goods wafted out of the sisters' house. "What's that smell?"

Ruby opened the door wider. "Opal's been baking. You want to come in?"

Suspicion made Monty back up. Recalling how vehemently she'd defended her sister, Monty didn't trust her not to mess with him some more. "Maybe next time."

"You don't know what you're missing," she sang out as he turned tail and fled.

Returning to his home, Monty tried watching TV while sitting with the icepack at his back. He could not stop thinking about Opal. Why? She wasn't at all his type. Superficial, adventure-seeking women were his dish of choice. They didn't influence his decisions and didn't detract from his career. He'd risen to his current rank faster than his peers for the simple reason that he'd had no distractions—no wife, no children. A woman like Opal could change all of that. Monty didn't want change. His modus operandi had served him well. Why shift gears at this stage?

And yet, Opal had glimpsed the deep-down, ugliest corners of his soul without flinching away. He had to admit, he admired her for that.

Heading straight to his kitchen, Monty found Sunny sitting by his bowl, glaring at him.

"Mmrow."

"I know. I'm only a little bit late today." He fed the cat, then stood there watching him eat. "Guess it's just us guys tonight." His gaze traveled with conjecture to his liquor cabinet. He thought about the half-full bottle of bourbon sitting in it. Opal would be understandably upset if he drowned himself in liquor again and tore his house apart.

Perversely, he crossed to his liquor cabinet, reached for a bottle, and unscrewed the top. A vision of Opal's back with its delicate shoulder blades brushed by a curtain of copper hair returned to him. If he didn't want Opal coming to his house in the dead of night to peel him off the floor and patch him up again, maybe he'd better not start.

With a sigh of resolution, Monty screwed the top back on and set the bottle back inside the cabinet.

CHAPTER 7

*M*onty neared Daytona at dusk. No thanks to a delay in his flight to Orlando, the car he'd reserved had been given to someone else. He had jammed his brawny body into the only economy-sized car available and had driven the last hour of his trip with the muscles in his back screaming. Opal's warning about sitting still for more than two hours at a stretch had been well founded.

If the pain in his back wasn't enough, the thought of facing Mikos's widow filled him with dread. His shirt stuck to his back as the AC in the tiny rental blew warm air at him.

Following the directions on his cell phone, Monty turned into a neighborhood of modest ramblers located just blocks from the ocean-front. Two young boys played whiffle ball in the street, blocking his approach. Realizing they had the same dark hair and olive complexion as Mikos, Monty parked along the curb, lowered his windows and turned the car motor off.

He tried to step out, but his limbs were like dead weights, keeping him from moving.

The sun had disappeared. The sky was washed in hues of violet. Mikos's boys, maybe six and eight years old, ignored their lengthening shadows and took turns swinging at the plastic ball while a fruit bat whirled overhead.

Mikos would never play with them again.

Just get out of the car, Monty. Get it over with.

He reached for the handle on his door and cracked it open. That same moment, light spilled across the lawn as a dark-haired woman stepped onto the porch. "Alex and Marcus, it's time to come in."

Both boys ignored her.

Their mother tried again. "It's too dark to play out here. Put the ball away and come into the house, now!"

"Five more minutes."

Monty heard defiance in the older boy's voice, read it in his body language.

Mikos's widow put a hand to her forehead. The weary gesture tugged at Monty's heartstrings.

With a vise around his chest, he watched her square her shoulders. She marched into the street and wrested the bat from the elder boy who, for a moment, looked ready to retaliate. But then the boy glimpsed his mother's expression and relinquished the bat. The threesome trailed quietly into their house. Mikos's wife shut the door.

Now was the time to go talk to her.

Only, Monty still couldn't move. Guilt burned in him like toxic waste. He shut the car door and started up the engine. With a tire-squealing U-turn, he fled the neighborhood.

The glow of neon lights lured him to the boardwalk. He paid seven dollars to park at the beach.

Kicking off his shoes and socks, he plodded toward the incoming tide, barefooted. The warm sand squished between his toes. He walked straight into the surf, where the shock of cold water hit his calves, his knees, his thighs, dredging up memories of SEAL training in Coronado. He did not stop walking until it smashed into his hips, nearly knocking him off his feet.

The Coronado Bay was colder at this time of year than the Atlantic Ocean. He and his fellow candidates were made to lie in the surf at dawn, clinging to each other while the waves crashed into them. It was a team-building exercise that taught them that together, they could endure anything.

Only, they hadn't. They'd been overcome by overwhelming odds and circumstances.

Would Mikos's widow understand that, or would she blame him the way he blamed himself? He would rather let the water close over his head than face her tonight. For the longest time, he battled the temptation to slip into the water and let himself drown. But the memory of Mikos's commitment to the mission had him turning around. Mikos hadn't given up; neither could Monty.

With his pants soaking wet, he got back into his car. He returned to Mikos's quiet neighborhood, got out and walked, still barefooted, to the front door. Hearing the banter of a television show host, he knocked.

A shadow blocked the light in the peephole. "What do you want?" He had to look suspicious, standing there in sodden pants.

"I'm a friend of Mikos's," he replied. "I was with him when he died."

The door cracked open. A dusky face peered out.

"My name's Monty." He put out a hand.

Her own hand was slim and small. Holding it put a chokehold on Monty's vocal cords.

"Victoria," she said. "Do you want to come in?"

"I'm all wet."

"Please." She opened the door wider.

Victoria found a pair of Mikos's sweatpants, long enough to fit him, and threw Monty's slacks into the dryer. Then the two of them sat across from each other in the dining room, where he spooned down the soup she'd insisted on offering him. The boys poked their heads out of the bedroom, but she shooed them away.

She waited for Monty to finish eating before demanding, "Tell me what happened."

He told her everything, not withholding the fact that he'd taken Chief Harmony's place. He braced himself for accusations, but they never came. She remained stoic right up to the point where he related how Mikos had passed out from lost blood, dragging Kelso down with him. As the rest of his story unfolded, her brown eyes filled with tears.

"Then he never knew what happened," she concluded, reaching for a napkin to cover her trembling lips.

"No, he never knew."

Her face contorted with grief as she nodded her understanding. Monty's composure slipped. The lump in his throat ached unbearably.

"Thank you for telling me."

Her gratitude shook him. His eyes burned. His vision blurred. "I'm sorry," he added, appalled to hear his voice crack. "I'm so sorry I couldn't save him."

"It wasn't your fault." Her eyes shone with forgiveness. Stretching a hand across the table, she covered his and squeezed. "Don't blame yourself. He died doing what he loved. How many people can say that?"

Monty nodded. Her humbling forgiveness kept his tears from drying.

Victoria offered him the guest room for the night, but Monty declined. Leaving an hour later in his dried slacks, he felt as if he'd been cut free from an enormous weight.

As he eased into his car with the intent of finding a motel, he felt the urge to talk to Opal. *You were right, Lieutenant,* he wanted to tell her. *That was good for me.*

Monty was back from his trip.

Opal parked her car in front of her house and smiled at the leering jack-o'-lanterns glowing across the darkness at her. He had faced them deliberately in the direction of her home so she wouldn't miss seeing them.

Apology accepted, Commander. Happiness warmed her as she peered into his windows. She hoped he'd gotten some closure after putting himself through that trip. As she got out of her car, she spotted a second vehicle parked beside his, and her happiness dimmed. The green Volkswagen belonged to yet another of his girlfriends, not the cat-sitter.

Opal's lips firmed. Scolding herself for feeling betrayed, she went to gather groceries from her trunk. At least with a woman over, Monty wouldn't be drinking himself into a stupor.

Loneliness enveloped her as she carried her groceries into her dark and empty home. Ruby hadn't left a single light on when she'd left for work. Flipping on switches with her elbows, Opal lit her way to the kitchen where she dumped her bags. Then she returned to the door, locked it behind her, and hung up her jacket in the closet.

While putting her groceries away, she cheered herself with thoughts of Steven Parks, the surgeon who had eaten lunch with her at work that past week. He was the kind of man she should be setting her sights on, not someone as complicated and tortured as her neighbor. Steven had promised to call her this weekend. Maybe she should check her messages.

Taking her cell phone from her purse, Opal carried it back to the kitchen. Her hopes stirred as she realized she had, in fact, overlooked a call from him, but he hadn't left a voice mail. Disappointed, she set her cell phone down and started unpacking her groceries. All at once, the landline in the kitchen rang. Opal looked up at it sharply. She'd been meaning to cancel her service for months now. The only calls she ever got were from telemarketers and political campaigners. But what if Steven was calling her home phone, having missed her on her cell phone? Both numbers were listed in the medical center's directory.

She crossed to the phone on the kitchen wall and snatched it up. "Hello?"

When the only sound coming from her phone was heavy breathing, Opal froze. With a gasp, she clutched the phone harder. "Hello, Eric," she said in a stern voice.

That prompted him to speak. "W-w-why're doin' this? Why? You're gonna...end up d-d-dead, like your father!" The call ended abruptly.

Opal stood in shock, rocked by the heavy beating of her heart. Eric had just threatened her. Hanging up, she collected her cell phone from the counter and accessed Special Agent Fitzpatrick's number. When her call went to voice mail, Opal left him a concise but shaken message, telling Fitzpatrick that Eric Novak had basically just confessed to killing her father.

She hung up and waited, suddenly conscious of how dark and quiet her house was. What if she wasn't alone? She strained her ears and listened. A muted sound seemed to come from upstairs.

Fear had her opening the drawer that contained her homeowners' association phone book. Opal flipped through it, then tapped out Monty's number, all the while aware that he had a woman over.

"Monteague."

Just the sound of his voice was reassuring. "Hi, this is Opal. Listen, I know you're busy, but something just happened, and I could use your take on it."

His leather sofa creaked. "What's wrong?"

She obviously hadn't hidden her fright well. "I just got a threatening phone call on my home phone. I know my timing is bad."

She thought he might offer up an excuse. Instead, he said, "Be right there," and hung up.

Opal pulled a notepad from the same drawer that held her directory and scribbled down Eric's exact words to her. Then she dashed to her porch to wait for Monty.

～

Monty found Opal standing on her front porch, arms locked across her midriff. "I'm sorry to bother you. I know you have a guest over," she said by way of greeting.

He glanced toward the car backing out of his driveway. "Tracy was just dropping by." Opal's call had given him just the excuse he needed to send the party girl on her way.

Opal gestured. "Please, come in. I wrote down exactly what the caller said."

Her kitchen still smelled of spices from whatever she'd been baking the other night. Several cloth grocery bags were folded on her countertop. Next to them was a piece of paper. She handed it to him, then gauged his reaction as he read it. Under the message was a phone number.

"This is the guy who's been harassing you," Monty guessed.

"Eric Novak. He acknowledged it was him. What he said to me was a threat, right? Plus, he basically admitted to killing my father."

Monty didn't bother correcting her assumption. "Was he your father's partner?"

"Yes, and a good friend, too. He's the one who stole the ricin, we think."

"And then murdered your father?"

"Yes."

"I thought you said the FBI was working on this."

"Not yet; not officially. But we were told to call if there are any new developments, so I did, right before I called you. Hopefully, Special Agent Fitzpatrick will get back to me."

"I hope so, too. Is there anything I can do for you while you wait?"

Opal shuddered. "Um. Yes, please. I thought I heard a noise upstairs. I'm sure it was nothing, but maybe you could check?"

Her vulnerability paired with the civilian clothing—soft, faded jeans and a pink sweater that highlighted her subtle curves—made him want to hug her. "Sure. Be glad to."

"Great." She led him toward her staircase in the foyer. "I'm so glad Ruby isn't here right now. She would be freaking out."

Like Opal wasn't? Monty led the way up the stairs while Opal trailed him, her expression alert. Her home was smaller than his, with the master on the second floor. Its classical décor, the tidy surfaces, and the light, rosy fragrance appealed to him. He peeked into her master bathroom, happy to see the plantation shutters closed. He looked under her bed—not even a lost sock down there—and inside of her walk-in closet, perfectly organized, just like his.

"Clear here."

Opal led him to the second bedroom. Ruby occupied what would have been a lovely guest room. She'd left the bed unmade, clothes on the floor. He checked under the bed and in the closet. Nothing here, either. "Better safe than sorry," he said to Opal, who was starting to look chagrined.

They went to the third room, which Opal used as an office. Like her bedroom, it was a pleasant space filled with bookcases and a desk.

"Would you like to see my father's journal?"

Monty looked over at the unexpected question. "Sure."

Opal opened the top drawer of her desk and withdrew a hardcover notebook. She flipped to the last few pages, then handed him the book and pointed. "Start reading here."

Monty scanned the entries as quickly as possible, given her father's quirky penmanship. The paragraphs were short and concise, signs of a logical thinker.

Tuesday, December 9. Eric's been acting differently ever since the ricin went missing. He must be worried Sonja isn't going to make it. Poor man. I know exactly how he feels.

Thursday, Dec 11. Eric is so distracted at work. I find myself going behind him to check that he's taking accurate measurements and documenting every step. He said his wife is getting state-of-the-art medical treatment. Still, I know he's worried about her.

Monday, Dec 15. Eric stepped away from his desk today, and I saw that he'd been checking his personal email, so I went to close it for him. There was an open message from someone I didn't know, citing the transfer of a lot of money. It shocked me. I wonder if Eric did steal the ricin and then sold it to someone. I printed out the message. Tomorrow, I'll ask him about it.

Monty looked up into Opal's anxious gaze. "Wow. And this is the final entry."

"Yes. There's a copy of the email folded inside the back cover."

Monty found it and skimmed its contents. "Sixty-four thousand dollars was wired this morning to the account specified," he read aloud. He looked up, reading apprehension in Opal's expression. No wonder the sisters were convinced Eric had killed their father. "How much time elapsed between your father's last entry and his death?"

"Less than two weeks. He died right after Christmas."

Two weeks was plenty of time for their father to have confronted Eric, then for Eric to have taken measures to keep their father silent. His message took on a more sinister aspect. Monty put the email back and returned the journal to Opal, who put it back in the drawer. "Well, I hope the FBI gets busy on this mystery," he told her. "You going to be okay waiting for the agent to call you back?"

"Oh, yeah. I'm good now. Really."

Her brave little smile didn't fool him for a moment. "When is your sister getting home?"

"Oh, an hour maybe. I'll be fine."

"You're sure?" He wasn't in a hurry to return to his empty house.

"Yes. I feel foolish for interrupting your evening."

"Don't." He realized he enjoyed being with Opal more than with Tracy, even under these strange circumstances. "Call anytime."

She seemed to flush. "Thanks."

Neither of them spoke as she led him back downstairs. He wished he could think of a reason to stay.

"Good night," she said, opening her door for him.

"Take care." He was stepping off her porch when he heard Opal's cell phone ring. Hopefully, that was the special agent calling her back.

Sitting in the windowless office of his penthouse apartment, Casey Fitzpatrick logged into the Trilogy platform used by the FBI to check his email. There it was, the information he'd been waiting for: a complete description of the original investigation over the stolen ricin. Fitz had requested it the same day he'd spoken with Ruby Bonheur.

Now Ruby's sister, Opal, was also getting harassed by their father's former colleague.

The fact that Eric Novak was so threatened by the Bonheur sisters suggested the man knew far more than he'd admitted to in the original investigation. When the ricin first went missing, all the employees at BioTech, including Danny Bonheur and Eric Novak, had been investigated as potential suspects, their bank accounts scrutinized. Contrary to the email printout tucked into the back of Daniel Bonheur's journal, referencing a large sum of money paid to Eric Novak into the "account specified," there hadn't been any large deposits placed in any account associated with Novak's social security number. He'd been dismissed as a suspect. Yet, he was evidently culpable somehow, or he wouldn't be so worried about a renewed investigation.

That didn't mean he'd killed his colleague, however. As Fitz had pointed out to an anxious Opal the previous evening, Novak's words could merely be interpreted as a warning. Nonetheless, he'd made himself a person of interest in the Bureau's eyes. Fitz was definitely reopening the investigation. His first course of action was to question Novak in person, but that turned out not to be so easy. Fitz had gone to BioTech, where Novak was still employed, only to find the man hadn't shown up to work for the past two weeks. His pay had been suspended. Nobody had seen him since.

Finding Novak required more resources at his disposal than Fitz presently had. He was forced to rely on the help of the Virginia Beach Police Department. Wondering if they had any updates for him, Fitz snatched up his cell phone and called the detective he'd spoken with just that morning.

"Hey, it's Fitz from the Bureau again," he said when Boswell Skags answered. "Any luck with picking up Eric Novak yet?"

"Ah, not yet." Skags was chomping on gum, making loud smacking noises. "Looks like he's laying low, but he's in the NCIC, so it won't take us long to locate him."

"I want you to call me if you pick him up."

"Whatever you say, boss."

Skags hung up on him, and Fitz heaved a worried sigh. The VBPD, like the FBI, was stretched pretty thin. He could only hope that between them and the Bureau, they could keep Novak's prediction from coming true. Nobody needed to die next, especially not the Bonheur sisters.

CHAPTER 8

*R*uby applied eyeliner with dramatic strokes, all the while scowling as she considered the likelihood of an unprofitable evening ahead of her. Opal was right. Waitressing was not a career—at least not in this oceanfront city. She couldn't live like this forever, with cash to burn one month, empty pockets the next.

The worst thing was subletting her apartment to a couple of friends because she couldn't afford to pay the rent herself. Could she trust them to care for her cherished stuff—her salt lamps, her colorful quilt, the framed painting of the house she'd grown up in? How long would she be forced by her financial circumstances to live like a gypsy?

Assessing the results of her heavy hand, Ruby realized she looked just like a gypsy. With a huff of annoyance, she reached for a tissue to tone down her makeup. But then the doorbell rang. Ruby froze, suddenly aware that she was home alone. Opal wasn't due in until six o'clock that evening, and, according to the police, Eric Novak was hiding from the law.

Peering out of the powder room, Ruby eyed the front door. The visitor was a man. She could tell as much by his broad-shouldered silhouette, visible through the oval glass insert, with a pink-washed sky behind him.

But he didn't look like Eric, who she remembered being tall and spindly.

Wetting her scarlet-tinted lips, Ruby tiptoed to the door for a better view. The man had turned to admire the sunset. All that she could see was a broad back and dark hair. There was something vaguely familiar about him. It definitely wasn't Eric.

As Ruby pulled the door open, the stranger turned. She gasped. It was the driver of the Honda Civic, wearing a white T-shirt and jeans, in lieu of a uniform. He looked even younger than he had the other day. She went to slam the door in his face, but he was faster than she was, jamming a boot between the door and the threshold.

"Go away!" Ruby pushed the door with all her might, but his boot held it open.

His gaze had fastened with incredulity on the logo emblazoned across her cropped orange T-shirt, paired with tiny black shorts. "You're a Showstoppers girl?"

It was none of his business. "Get lost or I'll call the cops."

He had the gall to laugh. "Oh, I don't think so. You didn't want cops to come last time, remember?"

"Look," she said, alarmed that the Joey-from-*Friends*-lookalike had gone to such lengths to find her, "I don't want you here. What part of get lost don't you understand?"

He folded his muscle-popping arms across his chest. "You owe me dinner to cover the cost of fixing my car."

Ruby's gaze swung to the car sitting at the curb. "It's already fixed," she noted, annoyed that he had the money to fix it, yet here she was pretty much broke.

"And you still owe me dinner."

His implacable tone belied the glimmer in his chocolate-brown eyes. He was laughing at her!

"I don't have time for this." Ruby glanced at her cell phone. "I'm going to be late for work."

"No problem. I'll go with you."

"You certainly will not!"

"Can I be of help?"

The familiar voice drew Ruby's grateful gaze to the neighbor as he cruised around the bushes in front of the porch and put a foot on the first step. Monty, as Opal called him, must have been about to slip into his hot tub. All he wore were his swim trunks, paired with a towel around his neck. Yo, no wonder Opal was in love with him!

Little Joey ought to have taken one look at the bigger man and fled. Instead, he turned back to Ruby and said incredulously, "Who is this?"

"I said, can I be of assistance?" The neighbor's tone was so cold that even Ruby shivered.

She rushed to explain. "This boy won't leave me alone. Now I'm going to be late for work."

Monty started mounting the steps to the porch. "Sounds like you'd better take a hike."

The brat totally ignored him. "Isn't he a little old for you?" he asked Ruby.

She rolled her eyes at his assumption.

Monty, who didn't like being ignored, asked Ruby without taking his eyes off Little Joey, "Is this the person who's been harassing you?"

Little Joey turned to face him, prepared to duke it out.

Ruby couldn't watch. "Hold up." She leaped outside between the pair. "No," she said to Monty, "this is just some kid who's mad because I back-ended his car the other day. This guy," she warned Little Joey, "is a Navy SEAL. You do not want to mess with him. Now leave me alone."

To her surprise, Little Joey snapped to attention. "Special Operator Second Class Tony Caruso, at your service, sir! I'm sorry, sir, I didn't realize."

What?

The menace went right out of the neighbor's posture. His expression turned pleasant. "James Monteague, Lieutenant Commander."

The two men sidestepped Ruby and pumped hands.

"Nice to meet you, sir. You live next door?"

"Yes, I do. What Team are you with?"

"Six, sir, DEVGRU."

"You don't say."

Ruby couldn't believe this was happening. Little Joey was also a SEAL. The odds were astronomical.

They both turned their heads to stare at her.

"She owes me a dinner," Tony explained to Monty.

"I am *not* taking you out to dinner!"

"Deal's a deal." Tony pulled a ring out of his pocket. "She even gave me this ring as a token of her honor."

Monty glanced at the ring, then frowned at her. "Does your sister know about this?"

Ruby snatched the ring out of Tony's fingers and jammed it onto her left pinkie. "I am twenty-four friggin' years old. I do not have to tell my sister everything!"

"Then act your age," he suggested, mildly. "You said you'd take him out to dinner."

Ruby threw her hands into the air. "Fine. We're going to Showstoppers. I'll pay for your dinner there."

The commander looked inquiringly at Tony.

The boy SEAL grimaced, like that wasn't his first choice. "That'll work," he conceded.

"See you around, Tony." With a nod at Ruby, Monty pattered barefooted down the steps to return to his hot tub.

Ruby glared at the upstart. "You'll have to follow me," she growled. "And try not to get me into any more trouble than I'm already in for being late."

He didn't make any promises, she noticed.

Between the boxing match on the widescreen TV and the action in the restaurant behind him, Tony didn't suffer a dull moment. He sat at the bar, jump-starting his five-course meal with an appetizer: raw oysters on the half shell.

As Ruby sashayed past him, he slurped the delicate meat from the shell as loudly as possible. She made a face of disgust and looked away.

An hour crept by, and Tony's appetite stirred enough to request an entrée. Torn between a bacon cheeseburger and snow crab legs, he ordered both, chuckling at the look of dismay on Ruby's face when she realized how much his dinner was going to cost her.

"Are you really going to eat all this?" she demanded when she brought him his food.

He couldn't resist teasing her. "Don't worry, *Bella.* I promise to leave room for dessert."

She blinked at his endearment, undoubtedly understanding it. "Don't call me that. You're just a child." She stormed off, leaving a cloud of sweet perfume in her wake.

Her words didn't faze him. Tony was used to being teased about his age. He was the youngest candidate ever to attend Basic Underwater Demolition/SEAL training in Coronado. That was where he'd gotten the code name that still stuck with him, Bambino, which meant baby in Italian. In spite of his nickname, he'd managed to prove he was any SEAL's match.

He'd been the man of the house from the tender age of ten. His home, on the south side of Philly, was surrounded by gangbangers and drug traffickers. He would've been trapped in that way of life, too, if not for his mother's illness. God had been waiting for Tony to ask for help. Since then, God had cleared the way for him, making all things possible—even winning over Ruby Bonheur.

Tony ate half of his burger before he set it aside and ordered Key Lime Pie. When Ruby served it, she thumped it down in front of him, obviously resentful of the bill he was ringing up.

"You want some pie?" He carved off the tip and held it up to her.

"No." She spun away to check on customers.

Too full to make a dent in his pie, Tony played with the whipped cream. Ruby glanced over at him while carrying a tray laden with half-empty glasses and dirty plates. Her toe caught the leg of a stool. The tray tipped. Tony cringed. Two cups toppled, spraying ice chips and soda all over the wall, but with a quick adjustment, Ruby righted the tray before the plates shared a similar fate.

"Good save!" Tony cheered, drawing a small thankful smile out of her.

"Ruby!"

Her smile vanished as the matronly manager descended. Ruby put the tray down and dropped to her knees to gather up the far-flung ice cubes.

"I knew that had to be you." The manager stood over her, lips pursed into a knot, not helping.

Ruby swept the cubes into one of the cups. "Sorry."

"Sorry doesn't cut it. If you drop anything else tonight, you're fired."

Tony expected Ruby to sass back. Instead, she called to the barkeeper's helper, "Can you toss me some paper towels?"

Feeling bad for her, Tony made a point to catch her eye. "Hey," he called, ignoring the manager's sharp glance. "If we never made mistakes, we'd never get better. I'm sure your boss knows that."

The boss in question shot him a peculiar look.

Ruby made a choking sound. He couldn't tell if she was grateful or contemplating murder as she dabbed the walls and then the rug.

Tony directed his attention out the windows. The sky had turned from pewter to black. The restaurant was beginning to empty. He looked back at the TV, catching the ninth round of the boxing match. Out of the corner of one eye, he saw Ruby take a biker couple's order. He thought he saw the old man put his hand on the back of her leg, just below her very-short shorts.

Tony waited for Ruby to come near him. "Did that old lech just grope you?"

She breezed past, not making eye contact. "I don't think so."

"What do you mean, you don't *think* so?"

She marched to the end of the bar where the bartender had set out two drinks for her. "It's no big deal."

"No big deal?" If Ruby was his little sister—Corinna—Tony'd make a really big deal out of it.

She breezed past him again with two Long Island Iced Teas. "Relax, Tony. I know how to handle it."

He had a hunch she did, but as she set the drinks in front of her customers, Tony kept an eye on her, just in case. To his astonishment, the sixty-something biker with a thin braid hanging down his back put his hand right where he'd put it the last time.

Ruby removed the hand, set it on the tabletop, and gave it a pat. *Good boy. Down, boy.*

She called that handling it? Tony stood. This was wrong.

As she doubled back with the couple's food orders, she intercepted his path. "Go back to your chair," she hissed, looking worried. "Don't you dare get me into trouble!"

"I'm just going to talk to him."

"Oh no you're not." She darted an uneasy glance at the manager who was standing behind the bar.

"Is there a problem, Ruby?" The woman's voice was like nails on a chalkboard.

Ruby shot her a fake smile. "Not at all."

"Actually, there is." Tony spun around to face the manager. "Do you allow your waitresses to be groped by customers?"

The unhappy woman sighed. "They're expected to deal with it."

"And I did," Ruby assured her. Shooting Tony a quelling glare, she continued toward the kitchen.

Tony resumed his seat where he watched the manager scrutinizing Ruby with a sour expression. How could anyone work in this environment? In his three years as a SEAL, Tony had faced down giants, but never alone. Every man on the Teams gave a 110 percent toward a common cause. None of that was happening here. It was Ruby doing all the work while the manager just stood there waiting to criticize her. Ruby deserved better.

Tony reached into his wallet and pulled out three crisp twenty-dollar bills. The next time Ruby passed him, she was slipping the bikers' meager tip into her pocket. He held out his twenties and said, "I'm ready to pay up."

She blinked down at the money, then up at him. Relief vied with skepticism. "Are you sure?"

"Yep."

"Okay. I'll be right back with your change."

"The change is for you."

He watched her swallow. All she managed was a nod.

As she put his money in the cash register, the manager came and stood next to her. Tony watched the woman, waiting for more criticism.

"Don't forget to tip the hostess and the kitchen staff. Twenty percent of your tip is six dollars." She held out a pudgy hand.

Ruby handed over six dollars wordlessly, then brought Tony his receipt. Over her shoulder, Tony saw the manager pocket the six dollars. He stepped off his stool and snagged Ruby's arm before she could get away.

"Hey, she just took that tip money for herself," he relayed loudly enough for the manager to hear. "Tell her you quit."

Ruby's widening gaze flew from him to the manager's reddening face. "I can't quit," she whispered.

"Sure you can. This isn't the place for you."

"You know what?" The manager went on the offensive, no doubt to deflect Tony's accusation. "You don't have to quit. I'm firing you. You've been a mess since the day I hired you."

Stalking into the kitchens, the manager departed, leaving Ruby sucker punched.

"It's okay." Tony held her stunned gaze. Having watched her stow her purse behind the bar when they'd first come in, he retrieved it. Then he towed a speechless and resisting Ruby toward the exit. "Come on, *Bella*. You don't need this place."

Cold air hit them as he hustled her out of the restaurant. "Do you have a jacket?"

Her jaw was set at a dangerous angle. "In my car." She dug into her oversized purse and came up with her keys.

Tony snatched them from her hand.

"Give me those!"

He held them out of her reach. "You're not driving anywhere right now." Spying what looked to be a sweater lying on the front seat of her car, he unlocked the driver's door and retrieved it, then shut the door before she could get in.

Her copper ringlets caught and held the light of the Showstoppers sign behind her. "I'm going to kill you!" she said through her teeth.

"Count to ten instead." He held up her sweater so she could put it on. "And then I'll let you hit me."

"Ugh." She wrenched the garment out of his hands and stormed ahead of him, threading her arms through the sleeves as she stomped across the parking lot toward an indoor shopping mall.

Tony took off after her. "Are you counting?"

"Ten!" She whirled without warning. He caught a fist in the gut and a cuff on the side of the head.

"Ouch, that hurt." He was impressed.

"I can't believe you just got me fired!" She shoved him for good measure. "Who do you think you are? I needed that job. Thanks a lot, you jerk!"

"No problem." Tony knew from experience you had to hit rock bottom before you asked for help.

Hearing her voice crack, Ruby fled across the parking lot, scattering the seagulls hunkered down for the night.

A car that was backing up blared its horn as she stepped into its path. The driver shouted obscenities. Ruby shouted one back.

How was she going to pay her rent now? There weren't any jobs near the beach at this time of year. She'd be crashing at her sister's place until springtime, providing Opal didn't kick her out first. She had to be tired of having Ruby around.

Heck, Ruby was tired of herself these days.

Tears of frustration stabbed her eyes. She was so intent upon putting distance between Tony and her that she didn't see the manhole cover sticking up above the pavement. She tripped over it in classic Ruby style and landed on her knees on the unforgiving concrete.

Hurt, she rolled over into a sitting position, bowed her head over her scraped knees, and willed herself not to cry.

The air shifted. "You okay?"

"Go. Away." She kept her head down so he wouldn't see the self-pity pooling in her eyes.

She sensed him hunkered next to her.

"Did you hurt yourself? Lemme look."

She lifted her head just enough that he could see her knees. He shifted so his shadow didn't block the light of a streetlamp. "Scraped 'em up good."

No kidding.

"Come on, I'll help you up." Grabbing her forearms, he hauled her to her feet. "Let's go inside." He gestured to the mall doors. "Maybe someone has Band-Aids."

Tony escorted her through one of the glass doors. The stores inside were all closed, except for a dimly lit Irish pub. Jerking free of Tony's touch, Ruby limped ahead of him into what was evidently a local's hangout. A handful of patrons glanced their way as she headed to a booth seat.

"I'll be right back," said Tony.

He was gone for ten seconds, enough time for her to verify that her pantyhose was shredded, and one knee was worse off than the other, with blood sliding down her leg. When Tony returned, he pushed into the space beside her and reached for her legs.

"Don't touch me." But then she saw the damp paper towels in his hands and she grudgingly submitted to his ministrations.

"Sit sideways." He patted his denim-clad thighs.

It wasn't like she had much choice with the table in the way. She swung her legs over his, noting that his thighs were like granite. He pressed the makeshift compresses to both her knees. "Better?"

"Better," she admitted. He had nice, tanned fingers and a surprisingly light touch.

A waitress stepped up to their table. "What can I get you?"

Tony looked up. "You guys have any Band-Aids?"

She flicked a glance at Ruby's knees. "I'll check."

Tony reached for the napkin dispenser at the end of the table and replaced the stained paper towels with clean, dry napkins. "You have beautiful legs." He shot her a smile.

Ruby steeled herself against his flattery, not to mention his Joey-from-*Friends* grin. "I don't know how to get this through your thick skull." She was growing weary of telling him this. "I'm not interested in getting to know you. I don't go out with guys my own age, let alone guys who are younger than me."

His chocolaty stare never wavered. Her words seemed to roll off him like water off a duck's back. "You still owe me a debt," he stated reasonably. "Who paid for my dinner? I did."

"Yeah, and then you got me fired by telling my manager that I quit!"

"Come on," he chided softly. "You deserve a better job than that, and you know it."

The assertion confused her. Ruby closed her mouth with a snap and considered her options. "Fine. I'll buy you a beer, how's that? Or are you even old enough to drink?"

"I'm old enough to die for my country." He managed not to tell her his age. "But I'd prefer a cup of coffee, with cream and sugar, please."

They both looked over at the waitress as she set two big Band-Aids on the table.

"Thank you." Tony slid them closer, then picked one up. "The lady's going to buy me a coffee with cream and sugar."

"And for you?" The waitress eyed Ruby expectantly.

She considered the meager tip money crammed into her pocket. Most of it was from Tony. "Just water for me."

"Coming right up." The woman moved away.

Ruby watched Tony as he stuck Band-Aids over both of her

banged-up knees. "You're good at that," she admitted when he was done. She swung her legs off his.

"I hope so. I'm training to be a medic."

She eyed him with surprise. "Really?"

"Yeah. I like it. I'm planning to go to med school one day. Uncle Sam's going to pay for it."

"Oh, yeah?" There had to be a brain that went with all that brawn for him to say that. "How long have you been a SEAL?" Not that she wanted to know him any better. She was just curious.

"Three years."

No way. "What? Were you like twelve when you joined?"

"Hah, hah. No, I was eighteen." He grimaced, realizing he'd just given his age away.

So, he was only twenty-one years old, three years younger than she was.

"And you don't join the SEALs," he added. "You're selected through one of the world's most rigorous training programs in existence. In my class, only 26 men out of 120 candidates graduated."

Wow. Okay, so that said something for him. Questions crowded Ruby's brain, but she swallowed them, not wanting to give him false encouragement.

Tony kept talking "When I was seven, I saw a documentary on the Discovery Channel about Navy SEALS. It looked like something I wanted to do."

"And now you want to go to med school." She had to say, the man was ambitious.

"Well, yeah. I like challenges. Which is probably why I like you."

He met her gaze suddenly. Ruby's breath caught at the intent expression on his face. "You're wasting your time," she insisted.

"We'll see. Of course, if I want to go to med school, I'll have to finish college first. Every semester I take two classes."

He *was* ambitious. "Good for you."

"What about you? Ever go to college?"

"Yes, I did." And she'd partied like a frenzied animal, not something she was particularly proud about.

"What'd you study?" he persisted.

"Journalism." *When I went to class.*

"And you graduated?"

"Yeah." Thanks to Opal who'd typed up many a paper for her and drove her to rehab until she got her act together.

"So, what're you doing waitressing? You should be on TV or radio or something."

"I could if I wanted to." Ruby dredged up her confidence. "I like the idea of snooping around, finding stories."

"You should do it. What's stopping you?"

"I don't know." To her gratitude, the waitress showed up with their drinks just then. The sooner Tony drank his coffee, the sooner they could go their separate ways.

Their waitress gestured. "Sugar's at the end of the table."

He thanked the waitress, then poured cream into his coffee while Ruby drained half of her water.

"I can picture you on the news." He reached past her to snag two packets of sugar, shook them, then poured the sugar into the cup.

Ruby sighed. He was young and dumb. He knew nothing of the world. "Look, no one's going to hire me," she told him in defiance of his confidence. "My grades were bad. I wouldn't have graduated if my sister hadn't helped me. She even lost a fiancé in the process." Aware that was sounding petulant, Ruby clicked her teeth together and fell silent.

Tony took a thoughtful sip, then put his mug down. "Know what I think? You've forgotten who you are."

Ruby bristled. "Don't talk like you know me better than I know myself. You don't know me at all."

He raised his eyebrows in surprise. "Sure, I do. You are an amazing child of God."

"Yo." Ruby hadn't seen that coming. "Don't tell me you're a religious fanatic."

"Not at all." He shrugged his broad shoulders. "I'm just stating facts here. You think you don't deserve a better life because you've made some mistakes. You've caused yourself and other people pain, but it doesn't have to be that way."

"Oh, boy." This twenty-one-year-old was behaving like an old, wise man telling her what to do. "Do you want another coffee?" Her temper flared yet again. "How many is it going to take for you to leave me alone?"

"Hmm." His eyes narrowed. "The repairs on my car came to 320 dollars."

Ruby swallowed hard.

He drew invisible numbers in the air. "At 2.50 a coffee, I'd have to drink…that's almost 130 of these babies." He saluted her with his mug.

Impressed by his mathematical ability, Ruby reassessed him. There was more to this boy-SEAL than met the eye. "You think you're pretty smart, huh?"

He shrugged nonchalantly, accepting what was obvious.

"So why didn't you go to college instead of SEAL training?"

His mouth quirked ruefully, and his gaze slid off to one side.

"Forget it," she added. "I don't even want to know."

"My mother got sick. She couldn't work anymore."

"Oh." Ruby immediately regretted asking him.

"I had a scholarship to wrestle at Penn State, but…" His sentence trailed off. "It worked out better this way."

She couldn't keep from asking. "Did your mother get better?"

"Yeah, she did."

"Well, that's good." Ruby thought of her own mother and then her father, and her heart folded over on itself.

The conversation lagged.

Tony sipped his coffee, then set his mug aside. "Did I say something wrong?"

"What do you mean?"

"You just dropped off a cliff there," he pointed out.

She gave up hiding her emotions any longer. She felt defeated and weepy, and she missed her beautifully decorated apartment, the one she couldn't afford to return to. "I'm just tired," she said shortly. "I want to go home."

"No problem." He slipped out of the booth. "Stay right here. I'll go get your car."

She stared at him, not understanding. "Why?"

"So, you don't have to walk." He was already on his feet, jingling her keys which were still in his possession. "Be right back."

"But I can..." In the blink of an eye, he was gone. Ruby cast her gaze around the pub feeling suddenly vulnerable. That feeling grew when she reflected that he'd gone off with her car keys. What if he decided just to dump her here? She hadn't been very nice to him.

A couple of minutes crept by. She paid the waitress and reapplied her lipstick, covering up the fact that she was nervous. But then Tony was back, reaching for her hand.

"I'm parked illegally." He helped her to her feet.

"I'm not a cripple," she protested. But the hand clasping hers felt so warm and steady that she didn't tug free. Besides, she felt wobbly on her feet for no reason she could come up with.

Her car was parked with two tires on the curb. He held the driver's door for her as she got in.

"Seat belt," he reminded her.

She looked up at him as she buckled herself. Was this it? Was he going to let her drive away and never bother her again? For some reason, the prospect was anti-climactic.

"If you want to see me again," he still held the door open, "you need to find me first."

"Who says I want to see you again?"

He ignored the question. "Put those sleuthing skills of yours to work. I have total confidence in you." With a wink at her, he shut her car door, turned away, and strode across the parking lot back toward his own car.

Ruby stared after him, utterly bemused. She wanted to lower her window and shout, "In your dreams, I'll find you," but that might sound a little childish. She had no intention of going to look for him, except to prove what she was capable of.

"Amazing child of God," she muttered, scoffing at his assertion. But deep in her chest, a yearning flickered. What if Tony was right about her?

CHAPTER 9

"*C*reepy."

Through her kitchen window, Opal watched the fog drift across her backyard like a flock of legless sheep. Of all the nights for the fog to be so thick, Halloween night seemed particularly apropos. It hovered above her lawn and amongst her bushes, making her backyard look like the setting for a horror movie.

As was her custom, Opal had donned her Roaring Twenties costume, complete with a black sequined dress, long black gloves, and a feathered headband. Decked out in her attire, she stood mixing the batter of her grandmother's legendary pumpkin bread, careful not to get any on her costume. Her hope was that baking would soothe her overwrought nerves as the search for Eric had yet to result in his apprehension.

Or maybe she was on edge because Ruby had confessed that morning that she'd lost her waitressing job. Opal sighed as she scraped the batter into a greased baking pan. Her little sister was never going to move out, let alone grow out of the partying phase. Dressed as a belly dancer, Ruby had taken off to a shindig hosted by a former college roommate. To her credit, she did seem more pensive than usual.

Opal transferred her baking pan into the preheated oven. That simple act reminded her that last year she had sworn to herself she'd be handing out candy with her husband-to-be by this date. Yet, here she was, alone on Halloween night, still relentlessly single. Her prayers for a life partner to come along hadn't been answered yet. Moreover, Steven Parks hadn't called at all lately, though he'd been as charming as ever at the hospital.

Opal's doorbell rang as she was setting the timer on her oven. Adjusting her hairband, she grabbed up her candy bowl and headed for the door. The toddlers awaiting her were so young they had to be prompted by their escorts to utter the magic phrase.

"Trick or treat!"

"How about a treat?" Opal kneeled to be at eye level with a Baby Yoda and a Cinderella, dropping candy into their plastic pumpkins.

As they left, she followed them out onto her porch, where she eyed the fog quilting the grass between her and Monty's homes. She was pleased to see his jack-o'-lanterns glowing on his front steps, a sign that he was handing out treats himself that night. The realization cheered her. She'd always suspected the tough-as-nails SEAL had a soft spot for kids.

The shrilling of Opal's cell phone drew her back inside. Adrenaline spiked as she eyed the unfamiliar number. Praying Eric hadn't discovered her cell number, she braced herself before answering, "Hello?"

"Hey, this is Steven." The friendly voice relieved her fears. "Did I catch you at a bad time?"

It was only seven-thirty. "Not at all. Where are you?" The noises on his end suggested a crowded party.

"I'm at a bar downtown. I was wondering if you'd like to join me. It's kind of a young scene, but the music's good."

"Oh." She was tempted, if only to say that she'd gone on a date. "But it's Halloween. I have to hand out candy."

"What, some little cowboy's holding a gun to your head?" He laughed at his own joke.

"No, but I get a kick out of seeing all the kids dressed up."

"Oh, I know what you mean."

"Would you like to come over here?"

"Uh..." He hesitated, and her hopes started to rise, but then he dashed them. "No, I'd have to ditch some friends. They'd be mad at me."

"I understand." His friends came first.

"How about later this week, though, like on Friday?"

"Friday's perfect." She tried not to sound too eager.

"Okay. I'll see you at the hospital before then. We'll talk some more."

"Sure. Thanks for calling." Opal hung up with renewed hope. Maybe God would answer her prayers for a husband after all.

For the next hour, it seemed as if every child in the neighborhood stopped by Opal's to soak up the attention they knew they would get. She passed out treats to a Mandalorian this time, a Wonder Woman, several Disney princesses, a cheerleader, twins dressed as Crayola Crayons, and a four-year-old firefighter.

At eight o'clock, the younger children vanished. With her candy bowl nearly empty, Opal heaved a sigh of relief. She checked on her bread and decided it needed to bake twenty more minutes. When the doorbell rang again, she opened the door without a second's hesitation.

Her smile froze. In lieu of a trick-or-treater, her stuffed scarecrow sat looking at her from the rocking chair, which had been moved to face the door.

"Okay." With a prick of fear, Opal lowered the candy bowl to the floor of her foyer and stepped onto her porch. Alert for signs of mischievous teenagers, she scanned the bushes around her house, only to realize that the fog offered concealment to anyone who might be lurking nearby.

She was returning the rocking chair to its original spot when someone bounded onto the stoop behind her. Opal turned and gasped as an adult-sized figure wearing a Green Goblin mask loomed next to her. He grabbed her arms and, to her horror, powered her back inside her home, then kicked the door shut.

Opal unleashed a belated scream. One minute she was thinking she was the brunt of a joke. The next, she was grappling with a stranger whose breath rasped through the slits of his rubber mask.

Monty was hoping the endless trickle of children had subsided when his doorbell rang. With a grunt of discomfort, he went to answer it. His back had begun to twinge again with any movement, making him long for one of Opal's massages. He found two adolescents standing on his porch but staring toward Opal's house.

"He scared the crap out of me."

"You think he's a friend of Miss Opal's?"

"I don't think so. I think he just shoved her into her house."

Monty froze with his bowl of Hershey's Kisses held out. "Who shoved Miss Opal into the house?"

One of the youths pointed toward Opal's lawn. "Some man dressed as a goblin. He was hiding in the bushes and scared us from her door. He just pushed her into the house."

Concerned, Monty shoved the bowl of chocolate at the kids and left his home, running through the knee-high fog to Opal's. His concern was probably unwarranted—a neighbor playing a hoax. But with Eric on the loose, he didn't want to assume anything.

Her porch light was on. Her door was closed. Not a goblin in sight.

But as he peered through the beveled-glass insert on her door, he could see a tall, dark figure shaking her.

Monty pounded on the door.

The Green Goblin's face whipped in his direction. Then the stranger wheeled away, fleeing down the hall toward the back of the house.

It was all the invitation Monty needed to go after him. He pushed through the unlocked door, passing a stricken Opal as he gave chase.

The man had fled through the French door in the family room, leaving it wide open. Monty tore through it, ran off Opal's deck and through her backyard. The sound of running feet had him chasing the goblin around the house. Fog swirled in funnels before him, letting him know he was close. Slowed by the sharp pangs in his back, he hobbled toward the street until he came to the sidewalk.

The footsteps had ceased. Monty stopped and listened, stilling his breathing, but all he could hear was the chatter of older children. Glow-in-the-dark night sticks bobbed here and there.

A car engine throttled suddenly, and Monty pivoted toward the sound. Brake lights flared as a car not fifty yards away from him squealed away from the curb. It sped recklessly out of the neighborhood with its headlights extinguished. Monty couldn't make out the plates. He watched helplessly as the car disappeared.

Ignoring the spasm seizing his back, he returned to Opal's via the front door and found her standing right where he'd left her, petrified by shock. He strode past her to close the French door. "You look like you've seen a ghost, not a goblin."

His attempt at humor got no response. He returned to assess her. "You okay?"

She looked like she'd stepped right out of Downton Abbey. She wore a shimmering black dress, complete with a fringe at the hem and matching silk gloves. A sequined headband with a white feather had slipped to one side. She pulled it off and laid it on the entryway table.

"I take it that was Eric?"

She nodded. "I've never been so scared in my life."

The impulse to hug her nearly got the better of him. Instead, he briskly rubbed her bare upper arms, finding her skin silky to the touch. "But you're safe now. I hate to admit it, but he got away from me. Can't exactly run like I used to."

Her gaze sharpened at his words. She searched his face. "Your back is killing you, isn't it?"

It touched him that she would think of his comfort. "I'm fine," he lied.

She gave herself a visible shake. "Wait, how did you even know to come over?"

"I heard some kids talking about a man in a mask. It sounded suspicious."

"I'm so glad you came." Without warning, she closed the gap between them, put her arms around his waist, and hugged him.

His right arm folded automatically around her. Caught off guard by how soft and sweet she felt, how she smelled of autumn spices, Monty kept quiet.

With a sharp inhale, Opal released him, stepping back with a self-conscious glance at his face.

"What did Eric say to you?" Monty asked.

Her brow puckered as she thought back. "He didn't make a lot of sense. First, he said he didn't kill my father. He said something about his wife being sick—he needed money to pay her doctor bills. I think I believe him, too. But then, who did kill my father?" She considered the question for a moment. "Then he became frantic and started shaking me and telling me that my sister and I had made a horrible mistake by getting the authorities involved. He said we were all going to end up dead."

Both the quaver in her voice and fear widening her eyes summoned Monty's empathy. "No one's going to die. But we need to call the special agent working on this case. Come have a seat." He coaxed her to the little table in her kitchen, pushed her gently into a chair, then set the cell phone he'd spotted on the kitchen counter down in front of her.

With a look of resolve, Opal consulted her contact list and put her call through. Listening to her relay what had happened to the agent, whom she called Fitz, Monty couldn't help but admire her strength. Even in this stressful situation, she was keeping it together. Ruby was right to have defended her so vehemently.

"They're on their way," Opal finally relayed, putting her phone down.

"They?"

"Fitz and a Virginia Beach police detective."

All at once her oven started to shrill. Opal jumped in her seat, betraying the taut state of her nerves, but then she got up and went over to it.

A mouth-watering aroma filled the air as she cracked the oven door. Moving with brisk efficiency, she grabbed an oven mitt, placed the loaf on the stovetop, and tested it with a toothpick.

"Perfect." She glanced over at Monty. "Would you like some pumpkin bread?"

His mouth watered. "Sure, why not?" They might as well eat while waiting for the authorities.

"It's going to be hot," she warned, reaching for a bread knife.

A minute later, she laid a plate with a buttered slice on the small table. "Have a seat."

As Monty sat down, she went to the refrigerator, poured him a glass of milk, and brought it to him, along with a fork.

"Aren't you going to have some?" he asked as she sank into the chair opposite him.

"I'm a little too nervous to eat. Please don't let that stop you. I'll have some later."

As he carved out his first bite, Monty waited for the intimacy of the setting to make him uncomfortable, but the feeling never came. He took a second bite, moistened it with a sip of milk, and went straight for a third.

He had to admit, "This is even better than my mother's. Please don't tell her I said that."

"Your mother?" Opal's blue eyes lit up with interest. "Where does she live?"

"In a Winnebago with my father. They're currently touring New Mexico, planning to hit up every state in the nation."

"That's wonderful!"

He thought he heard a hint of envy in her voice.

"Are they coming this way to visit you?"

"Yes, for Thanksgiving." Not that he had invited them.

She cocked her head at his unenthusiastic tone. "Are you not close to your parents?"

"Well, yeah. I'm an only child, and they're great parents, the best." Plus, he loved the fact that they were still in love with each other. All the same, he didn't want to hear their concerns about the recent tragedy, of which he'd told them the barest of details. Nor did he want to hear them hinting that it was time for him to settle down. Like he could just grab the next woman to come along and have the same perfect marriage they had.

"They're not used to seeing me all scrawny and scratched up." He uttered the only excuse he could think of. "I need to put on some weight by Thanksgiving."

"Have another slice of bread." Opal snatched up his empty plate and went to serve him more of it. "I wish I had two parents," she said at the kitchen counter.

Monty had only heard about her father's tragic death. "What happened to your mother?" He searched her face as she returned his plate to him and sank into her chair, looking sad.

"She died from a diabetic coma when I was a college freshman. Ruby was only thirteen."

Monty froze with his fork in the air. Her words had startled him. He regarded her, marveling that she'd turned out so squared away. First a mother's early demise, then her father's murder. Anyone else would be a mess, yet there Opal sat, composed and kind.

"I'm so sorry." He thought of his own terrible circumstances and his throat tightened. "How did you...?" He couldn't find the words.

"Get through all that?"

She had no trouble reading his thoughts, apparently. "Yeah."

"Well..." She broke eye contact and heaved a long sigh. "Two things helped, I guess. The first is that our grandmothers, both of whom were widowed, moved into our house and helped my father take care of Ruby."

"It took two of them?" He couldn't help the comment.

Opal smiled wryly. "Yes."

"Where are they now?"

"They live in Florida together. They became the best of friends."

"That's nice. And the second reason?"

She paused again, making him suspect it might be personal. "Um, I guess I'm just lucky. Whenever life gets tough, and I'm praying for help, I've always felt a still, small voice saying, *It's going to be okay. I'm still here.*"

The serenity in her expression shook him. What he wouldn't give to hear reassurance like that! "Whose voice?" He needed to hear her say it.

She shrugged and said simply, "God's."

Reflective, Monty forked a bite of his second serving into his mouth and chewed, scarcely tasting the moist morsel. Chagrin steamrolled him for having thought of Opal as anything less than angelic.

He put his fork down and swallowed hard. "Listen, I owe you an apology."

She shook her head. "No, you don't."

"Yes, I do. I misjudged you. I said harsh things to you that you don't deserve."

He covered her little hand and squeezed it, surprised by the warmth that stole up his arm and sped up his heart rate

"Forgiven," she replied. "Besides, if you hadn't come over tonight, who knows what Eric would have done to me."

The ringing doorbell had him pulling his hand back. Monty got up, joining Opal as she jumped up to answer.

At the door, they discovered that both lawmen had arrived at the same time. They both eyed Monty inquisitively.

"Thank you for coming," Opal greeted them. "This is my neighbor James Monteague."

Neither man wore a uniform. The ginger-haired gentleman

dressed in a burgundy suit with an orange tie extended a hand to Opal first. "Special Agent Casey Fitzpatrick. We finally meet."

At the rasping sound of his voice, Monty glanced at the man's neck, noting the scar there. Damaged voice box.

"Call me Fitz," added the agent, who extended a hand to Monty next.

Monty supplied his own moniker. "Monty."

Fitz gestured to the man next to him. "This is Detective Boz Skags."

The larger man had a scarred complexion and gum in his mouth. He nodded at the both of them, keeping his hands in his pockets.

"Please, come in." Opal invited them into the foyer where, with only a trace of her prior fear, she walked them through what had happened. "He was shaking me and telling me that we were all going to die when Monty burst through the door."

Both lawmen looked at him.

"Some kids alerted me to a man dressed as a Green Goblin," Monty explained. "I chased him out the back door and around the house, but he beat me to his car and took off. I have a back injury," he tacked on, humiliated by his inability to catch a civilian.

The special agent folded his arms across his chest. "Here's what I know about Eric Novak." He spoke primarily to Opal. "What he told you was true; he didn't kill your father. The original investigation into Danny Bonheur's death clearly states Novak was attending his wife's funeral the day of the accident."

"Oh." Opal's expression softened with compassion.

"Apparently, she'd been fighting cancer for years. Unfortunately, that ties into what Novak told you about needing money to pay for his wife's doctor bills. I think we can take his words as a confession that he *did* steal the ricin and, in exchange, the buyer or some third party paid off Sonja Novak's medical bills."

Monty didn't get it. "Then why threaten Opal?"

Fitz fixed green eyes on him. "Like I suggested to Opal the other night, he might not be threatening her, so much as warning her."

"About what?" Monty asked.

"Taking her evidence to the police."

Opal looked up at Monty. "Apparently, Ruby said something to Eric about Daddy's journal the first time she called him."

Fitz grimaced. "Apparently, Novak is concerned about a renewed investigation. The buyer, who must have trusted Novak to keep his identity a secret, now poses a threat to Novak, who's no doubt fearing for his life—and yours." He nodded at Opal.

The detective gave a loud sniff. "Yeah, I was about to say all that."

Opal heaved a sigh of understanding. "So, it's the buyer we have to worry about. That could be anyone."

Fitz nodded. "I can't see who paid off Sonja Novak's medical bills until I get permission to look at them. In the meantime, Skags here is going to arrange for round-the-clock protection." He turned to the detective for confirmation.

Skags cringed as if to say it was going to be difficult. "We'll do our best."

"How much longer before you get permission to look at those bills?" Opal asked Fitz.

"The warrant could come through any day. I'll let you know."

Opal smiled at the two men. "Thank you both for coming over."

Wanting to speak to the lawmen in private, Monty inquired whether they would like to go out back with him. "I'll show you the way Novak left."

"Sure." Skags handed his card to Opal while assuring her the security measures would be put into place as soon as possible.

Monty then led the two men through the French door, off of Opal's deck, and into her yard, where Skags strobed a flashlight across the lawn, looking for anything Novak might have dropped. By the time they'd rounded the house to stand in the front lawn, he'd found nothing.

Monty pointed to where the intruder had parked his car. "It looked like an older model Buick, definitely an American car, dark in color, but that's all I've got. I couldn't make out the tags."

Fitz turned to Skags who said, "Eric Novak drives a 2012 Buick

Regal. He's been moving from one motel to another, paying in cash. We figure he's running from the buyer. We'll pick him up soon enough."

The way Fitz slid his hands into his pockets, Monty could tell he wasn't so sure about that.

"Listen." Monty pitched his voice lower. "I know I'm just a neighbor, but I'm on leave at the moment, so I'm home most of the day, which makes me Opal and Ruby's first line of defense until you arrange for security. I'd like you to take down my number and keep me in the loop if you would."

Fitz pulled out his cell phone and took down Monty's contact information.

Skags just passed him a card. "You can call me. I'd best go now and put in that security request. Goodnight to you both." With a curt nod, he turned and trudged across the yard toward the white Pontiac parked at the curb.

Fitz also handed Monty a card. "Do you know, by chance, Lieutenant Strong from SEAL Team Six? He used to play tight end for the Dallas Cowboys."

Monty blinked. He hadn't mentioned to either lawman that he was a SEAL. "I've heard of Strong. Haven't met him yet, though. No."

"Hmm." The agent's keen eyes focused on Monty's scar. "That's quite a battle wound you've got there."

Monty was tempted to bring up the scar on Fitz's neck, but he held himself in check.

"Well, Miss Bonheur's lucky to have you next door. I'm sure we'll see each other again. Goodnight." Swiveling on his glossy shoes, Fitz headed toward the silver Lexus parked in Opal's driveway.

Monty followed his retreat with growing suspicion. The only way Fitz could have learned he was a SEAL was for Opal to have told him, in which case she had already shared his secret with somebody. Uncertainty undermined his high regard for his neighbor. Clearly, she wasn't the soul of discretion he'd thought she was. Before long, the whole world might know Monty's history. The media could be swarming his home by dawn.

He had intended to reenter Opal's house, to thank her for the bread and to reassure her that he'd be keeping a sharp eye out. All at once, he didn't want to. Turning his back on her door, Monty strode toward his own home, recalling that he'd left his place unlocked.

Disillusionment dogged his every step, deepening into something like anger. Opal had drawn him to her with her seeming integrity and genuineness. He'd thought he could trust her. But how else could Fitz have known he was a SEAL, if Opal hadn't told him? And why would he have commented on his scar unless he knew about the disaster, too?

Locking his door behind him, Monty stood a moment in his foyer, struck by the lack of enticing smells and the empty, less-than-welcoming feeling of his home. Opal wasn't perfect. No one was. But, for a little while, he'd been thinking he would like to get to know her better. Now he wasn't so sure.

"Huh." Casey Fitzpatrick lowered his iPad onto his chest, mulling over the news story he'd just read. He'd developed a habit of reading the news right before bed—not the smartest habit, since it often kept him awake and worrying. The article was about a chief of staff member found dead in his home, the cause of death unknown.

Fitz had never heard of the man. But, as the writer of the article had pointed out, his death was the fourth unexplained death of a military leader in the past eighteen months. Something about those words had niggled Fitz's intuition.

"People die all the time," he reminded himself.

He himself had almost died one year ago. He'd been tracking down the leader of The Entity, a group of far-right extremists stealing and hoarding weapons. A sniper had been waiting for him in his penthouse apartment, intending to kill him. Fitz, sensing him there, had fired in self-defense, managing to maim the man, but not before Fitz had been shot in the chest.

If not for the St. Michael's medallion his late wife had given him, Fitz would have died instantly. Instead, the bullet struck the medallion, which snapped, sending a piece of shrapnel straight into his throat. Now, he sounded like a gargoyle when he spoke, but things could have ended much worse, all things considered.

What were the odds that the cause of death in all four mysterious deaths was ricin—specifically the kind that had disappeared out of BioTech almost two years to the day? The first death had occurred shortly thereafter.

Fitz took his phone off the bedstand next to him and looked up the number of an acquaintance of his—a mortician by trade.

"Stan, it's Fitz," he said, cutting through pleasantries when the man answered. "You wouldn't routinely test for ricin poisoning in an autopsy, would you?"

"No, never." Stan sounded intrigued.

Fitz didn't explain. "I didn't think so. Thanks, I'll be in touch."

If the night were younger, he would've chatted a while, asked Stan about his much younger wife, but Fitz hung up with his imagination on fire. What would his supervisor think about his latest theory that the recently deceased chief of staff member had died of ricin poisoning? The SSA would demand a motive. That depended on what all four victims had in common, apart from having been top-brass military officers. It shouldn't be that hard to uncover.

Deciding he wouldn't sleep a wink with that question begging an answer, Fitz threw back his quilt, rolled out of bed, and headed for his home office.

CHAPTER 10

*R*uby frowned at her reflection in the antique mirror hanging over the marble-top dresser in Opal's guestroom. "To go or not to go?" The fact that she was still at home at seven o'clock on a Saturday evening was, in itself, a novelty.

Her black stilettos and high-waisted skinny jeans, paired with a cropped turquoise sweater that matched her eyes were suitable for a night on the town. Her friends were probably already at the bar with the cheapest drinks, waiting for her and scoping out the guys.

So, where was her enthusiasm to join them?

She probed her feelings, wondering at her reluctance. It had to be because Eric Novak was still at large. After what he'd done to Opal the other night, leaving bruises on her arms, maybe it wasn't smart to leave the house. On the other hand, Opal had a date tonight; she'd probably like for Ruby to leave.

"So, I'll go." She made up her mind.

But then she thought of Mark Minors who'd flirted with her at Katie's Halloween party a couple of days ago. He was a thirty-three-year-old stockbroker with a fast car, which meant that he ought to appeal to Ruby. Only, she couldn't help but feel like Mark had disrespected her, whereas Tony the boy-SEAL had called her a child of God.

Ruby swallowed the lump in her throat. *Find me.* The challenge Tony had issued was taunting her. It was annoying to admit, but Little Joey had gotten under her skin in an alarmingly short amount of time. She couldn't stop thinking of him.

A knock downstairs pulled Ruby back to the present. She left the room to get her first glimpse of Opal's suitor.

Like Opal's ex-fiancé, Steven the Navy surgeon was of average height, average build, with brown hair and blandly pleasant features. He bestowed a warm smile on Opal as he stepped through the front door. "I've never seen you in civilian clothes. You look nice."

"Thanks."

Ruby watched Opal touch a self-conscious hand to her hair. *Nice?* Ruby thought the compliment a little tepid. Wearing a gold blouse, black skirt, and cute black flats, Opal looked better than nice.

"This is for you." From behind his back, Steven produced a single long-stemmed rose, yellow for friendship.

Good choice, Ruby conceded.

"Oh, I love roses. Thank you." Opal took the gift and held it to her nose.

Ruby headed down the stairs, and they both looked up at her.

"This is my little sister, Ruby," Opal said, making introductions.

Steven couldn't take his eyes off her. "I've heard a lot about you."

Ruby didn't care for the innuendo in his voice. "I can only imagine."

"Aren't you going out?" Her sister sounded worried.

Ruby propped her hands on her waist. "I haven't decided yet."

"It's a Saturday night. When have you not gone out on a Saturday night?"

Ruby narrowed her eyes. "Don't worry. I'll stay out of your way."

"That's not what I meant."

Right, Ruby thought. "I'm just not sure it's safe with Eric on the loose."

Opal's confusion cleared, followed quickly by concern. "Oh, true. Maybe you should stay home."

Steven looked between them. "Eric?"

Opal put a hand on his sleeve. "I'll explain over dinner. Take this jacket off and I'll hang it up for you."

As Ruby started back up the stairs, a glance over her shoulder showed Opal putting Steven's jacket in the closet while her beau admired Ruby's backside. She resisted the urge to stick her tongue out at him.

Monty, the neighbor, had never ogled her like that, she realized, thinking better of him. Since rescuing Opal from Eric's clutches on Halloween night. Ruby's estimation of their neighbor had risen. Then, too, the realization that Opal had a crush on him made Ruby wonder if those two shouldn't end up together. She wouldn't feel so guilty about chasing off Opal's former fiancé if she could get Monty interested in her sister.

Deep in thought, Ruby spilled across the guest bed she'd been sleeping in. Discontentment gnawed at her as she considered all that Opal had done for her—helping her through college, cheering her through rehab. She'd been Ruby's lifeboat even before that, ever since their mother's death over a decade earlier. Their grandmothers had done a commendable job of filling their mother's shoes, but it was Opal who had backfilled the hole left in Ruby's heart, slowly and steadily, with a devotion she was just now realizing. Opal's devotion to her sister had cost her a fiancé. And now Opal was seeing a man who didn't deserve her.

Ruby flipped onto her back and sighed. "It's all my fault." Self-loathing made her stomach hurt. She needed to get a real job. She needed to return to her apartment with all of her candles and pillows and collection of cut glass.

Tony had a real job, the little twit. He probably had his own apartment, too.

"Ugh!" Ruby threw herself off the bed and stalked out of the guestroom into Opal's office. Tonight, she would come up with a résumé instead of going out and fending off Mark Minors. The thought alone made her feel better.

Opal's laptop was sitting on the desk, open and plugged in to a power source. Ruby plopped onto the ergonomic chair in front of it and typed in the password Opal had shared with her. She opened a browser and proceeded to search for a resumé builder.

An hour later, she sat back with a sense of accomplishment. The printer hummed as it spat out what she'd cobbled together—two-thirds fact and one-third fiction. Hopefully, when she submitted it, nobody would question the shades of gray or call up folks she'd listed as references.

Enough for now. Ruby stood and stretched. Tony floated into her thoughts again, prompting an itchy-under-the-skin feeling. *Find me.* The words taunted her. She knew she could if she set her mind to it.

She looked down at the laptop, thinking. She doubted she could find him with an Internet search. Navy SEALs knew to keep their vital records offline. Amongst themselves, on the other hand, Team members likely had a means of finding each other, which meant the SEAL next door could probably find Tony's address for her. But would he do it when she had chastened him soundly not too long ago? Doubtful.

"Hmm." She cast a considering glance at the computer, then stared at the wall in the direction of Monty's house. Did she want to find Tony badly enough to blackmail a Navy SEAL? After all, she knew a secret about him—one he didn't want anybody else to know.

Not a good idea, she decided. There had to be another way. Ruby tapped her painted fingernails on the edge of the desk. Opal had insisted their neighbor was a good guy. Maybe she could appeal to his nobler nature instead of holding information over his head. The first step was to find Monty's phone number, which she'd seen circled in some kind of address book down in the kitchen.

On an alleged quest for food, Ruby tiptoed down the stairs. Once in the kitchen, she spotted Opal and Steven sitting on the couch with a yard between them, watching a movie. Leftover food still sat on the stove. As Opal glanced back at her, Ruby headed toward it. Taking a plate from the cupboard, she helped herself to the last fillet of salmon, a spoonful of broccoli, and the rest of the rice.

As she warmed her plate in the microwave, she opened the drawer where Opal kept her appliance manuals. There was the address book for houses in the neighborhood. Ruby located Monty by his address and imported his number into her cell phone. Then she put the registry away and carried the heated plate back upstairs.

As she picked at her dinner, she rehearsed what she would say. Unable to eat any more, she set down her fork, drew a deep breath, and called him.

"Hello."

She could tell by his tone he thought she was a telemarketer.

"Hey, this is Ruby next door." She kept her tone light and friendly. Ignoring the astonished silence on the other end, she added, "I need to ask you a favor. You know that young SEAL who was over here the other day? I need his address and I was hoping you would find it for me."

The silence stretched on another few seconds before Monty said, "And why would I do that for you?"

To her relief, he sounded as much amused as irritated. She didn't want to have to blackmail him. "Um, because you're a helpful kind of guy. If you weren't, you wouldn't have scared off Eric the other night."

"I see. So, you're willing to take back some of the names you called me?"

"A few of them," she said stiffly.

"Well, thank you for that, but I don't think Tony Caruso would appreciate me giving you his address if he didn't want you to have it in the first place."

"But he does. He told me to find him, and now I am, but I need your help." She bit her lower lip, praying Monty would comply.

"I don't think so, Ruby."

"Wait," she cut in before he could hang up on her. "If you don't tell me, I'll make you."

A dark silence followed her threat. "Opal's been talking to you."

"Hah." She scoffed at his ignorance. "Opal's the last person who would throw you under the bus, Monty. I can't believe you still haven't figured that out about her."

"Then how do you know about me?"

He had picked up on her threat very quickly, but his menacing tone made her nervous. "I'm a trained journalist. I have a nose for stories, but I promise on my mother's grave I won't tell a soul about you if you tell me where Tony Caruso lives. That's all I want to know."

She could hear him breathing on the other end, reviewing his options. Then, in the background, something creaked, suggesting he was getting up. Hope thrummed in Ruby's chest as she waited. She heard clicking noises like he was logging onto his own computer. "Caruso," he murmured, confirming her suspicions.

"Yes."

"You got a pen?"

She cast her gaze to the ceiling. Old people! "Yeah, go ahead." She entered the address into her cell phone as he read it to her. *1005 Shore Drive.* The brat lived right up the street from her apartment complex, on the other side of the road, which meant it backed up to the ocean. "Awesome. Thank you so much. Your story is safe with me."

"It had better be." His growled words were a threat. "Whose car is that in your driveway?" he tacked on.

So, he'd noticed Steven's car. Ruby sought to whip up his jealousy. "Oh, Opal's got a date over, some surgeon she met at work."

Monty grunted. "How long has she been seeing him?"

He didn't sound too thrilled. "It's their first date, and hopefully their last. The man has a wandering eye."

Brooding silence was her only reply.

"Well, gotta run. Thanks for the info." All out of courage, Ruby hung up, then blew out a long breath. With a growing smile, she studied the address on her cell phone. She could get to Tony's place in just minutes.

"Gotcha," she murmured with satisfaction. Question was, what would she do with him once she found him?

Hearing movement downstairs, Ruby picked up her plate to return it to the kitchen. As she came down the steps, she was pleased to see Opal handing Steven his jacket from the closet.

"Thanks so much for coming. I didn't realize you were working tomorrow."

Steven was too busy watching Ruby descend the steps to say anything back. Opal followed his gaze to see what he was looking at.

"Nice meeting you, Ruby."

Steven's flirtatious tone was too much for her.

"I wish I could say the same, sir, but you came here on a date with my sister. Staring at me is inappropriate."

Steven laughed in awkward surprise. He turned to Opal for an explanation. When she simply raised her eyebrows, he backed to the door. "Well, goodnight." He let himself out quickly.

Ruby met Opal's taut expression. "I'm sorry. But you deserve better. That guy is a creep."

Without a word, Opal whirled, marching into the kitchen where she immediately started cleaning up.

Ruby followed her to put her dishes in the dishwasher. "I'm serious, Sis. Every time you looked away, he would stare at me."

Opal scrubbed viciously at the pan in which she'd broiled the fish. "If you haven't noticed," she retorted with an edge to her voice, "there aren't a lot of available men to choose from."

A knock came from the front door, causing both of them to fall quiet and look at each other. Opal turned off the water and quickly dried her hands. Ruby figured Steven had forgotten something. Trailing Opal to the door, she hung back so as not to be seen while still hearing what Steven would say.

"Oh. Hi, Monty."

Opal's startled greeting drew Ruby closer to the door.

"Hey, I'm sorry if my timing's bad." He still sounded surly from his chat with Ruby earlier. "But I thought I could install that lock for you if you bought it."

"The lock. Yes."

Joining her sister in the foyer, Ruby saw the reason for Opal's dazed response. Monty was dressed in a plaid flannel shirt, jeans, and boots that made him look like the Marlboro Man. In lieu of a cigarette box, he carried a power tool.

"Ruby." He sent her a nod and a hard stare.

"Um. It's in the garage." Opal started backing toward the laundry room that led to the garage. "I'll be right back with it." On her way past Ruby, she shot her a warning look.

But Monty already knew that Ruby knew his secret. Shooting him a small smile of thanks, Ruby hurried up the stairs, making herself scarce.

Her disappointing date forgotten, Opal carried the new lock, still in its packaging, back to the foyer, where she found Monty all alone. The serious expression on his face roused her compassion. She imagined he was doing everything in his power to ward off demons, even if that meant helping out a neighbor at almost nine o'clock at night.

"Good idea, bringing your drill." She gestured for him to follow her to her family room. "It might surprise you to know I own a power drill, but it's not charged."

Monty glanced toward her untidy kitchen. "Your date wasn't here very long."

How had he known she'd had a date? "No. He has to work tomorrow."

"Hmm. Any word yet on the Green Goblin's apprehension?"

She grimaced. "No, nothing. The police can't seem to find him."

"That's not cool." The frown he was wearing deepened. "The police should be out front protecting you by now."

"I've been told they're planning to start that soon." Opal unlocked the current deadbolt and stepped back.

Monty set his drill on the end table and cracked the door. "You don't have any pets, do you?"

Opal hugged herself against the cold sweeping in. "Just Sunny." She smiled as he frowned over at her.

His gaze drifted over her pretty outfit, giving her the impression that he liked the way she looked. "He's still coming over?"

"Now and then. He likes it when I make a fire." She gestured toward the fireplace.

Monty glanced toward her hearth and grunted. "Can't say I blame him." He then pried the plate off the deadbolt, exposing the screws underneath.

Opal watched his long-fingered hands as he adjusted the settings on the drill. She imagined him hiding from the Taliban by day, shivering in the cold at night as they hunted him. Compassion made her want to hug him, to tell him everything would be okay, but his grim silence kept a rift between them. She sought a way to relieve it, and her gaze alighted on his cowboy boots.

"Where are you from originally?"

He started to drill, ignoring her question until he'd lifted a screw out of the lock. "Nevada."

Nevada suited him. She waited for him to ask where she was from. When he didn't, she volunteered the information. "I grew up just thirty miles north of here, in a little town called Poquoson. It's on the bay." She tore open the box she was holding as the old lock came apart in Monty's hands. He set the components on her end table and took the new lock she held out to him.

She'd just about given up on getting a response from him when he asked, "Which do you like more, the bay or the ocean?"

Opal considered her reply, then shrugged. "Either one's good. I just need water and sunrises."

Monty grunted. "There are lakes in Nevada."

He was making an effort to be civil. But something had changed since Halloween night when he'd run off Eric, then spent time talking to the detective and to Fitz. He'd kept mainly to himself since then, not visiting until now. She hoped he hadn't slipped into a quagmire of depression.

Silence fell between them as he worked to align the two halves of the lock. His forehead knit with concentration. She longed to ask him whether he was struggling, if it would help to unburden himself on her, whether he'd thought about counseling, but none of that was any of her business, and Monty didn't seem predisposed to talk anyway. Maybe she would bring it up at his next PT appointment.

With a click, the new lock came neatly together. "There we go."

As he looked up, Opal handed him the power drill. He managed a small smile for her. Their fingers brushed in the trade-off, sending an electric impulse up Opal's arm to speed her heart rate. Monty met her gaze. He had felt it too? Probably not.

He bent over, drilling one screw into place and then the other. Eyeing the muscle-corded length of his neck, Opal wished she could massage the tension out of him.

Within seconds, the new lock was secured. "You got the keys?"

Opal lifted a pair of keys out of the box. "Right here."

"I'm sure you realize this, but don't leave the key parked in the lock and don't hang it anywhere close to the door." Monty transferred his drill to his left hand.

Her own hands were full of cardboard and plastic. She didn't want to let him get away, not without re-establishing the easy rapport they'd had the other night. "Thank you so much. This would have taken me hours." The open bottle of wine she and Steven had barely touched gave her an idea. "Can I reward you with a glass of wine?"

Monty followed her gaze, considering the bottle for a moment. "No, thanks, I'm trying not to drink at night."

Remorse shot through her. "I'm so sorry. That was thoughtless of me."

"Not at all."

"I have juice," she added, not expecting a positive response.

"What kind?"

"Cranberry." She held her breath, hoping he'd accept.

"I'll take some."

"Great." Opal tossed the packaging into her recycle bucket in the pantry. Conscious of Monty's silence, she washed her hands quickly before she fetched two small glasses from her cupboard, then poured them both a drink. It occurred to her that he wanted to ask her something but didn't know how.

They both took a sip in silence. Opal blurted the first thought to jump into her head. "Would you like to see a project I'm working on?"

"Sure."

Encouraged by his quizzical expression, she pushed past him toward her dining room. "It's in here."

Snapping on the light in the adjacent room, she showed him the thousand-piece puzzle she'd been working on for a month. It was two-thirds complete and took up half of the cherry tabletop.

Monty couldn't believe what the light of her chandelier displayed—not just a puzzle, but a scene he knew like the back of his hand. "This is Red Rock Canyon. This is where I grew up." She had to know that. That had to be the reason she wanted to show him.

"Are you serious?" Her look of surprise told him she hadn't known.

He bent over the table and touched a portion she'd completed. "Yep. I used to propel off this lip right here." He turned his head to regard her. "You just happen to be putting this together?"

"Well, yes. I have a passion for canyons. I love the colors and the wild, almost other-earthly terrain. I just couldn't live there." She shrugged. "No water."

"Right." No way was anyone that good an actress.

He had come over intending to help her replace her lock and then accuse her of telling her sister—not to mention Fitz—about his tragic story. Yet now that he was in her selfless presence, his suspicion had waned. But then, how had Ruby found out?

"May I?" He put his hand on a chair.

"Sure. I'd love your help." They each took a chair, sitting side by side.

Monty surveyed the puzzle pieces. He fit one under the lip of the overhang. Opal caught onto what he was looking for and slid several dark pieces closer to him.

"Thanks." The scene in front of him inspired a memory. "One night, I slept in a hammock, right here, two thousand feet in the air."

She turned wide eyes at him. "You're kidding me."

"Nope. Slept like a baby." He sighed at the memory, wishing he could sleep like that now, but sleep remained intermittent, fraught with bad dreams. He inevitably awoke in a cold sweat, calling out the name of one of his lost teammates.

"You don't sleep too well these days, do you?"

Opal's gently uttered observation made him frown at her.

"I'm working on it," he told her shortly. As she visibly withdrew from him, he regretted his bristling tone. "Thanks for your concern, though."

Several seconds of silence elapsed.

"I have some tea with chamomile that I take at bedtime," she said in the voice she used at work. "I can send it home with you, if you like."

He realized he would rather speak to the real Opal Bonheur than to his physical therapist. "Sure. Be happy to try it."

She shot him a tiny, grateful smile. Looking at her, it was hard to imagine her gossiping with anyone, not even her sister. Fitz must have heard rumors via his connection with Lieutenant Strong, the SEAL he'd asked Monty about. "Did you tell your sister about Operation Mother Eagle?" The accusation slipped from him.

Opal blanched but looked him straight in the eye. "No." Her full lips firmed. "Unfortunately, she caught me on my laptop reading an article about it, and she put two and two together. I tried to tell her she was wrong, but she could see right through me. Why? Did she say something to you?"

Her anxious tone assured him she was telling the truth.

"Do I need to speak to her?" Opal added.

"No. She promised my story was safe with her."

"When was this?" Opal seemed mystified.

"Earlier this evening. She called me looking for an address. Needless to say, I gave it to her."

Opal gasped, outraged on his behalf. "How dare she do such a thing? I'll make certain she keeps her word. I'm so sorry."

Her small hand clasping his forearm was all the assurance he needed that Opal was still the discreet and giving woman he'd come to know. "I trust her," he prevaricated. "And you," he added.

She removed her hand, visibly flushing. "Thank you."

They both looked back at the puzzle. A comfortable silence fell between them as they both found pieces that fit the area they were working on. To Monty's surprise, he felt an urge to tell Opal what had happened in Afghanistan. Why not, now that he knew he could trust her?

He began by explaining the objective—to save the Americans left behind. He then described how he'd taken Harmony's place because the chief had spiked a fever. Then he sketched a brief description of how everything had gone wrong. By the end of it, tears glistened in Opal's eyes.

Monty sat, no longer working on the puzzle but holding a piece in his hand. "Every day I ask myself if everything would have worked out differently if I'd just let Harmony go instead of taking over."

Opal shook her head.

"What if I did it for selfish reasons?" He articulated the question tormenting him. "Maybe I was craving excitement. I hadn't been boots-on-the-ground in years. I was rusty. Harmony might have done things differently. He might have kept our guys from dying—not to mention the ones on the helicopter."

Opal's hand covered his and squeezed, bringing him an inordinate amount of comfort. "I am sure your reasons weren't selfish," she insisted. "Remember how you helped out the pilot in our neighborhood who came back from Afghanistan paralyzed? That's the kind of man you are, Monty. You weren't thinking about yourself."

She'd called him Monty, like his closest friends did. It made him feel like he knew her well. "Thanks."

She kept her hand over his. "Have you talked to anyone about this? A therapist?"

Monty shook his head. "There's mandatory counseling, but the fastest way to sink your career is to tell the Navy shrinks too much."

She swallowed. "Am I the only person you've talked to?"

"Yeah." Self-consciousness made the scar on his cheek burn.

She gave his hand one last squeeze. Her grip was strong, as he knew all too well from her massages. "Thank you. You can talk to me any time."

The instant her hand was gone, Monty realized he wanted her touching him again. The realization annoyed him. Opal was his neighbor, the closest thing to a female friend he'd ever had. He didn't want to ruin that. Reaching for his glass, he drained it, then pushed his chair back. "I should get going."

She nodded, looking chagrined. "Puzzles aren't for everyone."

"No, this was fun. It's not the puzzle; it's me."

"Let me get that tea for you." She rose and lead him back into the kitchen where she snagged a box of tea bags from the panty. "I recommend a cup right before bedtime."

Monty took the box from her. "Thanks. I'll try it." He resisted the impulse to hug her as the memory of her soft, petite frame tempted him. He edged toward the hall, instead. "You're a good neighbor, Opal." He was so relieved not to hold her in suspicion anymore.

"So are you, Monty. Don't forget your drill." She picked it up and brought it toward him.

"Oh, yeah."

"Thanks for changing the lock."

"No problem." He headed for the door.

In the foyer, he ran into Ruby, who seemed to be standing there eavesdropping. He sent her another glare.

She pretended to zip up her lips, which nearly made him laugh, though he didn't.

Assured his neighbors were keeping his story to themselves, Monty let himself out, making sure to lock their door from the inside, lest the Green Goblin seek to pay another visit.

～

Stunned by the force of the car crash, Eric's instincts nonetheless told him to get out of the incapacitated vehicle, though he couldn't remember why.

Get out. Get out.

Through his shattered windshield, he saw spumes of steam escape the sides of his crumpled hood, rising like ghostly spires toward the branches of the tree he'd struck. A pine forest was lit by the headlights of a car idling behind him on the narrow, deserted road he'd turned down when he'd realized he was being followed.

The driver of that car was Eric's foe. Even concussed, he knew that much.

As he scuttled across the bench seat toward the passenger side, Eric fumbled in the glove box for his loaded gun. It felt like dead weight in his trembling hand. He pushed the groaning door open with his feet.

Panting with fear, disoriented, he rose from his battered Buick on knees that quaked. Blood coursed down his cheek from a cut on his brow. He squinted at the car behind him, unable to see the driver through the corona of the headlights. He raised a hand to block the streaming beams.

All at once, an arm looped around his neck, putting it in a vise. Fingers clamped over his, taking control of the gun. Eric struggled to free himself, but his attacker overpowered his best efforts, then lifted the 9mm pistol until the tip grazed Eric's ear.

"How much do the Bonheur sisters know?" growled a familiar voice.

Eric's confusion immediately cleared. Oh, yes, this was Ritter, the colleague who'd approached him two years ago with an offer he ought to have refused. The devil had tempted him, and he'd regretted his decision ever since.

"Answer me," Lyle Ritter snarled. "What did the younger sister mean when she asked how you sleep at night? What do they know, and what have you told them?"

"I-I-I..." Terrified, Eric realized Lyle must have tapped his phone. How else would he have known about Ruby's phone call? He tried to invent a lie but couldn't control his stammer any more than he could stop a cold wave of sweat from enveloping his body.

"Talk, you stupid shmuck. Something's got you spooked. Tell me, or I'll blow your brains out."

Eric didn't want to die. Ritter had let him live this long. Maybe he would let him go if he told the truth.

The constriction around his neck eased suddenly. In one breath, he sought to explain himself. "They found out D-Danny had a journal. He m-m-must have mentioned his susp—" The word *suspicions* was too hard to say. "I w-warned them—"

"Well, of course, Danny had a journal." Ritter's voice dripped with disgust. "You were his friend. You ought to have known that about him. I should have killed the both of you, not just him."

"No, p-p-please! I'll explain it all to them. I'll take the b-b-b-blame."

"That's right. You will." A thick, gloved finger took control of the trigger.

With a whimper of acceptance, Eric closed his eyes and pictured his late wife. *I'm coming, Sonja.*

CHAPTER 11

*I*f Ruby could have afforded 130 cups of coffee, she'd have ordered them at Dunkin Donuts and left them all on Tony's doorstep as proof that she'd found him. Since she didn't have the money, she figured she would knock on his door and show herself. Then he would know what a good sleuth she was.

Angling her rearview mirror, Ruby glanced at her reflection. Why had she taken such pains with her appearance? Was she just teasing Tony by showing him what he couldn't have? *That's not very child-of-God-like.* Ruby sighed.

She did look pretty, though. Her hair was a riot of copper ringlets. She wore a peach crop-top sweater, high-waisted skinny jeans with fashionable tears at the knees, and ankle boots that she'd had to grab out of a box in the trunk of her car. Layered over all of that was a cloud of irresistible perfume.

Obviously, she was toying with Tony, considering she wanted nothing to do with him. What kind of person did that make her? Not wanting to answer the question, she imagined the look on his face when she showed up on his doorstep.

A glance at the iPhone she was clutching told her his address was coming up on her right. A stiff November breeze rocked her car as she slowed before a row of beach houses built right along the coast. Granted, they were townhouses, but they were big and freshly painted in tones of peach, aqua, and pale yellow. Nobody Tony's age deserved to live right on the ocean, but there was his Honda under the carport of the end unit. Another foreign car was parked next to it.

Who else did he live with?

Growing nervous, Ruby parked in the driveway, buttoned up her cream-colored swing coat, and got out. She climbed fifteen steps to the front door, punched the doorbell, and waited, hugging herself for warmth. *What am I doing here?*

A soft thud inside was all the warning she got before the door swung open. Ruby regarded the pretty, young black woman in surprise. She ought to have expected it, but she hadn't.

"Sorry." She started to leave. "I think I have the wrong address."

"Who are you looking for?" The woman sounded friendly.

"Er..." Ruby turned back and spied a burly black man coming down the stairs. Relief washed over her. "I thought Tony Caruso lived here."

"He does." The woman's dimples flashed. "I think he's still out running on the beach, but why don't you come in and wait for him? He shouldn't be long."

"Thank you." Ruby stepped gratefully into the bright, warm foyer.

"I'm Natalie. Call me Nate." She held out a hand for Ruby to shake "And this is Theo."

Theo smiled, dazzling Ruby with a gorgeous smile.

"Theo and Tony work together," Nate added. "What's your name?"

"Oh, I'm..." Ruby wasn't certain who she was or what she did. "I'm just Ruby." She shrugged.

"Well, come on into the kitchen, Just Ruby. We have plenty of coffee and toast."

Shucking off her coat as she walked down a hallway, Ruby draped it over the back of the dinette chair in the open-concept kitchen. Both the kitchen and the family room boasted large windows with breathtaking views of the Atlantic Ocean. Today it looked tumultuous with white-capped waves and a watery sun smothered by scudding clouds.

"Wow, this place is amazing." Ruby ran an envious eye over the maple cabinets and quartz countertops. "Do you own it or...?"

"No, we all rent it together." Nate put a familiar hand on Theo's broad back. "Pour Ruby a coffee, will you, baby?"

"Sure." Theo turned to Ruby. "How do you take your coffee, ma'am? Cream and sugar?"

Ma'am? Ruby'd never been called that before. "Both, please." The couple's hospitality left her tongue-tied.

As she gazed out of the nearest window, sipping her coffee, she wondered what kind of nut would run outside on a day like this. As if conjured by the question, a hooded figure appeared over the sand dunes as he ran up a run of stairs coming from the beach. Ruby's heart started inexplicably to trot.

Seconds later, he arrived on the deck right outside the windows. His cheeks were wind-chapped, his dark eyes watering in the cold. She had to admit he was terribly good-looking. But then he chucked a wad of spit over the balcony, reminding her that he was flesh and blood and barely out of his teens.

In the next instant, he was slipping through the door. Catching sight of her, he drew up short, stunned but still capable of shutting the door. He stood there for a second, breathing hard. "Well, well." He broke into a smile. "Look who found me."

"Tag." She toasted him with her coffee mug. "You're it." She was pleased to sound utterly nonchalant.

"I'm it." He seemed to give the phrase some serious consideration. "I'm *it*," he said again. "Yeah, I like the sound of that. I'm *it*."

Ruby rolled her eyes. "In your dreams," she muttered, aware that Theo and Nate were witnessing their childish exchange.

Tony gestured at her. "Well, you're here, aren't you?" He pulled his sweatshirt off over his head.

Ruby stared. Beneath that baggy sweatshirt, he wore a long-sleeved Under Armor shirt. The sweat-soaked material stuck to his torso like a second skin, delineating every muscle in his shoulders, chest, and washboard abs. He certainly wasn't built like a boy.

"Give me a sec to shower off, and I'll be right down to join you." Tony winked at her. "Don't go anywhere." He turned and disappeared.

Listening to him take the stairs three at a time, Ruby turned back to her coffee and pondered her next move. If she stayed, it would mean she had given up resisting him. It would mean she was agreeing to his company. Was that really what she wanted? Surprisingly, the answer seemed to be, yes.

I don't have to date him, she reassured herself. *We can be friends.*

"Have some toast?" Nate slid a plate of freshly toasted and buttered bread in front of her.

"Oh, thank you." Ruby smiled self-consciously. She crunched into the first slice, turning her attention back out the window.

Memories of her childhood swept through her. Every Saturday in the summer, before her mother's death, her family would go to the beach. Ruby would sit at the edge of the sea; just sit and sink into the sand, becoming one with the ocean. How long had it been since she'd felt the surge and retreat of the waves, rocking her like a mother?

Lost in her thoughts, she didn't hear Tony's approach until his reflection filled the windowpane. She whipped around to find him standing next to her, having apparently set a world record for showering and dressing. He wore jeans, a long-sleeved burgundy T-shirt, and worn tennis shoes. A smile danced at the corners of his lips.

"How good are you at bowling?"

The question was so unexpected that it took Ruby several seconds to supply an answer. "I haven't bowled in years."

"You want to come? I have to be at the bowling alley in fifteen minutes."

She hadn't known what to expect, but bowling wasn't it. "Okay."

"Great." His smile was 100 percent boy.

As she came to her feet, he startled her by giving her a hug. Swallowed into a cocoon of warmth, she discovered she liked Tony's hugs. But then Tony dropped his arms and stepped back.

"I'll drive." He caught her arm and towed her toward the door.

Ruby glanced back at the other couple. "Bye, Nate. It was nice to meet you. Bye, Theo."

As they called back to her, Tony swept Ruby outside. He kept hold of her elbow as they descended the steps, no doubt thinking she might kill herself in her high-heeled boots.

"Just a head's up. I'm going to speed a little," he warned her, while opening the passenger side of his Honda. "Don't want to be late."

"Late for what?"

He didn't answer until he dropped into the driver's seat. "A tournament."

"Oh." The clean-car smell of his Honda distracted her. She noted the immaculate interior with a twinge of embarrassment. Her own car was a wreck, by comparison.

As he started the engine and backed fluidly out of the carport and around her car, she assessed the mileage on his dash. To her surprise, the car wasn't new. It had over sixty thousand miles on it, and it still looked like this. Maybe she should clean out her own car.

As Tony took off in the direction of the bowling alley, Ruby's eyes widened. He had not been kidding when he'd warned her about speeding. They flew up Shore Drive, hit a ramp in a tire-squealing turn and accelerated to eighty when they hit the expressway. For some reason, Ruby wasn't the least bit scared. Tony's haste exhilarated her. He kept two competent hands on the wheel while keeping his eyes peeled for cops.

"You're not worried about getting a speeding ticket?"

"Nah. Most cops will let you off if you tell them you're a SEAL. It's my senior chief I'm worried about."

Ruby frowned. "Why? How would he find out?"

"He's waiting at the bowling alley."

~

145

"You're late!" barked a male voice, booming out of the confusing blend of multiple conversations, rumbling bowling balls, and crashing pins.

Searching the crowd, Ruby quickly picked out the source of the voice. A broad-shouldered man in his late thirties with a streak of silver in his black hair was striding toward them.

"You missed the warm-up." He glared at Tony with eyes of such a pale hue they were nearly opalescent. "What part of eleven-hundred hours didn't you understand, Bambino?"

Ruby realized Tony had a nickname. She went to gauge his response and found him grinning. "Come on, Senior Chief, you know I don't need to warm up."

"You're a cocky SOB, Bambino. That's what I like about you." The senior chief peered past Tony, ignoring Ruby. "Where's Theo?"

"Theo's not coming."

"What? This is a tournament, for God's sake." A V-shaped vein appeared on the senior chief's forehead.

"It's not God's fault, McLeod." With affable authority in his voice, another man stood up from tying off his bowling shoes. Ruby gaped, awed by his size and his all-American good looks.

Mr. *Sports Illustrated* eyed Ruby with interest while asking Tony, "What's Theo doing?"

"Nate's got him looking at houses." Tony sent them an elaborate shrug.

"Unbelievable," muttered the senior chief on a note of disgust. "I knew a woman was to blame."

Ruby took immediate offense.

Tony threw an arm over her shoulder. "But I brought someone to take his place. This is Ruby Bonheur. Ruby, meet Lieutenant Strong and Senior Chief McLeod."

She forced a smile for them, then hissed in Tony's ear, "I haven't played in years. I can't be in a tournament!"

"We just want to play." Tony squeezed her and let her go. "We don't care if we lose."

"Speak for yourself," the senior chief muttered, but Lieutenant Strong cut him off.

"We need a fourth player, or we have to forfeit."

"So, we play with Ruby," said Tony, like the matter was settled. "Let's get our shoes." He drew Ruby over to the rental counter, where she grudgingly requested a pair of size sevens.

"I can't wear these," she protested when the clerk handed her what appeared to be clown shoes.

"Believe me," said Tony with a twinkle in his eyes, "no one's going to be looking at your feet."

That was possibly quite true. The bowling alley was chock-full of men, most of whom had military haircuts and incredibly broad shoulders. For Ruby, it might have been a social paradise, only the majority of them were pointedly ignoring her.

Tony hustled them back to their lanes. The atmosphere, complete with music from the fifties, put a spring in Tony's step. His enthusiasm was contagious. Ruby donned her clown shoes with rising excitement.

She watched Senior Chief McLeod place a pitcher of Gatorade and four plastic cups on the table behind them.

"His code name's Mako," Tony divulged, following her gaze.

As in mako shark? Ruby reassessed McLeod. With the silver streak slicing through his dark hair, a thick black mustache, and pale eyes, he looked just like a shark.

Tony pitched his voice lower. "But don't worry. His bark's worse than his bite. Or rather, his bite isn't all that bad," he amended to keep from mangling his metaphors.

"You're up first, Tony." Lieutenant Strong was dusting his right hand in powder. "And then you, ma'am." He nodded at Ruby.

Ma'am again. Weren't there expectations of behavior that went with that word?

"Here's a ten-pound ball for you." Tony set it in her lap. "Let me know if it's too heavy." He hefted his larger ball and stepped onto the wooden platform to launch it down the lane.

Ruby watched, enjoying the way he cocked his hips and took aim.

He stepped forward, bending his knees and swinging his arm in one athletic movement. The ball whipped down the lane, turned at the last second, and slammed into the pins, landing him a strike. Tony got two more turns, knocking down all of the pins on his second one.

The lieutenant high-fived Tony as he returned to his seat, grinning. "You're up," he told her.

Ruby's dismay rose along with her blood pressure. "I'm going to stink at this."

"Nah, just have some fun." To her astonishment, he placed a swift kiss on her cheek.

His audacity would have to be dealt with later. Feeling tense and exposed, with a hundred pairs of male eyes pretending not to notice her, Ruby gave it her best shot and landed a gutter ball.

"That's all right." Tony clapped encouragingly, even as the senior chief cast his eyes to the ceiling. "Try again."

Hot-faced but determined not to disgrace herself, Ruby waited for her ball to return. She aimed it with care, then tentatively released it. It rolled lazily down the lane, taking forever to near the pins, then toppled only a few of them.

She backed away from the lane, humiliated.

Tony grabbed her hand and pulled her toward their table. "Have some Gatorade and shake it off."

"I have to use the restroom."

"Sure." He slanted her a worried look before pointing. "It's over there."

With Lieutenant Strong and Senior Chief McLeod taking their turns, Ruby raced to the restroom, where she deliberated calling for an Uber to get back to her car. She realized she didn't want to let Tony down, so she washed her hands and returned to him.

He caught her eye. "Don't worry so much, *Bella*. Theo's not much better than you are. We'd still be getting the same score."

The screen over their area flashed a strike for Lieutenant Strong.

The man was incredibly impressive. He also wore a thick wedding band on his left hand. "So, you work with these guys?" she asked Tony.

"Yeah. LT's our operations officer and Senior Chief's our top enlisted, now that Master Chief's retired."

"He's scary," Ruby confessed as the man in question hurled the ball toward the pins, knocking all down but one.

"Naw. He's a pussy cat with fins."

An hour later, Ruby realized Tony might be right. The senior chief pointed out that she was improving with every turn, and that made her like him a little bit more.

For his part, Lieutenant Strong kept calling her ma'am, which she found dignifying. At the end of every turn, he held out a huge hand for her to slap.

She was feeling like one of the guys, a critical part of the team, and that astonished her, considering she'd only meant to prove to Tony what a super sleuth she was. It dawned on her that she'd wanted the upper hand in their peculiar relationship, but now they felt like partners.

~

"We're in second place," divulged Senior Chief McLeod two hours later. He'd just returned from a mini reconnaissance to discover their status among the contestants. "We're three points behind Team Ten." His opalescent gaze settled on Ruby and narrowed.

She got the message: *If we lose, it'll be your fault, woman.*

She couldn't let her team down. Ignoring the small voice in her head that insisted she would fail, Ruby summoned her determination. She'd played softball in high school. As a matter of fact, she'd been the starting pitcher. Bowling wasn't all that different. Maybe if she thought of the pins as home base and drove the ball straight across the plate, she'd have more success.

"Your turn, *Bella.*"

He'd called her beautiful several times now. She wondered if he spoke any more Italian. For the past two hours, he'd treated her like the queen of the bowling alley. He'd bought her nachos. He'd polished her bowling ball. He'd powdered her hand. She caught herself thinking he would sure make a sweet boyfriend.

Now was not the time for such irrational thoughts.

Focus and pitch to the plate. She carried her ball to the platform. Lining up on her lane, she hefted her ball, imagined it was a great big softball, and let loose.

The ball remained airborne for a moment. But then it hit the lane screaming. To her astonishment, it flattened all ten pins. Ruby threw her hands into the air and screamed with joy.

The senior chief and the lieutenant surged to their feet, roaring with surprise. Tony rushed at her, picked her up, and whirled her in a circle.

Clutching his broad shoulders and laughing, she realized she was happy in a way that she hadn't been in years.

"You're still up," he said excitedly. "Do it the same way!"

"Phew, okay." She shook off her happy jitters and went to collect her bonus points.

Tony stepped back, hushing the others into silence. Ruby envisioned home plate again, reared back, and let go. The ball did exactly the same thing as it had last time. With a scream of delight, she jumped into Tony's arms, locked her legs around him, and kissed him on the mouth.

What am I doing? It was perfect and perfectly wrong at the same time.

Stunned and confused, Ruby let her legs slip to the floor. She didn't know what to say in the face of Tony's growing smile.

"Now you get another turn," he informed her.

"Ruby, is that your phone ringing?"

Lieutenant Strong's question had her looking at her purse, then hurrying toward it. Her friends never called, only texted, which meant this had to be Opal. Indeed, it was. "Hello?"

"Hey, honey, I have news."

Opal's tense tone made Ruby sink into the closest chair, just in case. "What is it?"

"Eric Novak was found shot in the head on the side of a quiet road in Pungo. It was supposed to look like suicide."

"What?" Ruby let the awful news run through her. "You mean somebody killed him?"

At her question, Tony sat next to her.

"Probably. Detective Skags said it appeared staged. Eric's car had been nudged from behind and run off the road. It hit a tree. Skags found a second set of footprints, so he thinks Eric was murdered."

Murdered. The word echoed in Ruby's head. "By the same person who killed Daddy?" she whispered.

"Possibly. I need to know something, honey. Did you tell Eric that we found Daddy's journal?"

Ruby could feel the blood draining from her head as she thought back. "I think so."

"Detective Skags thinks you should come home, so the police can keep an eye on us."

The implication that the killer might be after them next was obvious. Ruby tried to swallow, but her throat was too dry. "Okay." Her recent elation was forgotten. "I'm on my way."

She thumbed her call to a close and sat a moment, processing Eric's fate. Was it her fault? If she hadn't called him in the first place and brought up the journal, he would still be alive.

"Ruby?" Tony put an arm around her shoulders. "What's wrong, *Bella?*"

"I have to go home." Feeling numb, she leaned over and untied her clown shoes. "I can't take my last turn."

"Why?" He sounded disappointed.

"It's just um..." The fewer people who knew, the safer it was for them. "I just have to go." She pulled off both shoes. "I'm sorry."

"That's okay. So long as you're not mad at me. You did kiss me first," he pointed out.

She straightened, looking over at him. "I don't want to talk about that. But, no, I'm not mad at you."

He grinned, said "cool," then sprang out of his seat to address Lieutenant Strong. "Hey, sir, something's come up, and I need to get Ruby back home. Senior Chief, you can bowl for her, right?"

McLeod clicked his tongue like it was a major inconvenience, but he was quick to snatch up his ball.

Lieutenant Strong approached Ruby with an outstretched hand, pulling her to her feet when she took it. "It was a pleasure meeting you, ma'am. I hope we see you again."

"Thanks." She managed a smile for him. "Y'all are fun. Even him." She nodded at the senior chief, who had taken her place on the lane.

"I'm focusing here," came the surly retort.

The threesome chuckled. Then she and Tony put their real shoes on, returned their rented shoes to the desk, and left the bowling alley. Troubled thoughts reentered Ruby's head, keeping her preoccupied. She couldn't summon a word of small talk. Luckily, Tony didn't seem to expect it.

She looked up to realize they were headed the wrong way—toward Opal's house, not Tony's condo. "Oh, but I have to get my car."

"No, you don't. I'll have it brought to you later today."

"But..." But then he would see what a pigsty her car was and wonder why the trunk was crammed with boxes.

"It's not a problem." Tony spoke with a quiet authority that made her stop talking. "Now, please, tell me what's going on. Who was killed, exactly?"

She hugged herself. How much should she tell someone who was not her boyfriend but was acting like one? She averted her gaze out the window. "It doesn't concern you."

The car got dangerously quiet.

As Tony approached the next intersection, he downshifted, his muffler roaring, and then executed a U-turn.

Ruby's heart started to race. Glancing at Tony, she found his jaw muscles jumping. "Where are we going now?" It occurred to her that she really didn't know this man at all. Somehow, she wasn't surprised to discover that he had a temper.

"Back to your car," he said on a reasonable but flat note.

Okay. She'd wanted that, but not when he made it sound like she would never see him once she stepped out of his vehicle. That prospect left her feeling unhinged.

As they screamed along a busy, four-lane road, bypassing a cemetery and hospital, Ruby struggled for something to say that would keep him dangling. Nothing witty or alluring came to mind.

Tony hooked a right and they were bearing down on his ocean-front condo. He whipped around her car, nosed into the carport, and turned his engine off. "When you're ready to share your life with me, let me know." He got out of his seat, rounded his car and, like a true gentleman, pulled her door open.

Ruby got out on leaden legs.

He stood intentionally in her way, forcing her to brush past him. Every nerve in her body flexed. The air seemed to crackle as memories of their kiss shortened her breath. *He's three years younger than I am!* she reminded herself. His wanting her to share her life with him just proved how immature he was. It was up to her to do the mature thing and walk away.

"Goodbye, Tony." She walked as proudly to her car as she could and slipped haughtily inside of it.

As she merged into traffic, she allowed herself a look in the rearview mirror. Tony stood at the end of his driveway, watching her drive off.

Ruby gave a whimper. He'd been nothing but sweet and courteous to her all morning. She'd been happier today than any day in recent memory. She didn't want to admit it, but she was going to miss Little Joey.

Still, she had bigger concerns than letting him down. Thoughts of impending danger rose in her mind like ocean swells. With Eric Novak dead, the obvious question was: Were she and Opal next?

CHAPTER 12

*M*onty wasn't so drunk that he couldn't walk home. Beneath a moonless sky, the invisible sidewalk felt as treacherous as the mountain pass where the Taliban had discovered the Americans before the SEALs could save them. He stumbled over cracks in the cement. Cars sped by him, headlights blinding him; taillights streaming.

The November air nipped at his ears and went straight through his jeans and sweatshirt. He *was* in Virginia Beach, right? Not wandering through the Hindu Kush in a delirious haze? The tang of the ocean and the smell of exhaust reassured him.

Why, exactly, had he hit up a sport's bar after working out at the gym? Oh, yeah, because he'd received a call from the head of SOCOM himself, informing Monty of his new orders. The news had gotten Monty so agitated he'd pushed himself at the gym, making his back hurt. Then, instead of going home, he'd stopped in at a pub a mile from his house, hoping to lessen both his pain and his angst with a stiff drink.

On his third shot of whisky, he'd realized that, even with a

Saturday night crowd pressing in on him, he was drinking alone, wallowing in self-doubt, and thinking, *What if I get more men killed?*

He'd looked around the bar, wanting consolation, a pretty face to help him forget the awesome responsibly looming before him. Eye contact and a receptive smile would get him what they always had. It never took a lick of effort on Monty's part to pick up a woman, usually just three words: *Navy SEAL officer.*

But a woman couldn't take away the cause of his concern. Nor did he want to be that guy anymore, the kind that went through women like they were breakfast cereal. A box might last him a week, or he'd binge on it for months, only to get sick of it. Really, the only woman who could help him sort out his thoughts about his new assignment, who could bolster his confidence and soothe his self-doubts, was Opal.

The realization had had him pushing aside his drink with relief. He'd paid his tab and left the bar. But then he'd had to walk the long mile to his house because he was too drunk to drive.

Dumb. Stupid. Idiotic. These and several other words occurred to him as he stumbled toward home. *This will be the last time I overindulge,* he swore to himself. He didn't need whisky to reduce his pain; he had a neighbor with a magic, healing touch who could do a much finer job.

By the time he neared his neighborhood, Monty felt better about himself. His pain had ebbed. Eager to see Opal and to share his news, he broke into an experimental jog. It didn't hurt any more than walking, and he would get to her house faster this way.

Soon, the pavement streamed like a dark ribbon under his feet. He swept into his neighborhood, turned onto the street where he and Opal lived, and tore past his home, cutting through Opal's yard toward the welcoming glow of her windows.

A column of light shot out of the darkness, blinding him. "Halt! Police! Get your hands up! Hands up now! Get your hands up and keep them up!"

Monty, who was conditioned to respond to threats, dove and rolled automatically toward the nearest cover—the bushes lining Opal's porch. Rising to his knees to assess the threat, he found himself spotlighted by the bright beam. The silhouette of a police officer approached him, barking orders and pointing a gun in his face.

"Hey, hey," Monty called. "I'm a friendly. Put the gun away."

The cop ignored him. "Put your hands behind your head and crawl out of there!"

It dawned on Monty that the police must have set a watch in the hopes of catching Eric. "I'm the neighbor," he explained, even as he shuffled out of the bushes. The fact that he hadn't seen the unmarked police car parked at the curb horrified him. Humiliation was the result of his oversight. He knelt in cold, damp mulch, reasoning with a nervous policeman, while every household on the street bore witness to what was going on.

The front door popped open. "Oh, heavens."

With relief, Monty watched Opal come flying off her porch in her slippers and bathrobe. Ruby stood at the door with a hand over her mouth.

"Ma'am, stay back! He could be armed."

Opal rounded on the wary officer. "This is not who you're looking for. This is my neighbor. For land's sake, stop yelling and waking the entire neighborhood!"

That's my girl. Monty wanted to cheer Opal for defending him.

"What was he doing running at your house?" The cop holding the light sounded skeptical. He blinded Monty again, pinning his spotlight on him.

"I asked him to come over."

Opal's white lie kept Monty from having to explain his behavior. She helped him to his feet, keeping a firm grip on him as if sensing his less-than-sober state. "Now turn off that light, and I'll introduce you."

To Monty's relief, the police complied. Opal introduced him to the deputy as Lieutenant Commander James Monteague, Navy SEAL. Their surly suspicion vanished in an instant. As the deputy groveled and conveyed his apologies, Monty commended him for their vigilance while Opal led him swiftly back inside.

"You've been drinking," she accused the instant she'd shut and locked the door behind her.

Monty peered around for Ruby but she seemed to have vanished.

"I know. I'm sorry. But that's why I'm here." He paused a moment. How could he convey his recent realizations without sounding like he was coming on to her? He wasn't, was he?

"Okaaay. Let's get you warmed up. You've been in the cold so long your cheeks are chapped. That's not good for your wound, you know."

She obviously still thought him under the influence, but, for some reason, her scolding made him feel special.

"Come on in the family room." She tugged on his arm. "I've got a fire going."

"Oh, I love fires, especially the outdoor kind, under a star-spangled sky in the desert." Squatting before the hearth, he held his fingers to the heat, lost his balance, and landed on his backside. "Oops." The flames mesmerized him, beating back the self-doubt he'd been wrestling with since the detailer's call. Hearing Opal in the kitchen, he looked over his shoulder as she brought over two mugs.

"Here, drink this." Handing him one, she lowered herself onto the hearth rug next to him.

Monty recognized the fragrance and flavor of the same chamomile tea given to him the other day. As he sipped it, he eyed Opal over the rim of his mug. "You were headed for bed." She wore a familiar-looking flannel robe over cream-colored pajamas.

"I wouldn't have been able to sleep anyway."

There was something in her voice. He lowered his mug. "Why, what happened?"

"Eric Novak's dead."

It took Monty a second to remember who that was. "The Green Goblin? How'd he die?"

"He was shot in the head. It was supposed to look like a suicide, but his car was run off the road, and another set of footprints was found on the scene."

A shiver ran through Monty. In other words, *murder.* "The one who bought the ricin killed him," he guessed. "Who else would have a motive?"

Opal nodded. "That's our guess."

"So that's why the cops are out front. 'Bout time." He ran a hand through his hair, then searched her face for the fear she had to be feeling.

There it was, in the tremulous smile she sent him. He wanted to hug her for being so brave.

She cocked her head inquiringly. "You were about to tell what had you running up to my door at ten at night."

She looked so pretty in the firelight; he couldn't remember why he'd ever thought her plain. "Oh, yeah. I got new orders today."

She seemed to brace herself. "To where?"

"Right down the road. Dam Neck Naval Annex. Team Six has been looking for a new commander for almost a year. Their last one is sitting in a federal prison."

"Oh my gosh. What did he do?"

It took Monty a second to remember. "Oh, yeah, he was part of that vigilante group called the Entity. He used his position to steal weapons before his Team could interdict them. Then he hoarded them, supposedly in the best interests of the country."

Opal sighed. "Everyone thinks they're doing the right thing."

Monty shook his head. "That doesn't excuse his behavior. You don't get to take over national defense just because you're worried. You get to vote, same as everyone else. That's the way our country works."

"I agree." She cocked her head. "So, who's been running Team Six since the corrupt commander went to jail?"

"Their XO, Lieutenant Mills." He told Opal what the admiral at SOCOM had told him over the phone. "Mills spent a year in a Venezuelan prison after the warehouse he was reconning with his SEAL squad exploded. Everyone thought he'd died in the explosion. A year later, he escaped and made his way home."

Opal's eyes widened. "Oh, my gosh. Yes, I know him—*Jonah* Mills.

We prayed for him at church all year long, and then, one Sunday, there he was with his wife and daughter. Eden teaches fitness classes on Dam Neck. I treated her once for a hamstring strain."

"Small world," Monty marveled. Then, recalling his misgivings, he stared down into his tea.

Opal kept quiet, waiting for him to say more. "Aren't you happy with your orders?" she finally prompted.

He couldn't look at her, so he stared into the fire. "It's a lot of responsibility."

She waited again, her silence wrapping around him, giving him time to voice the fears he'd been battling since the admiral's call.

"I think about what happened when I took Harmony's place. My decisions cost the lives of fifteen men. This time I'll be in charge of a hundred." He pushed his reservations through a tightening throat. "And every one of them knows what I've been through. Half of them probably blame me."

"Oh, Monty." Laying her mug aside, she scooted closer and linked her arm through his. "What happened in Afghanistan would have happened regardless of who led the rescue operation. I'm sure your teammates understand that. You can't let that tragedy define you. All you can do is learn from it."

He thought back over his experience. "I did learn from it. I learned I'm just as human as the next guy. I can make mistakes. I can die from hunger and thirst just like the rest."

"That's not such a bad lesson."

He recalled his torment. "I remember praying for the first time since I was a kid."

"You used to pray?" She smiled at him with wonder.

"All the time. My parents sent me to a church-affiliated private school. I was taught that God loved me, and I could rely on Him for everything. And I did, back then." He fell silent. When, exactly, had he blocked God out of his life?

"You can always start praying again."

The murmured suggestion filled him with a sudden deep desire to cast his burdens onto someone else's broad shoulders. "That sounds really good."

"And I'll pray for you, too. What should I pray for?"

He considered what he needed most. "For wisdom and the grace to do what's right. Always."

Her eyes grew shiny. "Those are good things to pray for."

He was enjoying the feel of her tucked close to him. Peace like he hadn't felt in weeks, if not years, filled him. Wanting to thank Opal for bringing it to him, he ducked his head and dropped a grateful kiss on her lips.

Her in-drawn breath let him know he'd caught her by surprise.

"Sorry," he said, though he wasn't. Not at all. Her mouth was soft and sweet and oddly familiar. Testing his luck, he kissed her a second time.

He thought she might pull away. Instead, her lips softened, and the room started to spin. Intoxicated for reasons other than the whiskey he'd drunk earlier, Monty checked his behavior and pulled away. Opal wasn't like the women he dated. At the same time, the splendor of that simple kiss took him by surprise. But he still wasn't about to take advantage, not even with the look of disappointment on her face.

"I should go," he said.

She scooted away from him and nodded at his mug. "Drink your tea first. It'll help you sleep."

He downed his drink in three long swallows, then clambered to his feet, a little steadier than he had been. "Call me for any reason. I'm right next door, you know."

"Oh, I know."

Her poignant tone made him hope he hadn't misled her. "I'll let myself out. Goodnight." He left his mug in the kitchen then headed for the hallway.

She trailed him, keeping her distance. "Goodnight"

His back twinged as he shut and locked her door. With a wave for the police who sat in their undercover vehicle, Monty headed toward his dark, lonely home. *But I won't be alone from now on.* God, he vowed, was going to be part of his life going forward. He had thought he could do everything on his own, and look how that turned out.

~

Opal turned back to the fire as soon as the front door closed. Her lips still tingled from Monty's kiss. What on earth had compelled him to do that? He wasn't that drunk—certainly not as bad off as the night she'd patched him up. Was he starting to have feelings for her? Hope fluttered in her chest. Now that he knew he had been assigned a job right up the road, might he consider dating her?

"Please," she whispered, giving voice to her deepest yearnings. But then common sense prevailed. He'd kissed her for the same reason he'd kissed her the first time. Monty was used to a certain lifestyle, and drinking lowered his inhibitions. Too bad for him; Opal had no interest in shallow relationships.

Crouching before her fire, she closed the glass doors of her hearth to stifle the flames. If only she could put out the embers in her heart so easily.

~

Ruby exited the WAVY Television Studios with confidence in her stride. *I got the job!* She tamped down the urge to do a happy dance.

The police escorts waiting for her by her car were watching her approach. She drew herself up, squared her shoulders, and walked like the professional she was, briefcase in hand, to her car.

The Human Resources office had called her for an interview on the same day they'd received her résumé. They were looking for a field reporter—young, attractive, articulate, and tenacious.

"I'm your girl," she'd told her interviewers: the station director and the news anchor, both men. Ruby had crossed her legs just so, drawing their attention to her slim calves and proving—once again—that it wasn't what you knew but how you carried yourself. All those years of taking drama back in high school had paid off. Not once did they realize that beneath her periwinkle-blue wool suit that she was suffering through cold sweats.

"We'll call you this afternoon with an official offer," the news anchor had promised her. "But I can tell you right now you will love working for this station. I've been happy here for twenty years." He'd pumped her hand enthusiastically, his gaze dropping with curiosity toward the cameo of Great-Grandma Ruby she'd worn for luck.

She wasn't sure she was all that qualified for the position, but what did it matter? They were going to pay her a decent salary, *with* benefits. Not only could she afford to pay her rent again, she might even buy a new car!

Best of all, Tony might just see her on the news.

She envisioned him slapping his forehead. *Oh, man, I used to know that woman!* Yeah, and they might still have been friends, too, having a great time together, if he hadn't given her that ridiculous ultimatum about sharing her life with him. What an idiot! Like either one of them was ready to settle into a long-term, monogamous relationship.

Sure, maybe he had a career and his whole life figured out. Maybe he acted like the responsible adult, with a thing or two to teach her about growing up. But those days were over. Ruby Bonheur was getting herself together, and she was dying to tell him all about it. She didn't want to wait for him to see her on TV. She wouldn't get to witness his regret that way. No, she wanted to rub his nose in it this very minute—*without* having to share her life with him.

Slipping into her car, Ruby took her cell phone from her purse and looked up his number—the one she'd discovered while he was taking a turn bowling. She'd pounced on his phone before his screen locked and queried his number with a short but effective search. She dialed that number now, while gazing at the fountain in the man-made pond next to the station.

Planning to leave a message, she was caught off guard when he answered.

"Yo, this is Tony." He sounded full of energy and impossibly young.

Just the sound of his voice made her happier. She wanted to see him again.

"Hey, it's Ruby."

"Ruby? How'd you get my number?"

He didn't sound too upset that she had it. "That doesn't matter. I just wanted you to know I got a job. I'm going to be a field reporter for Channel Ten."

"Well, well, well." There was a smile in his voice. "I never doubted it."

His friendliness warmed her. She gave him some of the credit. "Thanks for pushing me."

"When do you start?"

"I'm not sure. Next week, I think."

"That's awesome. You deserve a good job."

She wanted to see him. "I'm surprised you answered. Aren't you at work?"

"I get off early on Wednesday so I can go to class."

"Oh." Her hopes fell. "Well, I don't want to make you late." She didn't want to hang up either.

"Actually, I was thinkin' of skipping class today and taking my Harley for a ride."

The underlying invitation took her breath away. "You do not have a Harley," she retorted.

"Yeah, true, but Chief Wade does, and he said I could drive it once a week while he's off in Oklahoma.

She had no idea who Chief Wade was. "Cool." Visions of the wind blowing through the tight weave of her suit tantalized her.

"Wanna go for a ride?"

"Um..." Yes, but she had a slight problem. Slidel and Holmes, her police escorts, would pitch a fit if she tried to hop on a bike with a total stranger. Her mind raced for a way to shake them loose. She made a quick decision. "I need you to pick me up somewhere."

"Sure. Like where?"

She gave him directions to a boutique on the oceanfront. "Meet me in the alley behind the store, at the employee entrance." As she slipped into her car, she eyed her escorts in her rearview mirror.

"Okay." Tony's tone was suspicious, but he didn't ask.

"I'm still in Portsmouth," she added, hauling on her seat belt before Tony could remind her. "I'll need twenty minutes to get there."

"See you in twenty," he said, and the phone clicked in her ear.

It was Monty's fifth physical-therapy session. As Opal eased her thumb into the serratus posterior inferior to the right of his spine, she savored the velvety texture of his skin and the density of his muscles. The memory of his kiss the other night made her touch more lover-like than professional.

Catching herself, Opal made a conscious effort to distance herself emotionally. Monty should not have kissed her at all, not if he hadn't meant it. Ever since, she'd caught herself daydreaming about the possibility of a future with him, which was likely never going to happen. She was setting herself up for heartache.

She cast about for a safe subject. "How's—ah—how's the turnover at your new job going?"

Monty grunted, betraying reluctance to talk. "It's good. I decided to meet the men at the top of the wall. Sort of catch 'em off guard during their PT time."

"The wall?"

"It's part of the obstacle course."

"Oh." His low, sleepy voice sounded like a lion's rumble. It made her want to stroke his hair, the color of autumn oak leaves.

"You want to come to my swearing-in ceremony?"

His invitation caused her heart to leap with hope. Was he asking her to come as his neighbor or something more? "Sure, when is it?"

"This Friday at noon. Please don't stop."

She continued her massage, only too happy to bring him relief.

"This Friday." She consulted her mental calendar. "Gosh, you'll be back at work before you know it."

"Yeah." His short answer betrayed a portion of the fears he'd shared with her the other night.

"You'll do great." She smoothed her thumbs along the healing muscle.

"Don't stop praying for me."

The request touched her. "Of course."

"I have a feeling God answers your prayers."

"Hmm." She thought about his words for a moment. "I think He answers anyone with a repentant heart who reaches out to Him."

"Even me?"

"Especially you... if your heart is repentant."

As Monty lapsed into silence, she concentrated on softening the tightness running parallel to his spine. His softly spoken words were barely loud enough for her to hear.

"I couldn't get any more repentant."

Tears of compassion rushed to Opal's eyes. *Oh, Monty.* She found herself bending over him, laying her cheek on the back of his shoulder, savoring his woodsy scent, hugging him. It was highly unprofessional of her, but the Spirit didn't make mistakes. A passage of Scripture popped into her head, so she murmured it. "If we confess our sins, then He is faithful and just to forgive us."

A rapping at the door saved her from any subsequent embarrassment. Opal straightened. "Yes?"

Monty lifted his head as the corpsman peered inside. "Ma'am, you have an urgent call on line three from an Officer Slidel."

Alarm tightened Opal's scalp. She met Monty's look of concern before hurrying from the room.

Minutes later, she was standing in her office, gripping the back of her chair, when Monty appeared at her open door, fully dressed in the NWUs he'd worn to the obstacle course.

"Everything okay?"

Worry kept her throat tight. "Ruby's missing. She disappeared out of a boutique on Atlantic Avenue."

Monty held her terrified gaze for a moment, then stepped into the room and tugged her away from the chair, into his arms. With a stifled whimper, Opal sagged against him, grateful for his consolation.

"Don't jump to conclusions." His chin bumped the top of her head as he spoke. "Check your text messages. She might have just pulled a fast one on her watchdogs."

That thought had not occurred to her. "You're right." With reluctance, she eased away from him and retrieved her cell phone from her purse tucked into the back of a cabinet. "There's a voice mail from Ruby!" Hope rose in her as she put it on speaker so Monty could overhear.

"Hey Sis, it's me. Listen, don't worry about me, okay? I just need a break from these clowns who are getting on my nerves. I'll be with Tony. He's a SEAL, remember? You know he can take care of me. Oh, and by the way, I got the job! Wahoo, time to celebrate, huh? I'll be out of your hair in no time."

Opal sent Monty a wry smile as she put her phone back. "Now I feel foolish for assuming the worst."

"Told you. Ruby's tougher than you think. No one's going to catch her by surprise."

Her thoughts turned to Ruby's escort. "Do you know this Tony? He's not in Team Six, is he?"

"Actually, I met him on your front porch a while back. And, yes, I saw him at the obstacle course this morning."

She turned back to Monty, confused. "Why was he at my house?"

"To see Ruby, I guess. I heard her telling him to get lost, and, thinking maybe he was Eric, I popped over to confront the guy. Instead, I met Tony Caruso, who claimed Ruby had hit his car and promised him dinner by way of payment."

"Oh, dear." Opal marveled that Ruby hadn't told her anything about this occurrence. "Well, thank you for checking on her."

"My pleasure. The kid was polite and persistent. If he's on Team Six, he's got to be squared away. You have nothing to worry about."

"The kid? Just how young is he?"

"Younger than Ruby. I'd say about twenty or so."

"Twenty! Ruby's never gone out with a younger man."

Monty shrugged. "There's a first time for everything."

His gaze locked on hers as he said the words. Was he thinking about himself now? The two of them?

Monty broke the silence. "As soon as I know more, I'll get you the details about the swearing-in ceremony." He backed toward the door.

"Great." She tried not to beam at him. "I look forward to that."

He paused with a hand on the doorframe. "I only have one appointment left with you, next week. You sure that's enough?"

"I'm happy to extend your therapy if you think you need it."

His slow smile made her stomach cartwheel. "Free massages. That's going to be hard to resist."

"You'll be too busy once your job starts."

"You're probably right. Could I schedule as needed?"

"Of course."

"Great. See you." He patted the wall and vanished.

Opal stared at the empty door. Monty had definitely been flirting with her. Or was he just being friendly? It was hard to tell. She hoped he understood she wouldn't indulge in a frivolous fling, not even with a man she'd worshiped from afar for years. With Opal, it was all or nothing. She heaved a sigh, wishing she weren't so straightlaced. "It's bound to be nothing, then."

CHAPTER 13

Tony knew trouble when he smelled it, and when Ruby Bonheur slipped out the back door of the jewelry boutique smelling like a million dollars, he knew he was going to have to face temptation like he'd never faced it before. What's more, if he wanted Ruby to take him seriously, he would need God to give him the words.

Wearing a periwinkle suit and heels so high they qualified as weapons, she couldn't have been more unsuitably dressed for a motor-cycle ride. At least her golden-red hair was confined into a bun so it wouldn't tangle into knots. Wearing pearls and cream-colored stock-ings, she could have knocked his socks off.

"Hey." He sidled up next to her in the designated alley. "Aren't you that famous reporter I saw on the news last night?"

She went along with his game and struck a pose. "Yes, actually, I am."

"Cool." He handed her a spare helmet. "How's about that ride?"

"Don't mind if I do."

"Who are you hiding from?" he demanded as she squashed it down on her bun and latched it under her chin.

"I'll tell you later." Her turquoise eyes glimmered like gemstones. In the next instant, she was hiking her skirt up to jump on behind him. Whatever she was up to, she was enjoying herself. "Just get me out of here, fast."

Calculated risks were an everyday affair for Tony, but he feared there wasn't much calculating going on in his head as he squealed out of the alleyway with Ruby plastered to his back.

Ruby wasn't thinking long-term when it came to them. There had to be something he could say, something he could do to open her eyes to their potential as a couple.

You gotta help me out here, God.

Driving straight into a chilly breeze, Tony's eyes watered as he zipped up Atlantic Avenue. He went just fast enough to meet Ruby's expectation of adventure, while taking no risks with her life. Until he'd seen how she was dressed, he was thinking he could take her to First Landing State Park, but that option was out. So, where could they go?

As they headed north, away from the boardwalk, the tops of two lighthouses rose into view in front of him. All at once, Tony knew their destination. God sure was clever sometimes.

Ruby peered over Tony's shoulder as he veered off the main road. Downshifting, he drove them along a residential street that dead-ended at a gate complete with chain-link fence and guards toting M15 rifles. Tony slowed to a stop at the gatehouse and stood to take his wallet from his pocket.

"What is this place?" she asked as he handed his ID to the guard.

Tony glanced back at her incredulously. "How long have you lived here?"

She gestured at the sign behind the guard. "I mean, obviously, it's Fort Story, but why have you brought me here?"

"You'll see." He put his wallet back in his pocket and sat back down. "Hold tight."

She hugged his lean waist tightly, but he took off slowly, motoring at a sedate speed past gnarled bayberry bushes and grass-covered sand dunes. The two lighthouses rising into the sky dead ahead looked like something off a postcard. He wasn't going to take her sightseeing, was he? After taking her bowling the last time, she didn't know what to expect from him.

They zipped into a parking lot for the lighthouses but didn't slow down. Tony drove around the newer lighthouse with its white-and-black checkered design toward the old brick lighthouse built atop an overgrown hill.

"It's open to the public now," he called over his shoulder.

Oh, joy. He *was* taking her sightseeing.

Instead of parking, Tony drove them straight into the vegetation and up a narrow footpath. Ruby had to hang on tight as they bumped over roots and fishtailed on the sand. At the top of the hill, he nosed the Harley into a grove and killed the engine.

"Shhh," he said, turning his profile to whisper to her. "Listen."

Ruby listened, but all she could hear was the roar of the surf, the sound of leaves rustling, and the call of seagulls.

"All clear." Tony got off the bike first, then helped her to dismount. He unlatched her helmet for her, then stowed both his and hers in the compartment by the back tire.

The excitement shining in his dark eyes made Ruby feel like something wonderful was about to happen. Maybe sightseeing wasn't the worst thing they could do.

Her high-heeled shoes became the object of his scrutiny.

"I'd better carry you."

That was all the warning she got before he picked her up, so high off the ground that she flopped over his shoulder like a sack of potatoes.

"Hush," he said as she voiced her concern.

"Put me down."

"I will." But he didn't. He ran out from the cover of the dunes with her bouncing on his shoulder, jogged up several steps, and then put her down. She found herself beside a wooden door with a padlock on it.

Ruby eyed the padlock while tugging her suit back into place. "I thought you said it was open to the public."

"Just on weekends. No worries, though. I got a key."

"You don't have a—" She paused as he opened his wallet and took out a set of small metal rods. "What the—?"

"A memento of my past life." He caught her eye. "I don't do this anymore. I just want to illustrate where I come from so you know you're never too far gone."

What the heck was that supposed to mean? She didn't ask because he'd started to work one of the picks into the lock like he was seriously going to open it. She cast a wary eye at their environs, but they were utterly alone. Excitement quickened her pulse. They could get into trouble for this, couldn't they?

With a click, the lock fell open. Tony put away his pick set, swung open the old wooden door, and pulled her into a dank, dark stairwell.

"You're crazy," she hissed as he shut it behind them.

"No argument there. Start climbing. I'll be right behind you."

A spirit of adventure gave her the energy to tackle the wrought-iron staircase. Sunlight shone through the narrow windows cut into the thick brick every twenty feet, allowing her to see each step.

"There'd better be a good reason for this," she huffed minutes later.

"There is. Just be careful."

Like she would hurt herself with him dogging her every step, ready to catch her if she fell. By the time Ruby's head crested the upper landing, she was perspiring in her wool suit. The view startled an exclamation out of her as she stepped into a circular room. The entire space was enclosed by a glass dome that offered a panoramic vista of the cape. The new lighthouse loomed nearby, with a cluster of outbuildings at its base.

"Have a seat." Tony, who wasn't the least bit winded, drew her toward the side with the best view and pulled her down on the cement ledge next to him.

Still breathing hard, Ruby took in the view. Contrary to how modest the structure had seemed from the outside, it felt like they were way up in the sky. The ocean cast a blanket as far as the eye could see, moving through a spectrum of blues and grays as it mingled with the waters of the Chesapeake Bay.

"Amazing." She'd never seen the coast from this perspective.

Sensing Tony's scrutiny, she turned her head to find him studying her reaction. The thought occurred to her that he had brought her all the way up here to kiss her. She really hoped he would, so long as he didn't bring up the share-your-life-with-me subject.

"You're beautiful," he stated.

"Thanks." She knew she was pretty, but Tony made her feel like she was special, too. She expected him to kiss her then, but he shifted so that he was facing the view and not her.

"Lemme ask you a question."

"Okay." She turned back to the view that was now fully absorbing him.

"Who do you look to for help when your world falls apart?"

Had he seriously brought her here to talk? With a pinch of discomfort, Ruby searched herself. "To my sister, I guess." She shrugged.

"She's your rock, huh?"

Ruby had already realized as much. "Yeah. What about you?" She lobbed the ball into Tony's court.

He kept his eyes on the view. "I didn't have an older sibling. My dad took off when I was ten, but I never looked up to him anyway. He wasn't the best father."

The confession caught Ruby off guard. She'd been thinking of her own hard luck, not realizing Tony had a similar story.

"I thought I could do better. I tried to be the man of the house, started working odd jobs to help my mother out. Philly is a rough city for a kid to grow up in. I'm not proud of some of the stuff I did to earn money."

Ruby stared. Wait, was perfect Tony Caruso not so perfect after all?

He nodded. "Oh, yeah, by the time I was fifteen, even though I was a good student in school, I was a hustler on the streets. I didn't know any different. I thought selling dope and breaking into houses to steal things was the only way to make it. But then God opened my eyes."

God again. But he seemed to really believe what he was saying. "What do you mean opened your eyes?"

He finally regarded her with an expression that made him seem suddenly older. "My mom started having heart problems and ended up in the hospital. Up to then, she'd been my only constant, like Opal is for you. But there she was, in the hospital, looking like she was going to die, and I thought, What am I gonna do without her? How'm I gonna take care of my little sister, Corinna, who was just twelve at the time? My life felt out of control. Scary. One day, when I was visiting the hospital and Ma was sleeping, I saw a Bible on the table next to her, so I picked it up and started reading. Hah." He laughed like he still couldn't believe it. "It was like God was in the room talking directly to me. Next thing I knew, I was on my knees, praying my heart out, asking God to heal my mother, to make me a better man. After that night, everything was different."

Ruby kept quiet. She and Opal had been raised in a faith-filled household, but when their mother died, Ruby's faith in a loving God had faded. When their father died next, she'd wondered how Opal could keep on believing.

"My mom got state-of-the-art treatment, and in two weeks she was back home with us. That's what got me interested in being a doctor. Corinna got accepted to a school for the arts—she wants to be an actress—and that school keeps her busy and off the streets. Best of all, I got a whole new outlook on life. Suddenly no challenge was too big —not even those medical bills from the hospital. Every time I came to a dead-end, a door would open. God has been amazing to me."

A peculiar weight pressured Ruby's chest. The urge to cry caught her off guard. She averted her face, pretending absorption in the view. What Tony had described couldn't be real. It couldn't be that easy to walk away from your past and start over again.

"You want to try it, Ruby?"

His hand covered hers, warm and inviting. A current of electricity seemed to flow into her bloodstream.

She wrested free, a little frightened by his zeal. "Is this the only reason why you brought me here? So you could convert me to your religion?"

The glow in his eyes immediately dimmed. She felt like she'd smacked him and immediately felt guilty for it. "I'm sorry. I didn't mean it like that. It's great that you're on the right track now and God's looking out for you, but I'm not interested."

"You're not interested." His dark eyebrows pulled together. "Hmm." He looked back outside.

Silence fell between them, broken only by the distant boom of the waves hitting the shore.

Ruby suffered immediate doubts. She had just gotten to the point where the thought of dating Tony held a certain appeal. She enjoyed his company. She didn't want their relationship to be over just yet. "Maybe I just need more time."

His relief was obvious. "Of course. Take all the time you need. So…" He threw a companionable arm over her shoulders. "You want to tell me what's going on that has you meeting me in alleyways?"

"Oh." She resigned herself to tell him. "It all started with my dad's death two years ago."

Tony went still. "Hasn't been that long."

"No. It was deemed an accident, but Opal and I knew all along he'd been murdered."

"Murdered!" His hold tightened, making her feel comforted and safe at the same time. "Right before his death, some ricin disappeared from the company he was working for, BioTech. My sister and I found entries in my dad's diary suggesting he suspected his friend and colleague. He probably confronted Eric, but they were friends, so my father didn't report him right away. He went on a business trip to West Virginia, where he was hit from behind and drove off the side of the mountain."

"Poor *Bella*," Tony crooned.

"Once Opal and I discovered Daddy's diary, we realized he was murdered. I made the mistake of calling Eric and accusing him. Next thing I knew, Eric was harassing me, then my sister. We figured he was the one who'd gotten Daddy killed, but then Eric was just found dead, shot in the head, so it probably someone else who killed him and Daddy, both. That's why police are protecting Opal and me. And that's why I had to meet you in an alley. I had to get away from them for a while."

Tony tipped her chin up so he could look her in the eyes. "You're serious."

"Yeah. You think I'd make all that up?"

Worry drew Tony's eyebrows back together. "Does your sister know where you are right now?"

"I told her I was with you and that you're a Navy SEAL, so I'm safe."

Tony blinked his impossibly long eyelashes. "I don't like the idea of you in danger."

The words warmed her. "I don't like it either."

"Would you mind if I kissed you right now?"

About time! "Just this once." She didn't want to sound too eager. After all, she might still decide Tony Caruso was way too young, and she might kick him to the curb before his obsession with her spiritual state became an issue.

"Well, hello, Miss Bonheur."

Opal looked up from the program for Monty's swearing-in cere-mony to find Special Agent Casey Fitzpatrick standing over her in a royal-blue suit and a yellow tie.

"Oh, hi." She sent him a quizzical smile and glanced around. "What brings you to this occasion?"

The special agent took the seat next to her while gesturing to a tall, redheaded woman standing amidst a knot of sharply dressed SEALs. "I'm friends with Charlotte Strong, wife of the operations officer. Last year, I convinced her to attend the FBI Academy. Now she works in the same field office I do."

"Really?" Intrigued, Opal admired the striking woman.

Fitz nodded. "She and her husband, Lucas—he's the big guy—were instrumental in my investigation and prosecution of the previous commander."

Opal's conversation with Monty the other night came to mind. "You were the one who caught the corrupt commander?"

"Not by myself. I couldn't have done it without those two, plus another SEAL named Saul Wade. I hear he's tending to some land he inherited in Oklahoma." Fitz shifted his focus toward Monty, who stood on a small stage with the acting commander, Jonah Mills, and the base admiral. "It's about time someone takes Dwyer's place." Fitz cut his green gaze to Opal. "Do you know what James Monteague was doing before this?"

The question sounded casual, but Opal could tell he was either fishing for information or wanting to know if she knew something he was already aware of. To her relief, the recording of a marching song began to play, sparing her from having to answer. The room fell silent as the color guard marched up the center of the room with flags, prompting those seated to stand.

Opal, having picked a seat near the stage, kept her eyes on Monty. Senior enlisted personnel had lined up on one side of the stage, while senior officers, including the tall, handsome husband of Charlotte, lined up on the other. At the back of the room, junior SEALs stood shoulder to shoulder as they lined the wall. One of them had to be Ruby's new friend.

Once the Pledge of Allegiance was spoken and the flags placed in their stands, the admiral stepped toward the mike. "Family and friends, please be seated. Operators, at ease."

A general rustle occurred as the civilians sat, and the SEALs assumed a parade-rest stance. Opal knew what to expect next as the procedure was the same as at any swearing-in. In a dry, succinct voice, Admiral Holland launched into a speech praising the accomplishments of the executive officer, Jonah Mills. Opal glanced toward his wife, Eden, whom she'd greeted when first arriving. The blond fitness instructor hadn't been pregnant when Opal had treated her for a strained hamstring. Opal had congratulated her on the baby that looked to be due shortly, and Eden had introduced Opal to her teenage daughter.

"These kinds of functions need to happen more often," Miriam had stated.

"She's missing school," Eden had explained.

Both mother and daughter were now gazing raptly at their SEAL. Jonah Mills stood at Monty's side, both men nothing short of impressive in their winter dress blues.

Imagining what it must be like to be married to a SEAL, Opal suffered a moment's envy.

The admiral turned to Monty next, highlighting his achievements that were also printed on the back of the program. Not only was he the leader of his ROTC program at UNLV, but he'd been the honor graduate at BUD/SEAL training, class 232. Recalling his worries about the opinions of his subordinates, Opal searched their expressions. She could see nothing but respect and acceptance on their faces. Certainly, no one seemed to condemn him for the Mother Eagle disaster.

Her gaze swung back to Monty, who'd cut his hair recently. The shorter style gave him a harder edge, as did his serious demeanor. This was not the playboy neighbor she'd known for years. The words he'd spoken the other day popped into her thoughts. *I couldn't be more repentant.*

With impeccable posture, he stepped forward, joining the admiral and the acting commander at the podium. In minutes, the leadership of Team Six was transferred from Jonah to Monty and sealed with a three-way salute. Then Monty was given the mike to address his new team members.

"You know, I used to believe that I could do anything. I could beat any opponent in any competition and come out on top. Nothing could stop me. Nothing could knock me off my pedestal."

A knot swelled in Opal's throat as she realized where his speech was going. He was addressing the elephant in the room, putting to rest the reservations his men might have about relying on him for leadership.

"I've since realized that the mighty will fall. That the first will be last." Silence filled the room as if everyone held a collective breath.

"Who among you wants to be great?"

His gaze shot toward some SEALs at the back of the room who must have raised their hands. He cracked a slight smile and nodded in acknowledgment. "Then here's my advice: Be a servant to every brother, everyone you know. If you want to be first, be the last man out. If you want to be remembered, touch the lives of those around you, not just your teammates. We're not invincible. We're not immortal. But we are united, supportive, collectively strong. So, yes, I'm your new commander. But, more than that, I am here for you any time, any day, anywhere."

Opal's heart had swelled with so much love and admiration that the buttons on the front of her work uniform were in danger of popping.

Monty thanked the attendees for coming, then stepped back. For a long second, nobody reacted. Then, with simultaneous zeal, every SEAL in the room bellowed, "Hooyah, Commander Monteague!" The guests clapped and stood, adding their own cheers.

As she joined in, Opal wiped away the tear sliding down one cheek. Monty had innate leadership, not to mention charisma. It wouldn't take long at all for his men to believe in his integrity, if he hadn't already convinced them.

Lieutenant Mills led him offstage for a Pass in Review, in which Monty would be formally introduced to men he'd already met under less formal circumstances. The admiral spoke into the mike, inviting family members and guests to partake of the cake and punch.

Fitz caught Opal's eye. "Well, better head back to the office."

"Wait." She caught his sleeve before he got away. "What's happening with the investigation?"

"Oh, I meant to call you. I got permission two days ago to access Sonja Novak's medical bills." He glanced around, then leaned closer so no one else could hear him. "Interestingly, they were all paid off by an anonymous source. My analysts are trying to put a name to the source, but it isn't easy. The funds were exchanged from cryptocurrency to cash, making it difficult to trace."

"So, you haven't discovered who bought the ricin from Eric."

"No. And there's more." Fitz pitched his voice even lower. "There have been two deaths in the past eighteen months attributable to ricin poisoning. Both men were upper-brass military. I'm waiting to hear from a coroner about two more."

Opal widened her eyes. "Someone's been poisoning senior officers?" She kept her voice at an incredulous whisper. "Why would anyone do that?"

He spread his hands. "When I know that, I'll have cracked the case."

"Oh, gosh. This just keeps getting worse." Opal folded her arms to quell a shudder.

"The payoff of Sonja's bills should have been caught two years ago. But don't worry. We'll get to the bottom of it." With a pat on her shoulder, he crossed the room to share a word with his new colleague, Charlotte.

Opal wandered to the punch bowl and helped herself to one of the cups already filled. Sipping it, she admired the enormous sheet cake with WELCOME LCDR MONTEAGUE written in red, white, and blue frosting, but having eaten lunch just a short while earlier, she couldn't bring herself to take a precut slice. Monty was still busy meeting his teammates. Opal eyed the view through the window and decided to step outside.

The officers club on Dam Neck Naval Annex stood some distance from the beach, with the ocean just visible above the grassy dunes. Braving a cold inland breeze, Opal moved to a patch of sunlight while standing on tiptoe to see over the sand dune. Cobalt waves bucked and tossed as if mirroring her thoughts about the ricin. To think that someone was using it to kill high-ranking officers!

Who would do that, and why? Now that Eric was dead, would they ever find the person responsible? More urgently, was the killer a threat to Ruby and her?

Sensing someone coming up behind her, Opal whirled to see that one of the senior enlisted who'd flanked the stage during Monty's ceremony had just joined her outside. Pinned in place by his translucent gaze, Opal marveled that his combination cap remained stuck to his dark head as he drew up next to her.

"Do you swim?" His question was uttered in a gruff voice that betrayed a quaint dialect.

"Of course." She marveled at the sheer number of service pins vying for space above his left pocket. He hadn't introduced himself, but his name and rank were readily apparent: Senior Chief McLeod. He appeared about a decade older than she was, with a handsome, weathered face, thick dark mustache, and eyes of such a pale hue they seemed almost colorless as they drifted over her.

Opal felt less than attractive in her khaki linen skirt and pumps.

"Women have an easier time treading water than men."

She found his observation strange. "Because they have more body fat?"

"Yes." He slanted an appreciative look at her figure.

Opal's face heated. Gosh, if only Monty looked at her like that, she'd have it made.

"Take a look out there."

She followed his pointing finger toward the ocean.

"Y'see that column of water that looks sandy? The waves are lower there."

Opal had to stand on tiptoe to see it. "Oh, yes."

"That's a riptide." He faced her suddenly. "One minute you're swimming near the beach, the next you're being sucked out to sea."

The ominous words sent a shiver down Opal's spine. Of course, it was November, and the weather was far from tropical.

"Do you know what to do," he quizzed her, "when that happens?"

Were they talking about something more than riptides? She tapped into her Red Cross training. "Um, stay calm and swim parallel to the shore?"

He didn't smile, but she got the impression that he was laughing at her. "What if you're not strong enough to escape the ocean's pull?"

His eyes were mesmerizing. "I don't know. I don't swim in the ocean all that much."

"Afraid of sharks?"

He was definitely laughing at her. "Aren't most people?"

He stuck his hand out suddenly. "My name's Amos."

"Opal." His hand swallowed hers completely, making her weak-kneed. She realized when he didn't immediately let go that he'd been flirting with her.

"Water's a little cold, or I'd take you for a swim right now." His thumb stroked the underside of her wrist, where he could no doubt feel her pulse.

With a nervous laugh, Opal tugged her hand free. The man was too much. To her relief, she heard the door squeak open, and Monty strolled toward them with a guarded look on his face.

Amos turned to acknowledge his approach. "Sir."

Monty gave him a hard look. "Senior Chief." He turned his attention to Opal, no doubt noticing her heightened coloring. "Did you get some cake?"

"I had to pass. Thank you for inviting me, though. The ceremony was well done, not too long, not too short. And your speech was perfect." She shut her mouth, aware that she was gushing.

"Thank you. Are you heading home now?"

Home? He made it sound like they lived in the same house. "No, I have to go back to work."

"But you'll be over tonight for the party, right?"

"Of course." Opal couldn't wait to be in the midst of one of Monty's famous parties, her first time ever to be invited.

"What about you, Senior Chief?" Monty's tone lost some of its warmth. "You should've received an invitation."

"I did. I'll do my best." Amos's mustache lifted in a semblance of a smile.

Monty reached for Opal's arm. "Come back in and try the cake, at least. It's bad luck not to have some."

She got the impression he was taking her away from the senior chief. The suspicion that he might be jealous lifted her spirits. Was it too much to hope the kiss he'd given her the other night hadn't been a thoughtless impulse?

"Could you point out Ruby's friend to me?" she requested as they stepped inside.

"Sure." Monty searched the crowded room. "There he is. I'll introduce you."

Several pairs of eyes tracked them as she accompanied Monty across the room. *This is how it would feel to be his wife.*

She wrested herself from the frivolous thought as Monty drew her toward a handsome young man laughing with his teammates.

"Caruso."

He turned and sobered immediately, but recognition lit his features, letting Opal know he'd already identified her.

"This is Opal, Ruby's older sister."

"Ma'am." The SEAL bestowed her with a blinding smile and held out his hand. "Ruby thinks the world of you, and I can see why."

Stunned, Opal accepted his handshake slowly. She'd never known Ruby to pursue a man in the military, let alone one so young. But he'd sold her in his first sentence. "Thank you. I hope to see more of you."

His grin widened. "That makes two of us."

She was tempted to ask him whether Ruby had made amends for back-ending his car, then decided to stay out of it.

Monty interjected, "Why don't you come to my party tonight, Caruso? Bring Ruby as a date."

Opal cast Monty a grateful look.

"Thank you, sir!" Given the young man's surprise, junior enlisted weren't normally invited. "I'd be honored."

"Just come and have fun. No honor required."

Tony met Opal's gaze. "I'll see you there, ma'am."

"Great. Good to meet you, Tony."

As she and Monty turned away, Opal smiled regretfully. "Thank you so much for inviting me, but I need to get back to work."

He nodded. "It means a lot to me that you came."

Not as much as it means to me. Suppressing the telling words, she returned his nod, spun on her pumps, and left the room, heading for the coat closet.

CHAPTER 14

*P*lucking up her courage, Ruby locked up behind her as she left Opal's to attend Monty's party. Opal was already there, having left early to help him set up. Who was going to break in with a police car parked at the curb? Ruby locked up all the same, then slipped the key into her bra since her dress didn't have a pocket. She'd left her coat behind—no need for it since Monty's house was right next door.

Going to a party full of middle-aged Frogmen held as much allure for Ruby as a trip to the dentist, but since Tony had texted to say he would be there, she knew it couldn't be as boring as it sounded. Just for him, she'd put on her prettiest dress and stuck a leopard-patterned bikini in her pool bag, thinking she might talk him into jumping into Monty's hot tub—not that she would have called Tony her boyfriend at this point. But, recalling his kisses at the top of the lighthouse, she had to admit she couldn't wait for him to kiss her again.

Her anticipation mounted as she waved at the police while coming off the porch, then hurried across the lawn toward Monty's home. She could hear techno music pulsing through his walls. People still listened to that stuff?

She was in Monty's yard when a silhouette detached itself from the trunk of the maple tree, startling her.

"Whoa." Ruby scuttled sideways, then recognized Tony and beamed. "Hey!" Her smile vanished as she took in the jungle-green fatigues he was wearing. He wasn't dressed for a party.

"Sorry." His signature smile was absent. "Didn't mean to scare you." He shifted, so the lights from Monty's house fell on her. "Wow, you look gorgeous."

"Thanks." Her red silk dress, reminiscent of a traditional Chinese qipao, was meant to help her forget the stresses of her new job. "Why are you dressed like that?"

He grimaced. "I can't make it to the party, *Bella*. I came to tell you that I'm going wheels up."

She braced herself for the worst, while admitting, "I don't know what that means."

"It means I'll be gone. Can't say where, can't say why."

Her expectations of a carefree evening evaporated in an instant. "Why does that sound so dangerous?"

His cocky smile made a brief appearance. "Well, I'm not exactly in the Boy Scouts. We SEALs take camping to a whole new level."

She suffered an overwhelming urge to cry. She'd worked so hard all week, learning the ins and outs of her new job. Having fun with Tony this weekend was supposed to be her reward, and here he was, telling her that he was going away.

He reached for her hands, holding them securely. "I met your sister at the swearing-in today. She's really nice."

"I know. I was invited, but I couldn't get off work." She clung to him, her disappointment mounting.

"So, how's the job situation? Better yet?"

"It's okay." It was only because of Tony that she'd made it through the first few days. How was she supposed to get through this transition phase without him around, cheering her on, telling her every day that anything worthwhile was always difficult at first? "I'll be moving back into my apartment soon." At least she was compensated for the added responsibility.

Tony frowned. "Don't you need to stay with your sister so the police can guard you? I tried walking up to your door just now, and they drove me away."

"They're so annoying. I got lectured for ditching them the other day."

"Well, it's for your own safety."

She rolled her eyes. "You're one to preach about safety. You can't even tell me where you're going. Can you at least say how long?"

"Sure, not too long. Couple of weeks. Here, I brought you something to read while I'm away."

In the fickle lighting, she made out a book as he passed it off to her. "What's this?" She was glad to see it wasn't a Bible.

"It's called *The Power of Positive Thinking*. It's been around for decades. Read it. It'll make your whole life better."

She frowned down at the yellow cover, doubting that was possible. Her life seemed a whole lot worse suddenly, with Tony going—what had he called it—wheels up?

Making a sudden decision, Ruby flung her arms around his neck and hugged him hard. "I want to date you," she blurted in his ear. "Please come back to me safe and sound."

To her delight, he did more than hug her back. He rocked her like a baby. Then he turned his head and caught her lips in a kiss that curled her toes within her beaded Chinese slippers. What a moron she'd been! To think that all this time she could have been kissing Tony, instead of playing hard to get. Suddenly it didn't matter that he was three years younger. She wanted to share her life with him—well, at least *this* part of her life.

He ended the kiss with a groan, stepping resolutely away from her. "I really have to go."

Fear coiled tentacles around her heart. Wouldn't it be just her luck that something awful happened to him? "Please, be careful."

He stretched out a hand, stroked the side of her face, then backed away. "I'll be all right. Read the book, you'll see. Ciao, *Bella*."

"Ciao." She'd gotten used to them saying *Ciao* over the phone. This time it felt far more permanent. Hugging the book he'd given her, Ruby watched him walk away until he slipped inside of his Honda. The engine revved and the lights blinked on. She stared after it until his taillights disappeared.

Reminded of the day she'd watched her father take off on his business trip, Ruby gave a whimper. Daddy had never come back. If Tony didn't return soon, she was sure she would never smile again.

Sitting in Monty's hot tub under a string of lit Edison bulbs, Opal thought of the time her father had taken her fishing out in the Chesapeake Bay. The blue fish she'd hooked had weighed almost as much as she did. She'd needed her father's help to reel it in.

Daddy wasn't alive to help her right now. And the fish she'd snagged on her latest lure was the size of a shark.

Help! she longed to cry, but she was a grown woman, fully capable of telling the shark in question to back off. Only he was underwater, showing her how long he could hold his breath so she couldn't use her words. All she could do was inch away from his mustache as he started nibbling her toes. Perhaps if she weren't wearing the hot-pink bikini Ruby had insisted she borrow, she wouldn't feel like Amos McLeod's next meal.

Why was the man so overwhelming? The couple Opal had intended to join had taken one look at his daunting features and abandoned the hot tub, leaving her alone with him. Amos had promptly pointed up at the night sky, much as he had at Monty's swearing-in, and had asked if she knew what star he was singling out—one of the few they could see because of the bright bulbs overhead.

She'd hazarded a guess. "The North Star?"

"Nope. It's not a star at all; it's the planet Mars."

To her astonishment, Amos had recited her a poem about Mars, the god of war, ever-present, throughout human history.

"That's eloquent." The lyrics had, in fact, disturbed her. "And you have it all memorized!"

"Hmph." His small smile, disguised by his mustache, had made her wonder if he hadn't written the verses himself.

"Do you like babies?"

She'd laughed at the unexpected question. "Of course. Who doesn't?"

"Some people don't. I had a baby once, a son."

With a gift for storytelling, he'd relayed how he'd come home from a fourth tour in the Middle East, anticipating his reunion with his six-month-old, whom he'd last seen at the baby's birth. Only he'd found his house completely empty. His wife had left him, taking baby—the center of Amos's universe—with her.

Opal had stared at him, sensing devastation in his gruff confession.

"I've been hunting for him for over five years now, using five different detective agencies. None have managed to find him."

"I'm so sorry." She had understood Amos better at that point, especially when he'd told her she would be a good mother. The poor man just wanted children and considered her a candidate to give him one!

When their conversation lulled, he'd said out of the blue, "Did you know I can breathe underwater?"

She hadn't believed him. "Really?"

His pale eyes had glinted. "I'll show you." That was when he'd submerged himself, many long minutes ago.

Apparently, he hadn't been lying. Up to the point where he'd begun nibbling on her toes, she'd enjoyed herself, a little. He was unusual, that was certain. With his quaint dialect and obvious intellect, he might even be attractive to some. For herself, she merely felt sorry for him and somewhat flattered that he recognized she would be a good mother.

But Opal was more aware of Monty's response to her being alone with Amos than she was of Amos himself. Given the number of times

Monty had stalked by the glass door to look at them, one might conclude he was jealous. Opal prayed that was the case and that he would intervene soon, before she had to muster the courage to check Amos's expectations.

To her relief, he finally came up for air, breaching the water's surface with stealth that drove home what he did for a living.

"I guess you *can* breathe underwater." Her voice sounded high and thin. She reached for her towel, sending the signal that she was getting out.

"I cheated." He sat smoothly on the ledge close to her. "I sucked air out of the jets."

"Oh." She laughed at his ingenuity while scooting several inches away. "I didn't realize that was possible."

"Anything is possible."

She gulped as he laid an arm along the back of the tub. To anyone catching sight of them, it would look like he just put his arm around her.

For the past twenty minutes, Monty had watched Opal with a protective eye. Amos McLeod, apparently oblivious to the message Monty had sent him earlier that day, had started chatting up Opal the instant he arrived at the party. When he'd talked her into joining another couple in the hot tub, agitation had slipped under Monty's skin.

Opal was a grown woman with every right to flirt with whomever she pleased, but those two were looking far too cozy out there.

He'd wrestled with himself. It wasn't like Opal was his girlfriend. Indeed, Monty had invited Tracy over to fulfill that role. But Opal was his friend and his neighbor. She was also good and kind and deserved nothing but the fullest amount of respect. And from what Monty could see, Amos was moving way too fast for respect to even be a factor.

Granted, Opal was one of only two single women in the room, but why did he have to go after *her*? Monty's blood pressure had risen steadily as he kept an eye on them. The urge to halt his senior chief's advances was gnawing at him. He had to do something, but he didn't want everyone else at his party witnessing what might become an ugly confrontation.

He glanced at his watch. The party had gone on long enough. He was tired and irritable and certainly not enjoying himself. In desperation, Monty turned to his new operations officer, Lieutenant Strong. "Lucas, I need to ask you a huge favor."

"Sure, anything, sir." The former NFL tight end, taller than Monty by a good three inches, smiled down at him.

"I need you to help me clear my house in five minutes. Party's over."

Lucas's smile vanished. He glanced astutely out the window Monty had just been looking out of. "Five minutes, sir?"

"Yes."

"But—" Lucas gestured to Tracy, who was showing off her best side while playing foosball with the lieutenant's wife. "What about her?"

"Everyone," Monty repeated, grateful that Jonah Mills had left a half-hour earlier. The man who'd run the Team in the absence of a commander might think him imbalanced for what he was about to do. Maybe he was. "I'll be in your debt. I know my request is a strange one."

Lieutenant Strong blew out a breath. "Can I talk to my wife first?"

"Sure." Watching the tall man converse with his impressive wife, Monty counted the beats of his hearts. All at once, Strong raised his voice over the techno music. "Listen up, people. The CO's not feeling too well, so the party's moving to my house."

Perfect, Monty thought as several people expressed their disappointment. Grateful to Strong for his cooperation, Monty started backing toward his bedroom. "Thank you all for coming. Don't want to get anyone sick."

Charlotte, Strong's wife, joined the mobilization effort. "Hop to it, people. Recycle all bottles. Drain any red cups before you put them in the trash. Designated drivers, raise your hand. If you've been drinking, go with one of those two, or I'll arrest you myself."

Several people chuckled at the thought of an FBI special agent making a DUI arrest.

"Monty, wait!" Tracy rushed up to him before he could shut his door. Professing profound disappointment, she hung on his neck and pouted.

Monty realized with a twinge of his conscience that he'd completely ignored her that evening. Sure, she was attractive, but they had nothing to talk about. "Listen, it's better to be safe than sorry. I don't want to get you sick, either." He pried her off him and gently pushed her away so he could close his door. He would break up with her another day.

Locked in his bedroom, Monty paced back and forth. Had he lost his mind? Offending his senior chief before they'd even begun working together wasn't the smartest thing to do. Amos might assume that Monty was drunk, but he had sworn off alcohol since the night he'd run across Opal's lawn and nearly gotten shot.

So where was his anger coming from? And was it warranted? Maybe Opal wanted to be courted by his senior chief. Then again, she had no idea—and he had only just heard it himself from Jonah Mills—that Amos was an excellent NCO but he hated women. So, no. Monty wasn't going to stand aside and let Amos woo Opal, only to trample her tender feelings somewhere down the road. He was going to make it clear that Opal wasn't available.

What if Amos didn't like that? The senior chief was built like a bull with a hard edge to his character that made him a dangerous enemy. Monty drew several deep breaths to lower his blood pressure.

At last, Strong bellowed, "Clear," allowing Monty to take action.

Summoning his self-control, he left his room and went straight to the back deck, where Opal and Amos were so caught up in each other that they had no idea the party was over.

As Monty stepped onto the deck, Opal sprang out of Amos's arms like a jack-in-the-box. The senior chief leveled his silvery gaze at Monty, noting his rigid stance. His gaze plumbed the house next, noting the lack of guests.

"Oh," he said.

"Everyone's gone home." Monty fought to keep his tone causal. He watched Opal lunge for a towel and stand up. Her cheeks were as pink as her bikini. As she stood clutching the towel, Monty unplugged the Edison lights to afford her some modesty, but not before enjoying a glimpse of her slim waist and flared hips.

He turned off the tub's jets next. Opal clambered onto the deck, but Amos took his time. He rose from the water like Poseidon himself. Rivulets streamed over his powerful trunk, glinting like rivers of mercury as he swung his feet to the deck. Then he reached for his towel and briskly rubbed himself.

All the while, his gaze swung between Monty and Opal, as if trying to determine their relationship. "Thank you for the conversation," he said to her without looking at her.

Opal shot Monty a defiant glance. "You're welcome."

Still dripping wet, Amos slung his towel around his neck and scooped up his carefully folded clothes. "Good party, sir." With a curt nod, he walked off the deck in just his swim trunks. He strode off into the dark, heedless of the cold, bound for his vehicle out front.

Monty felt some of his tension abate. Obviously, the man hadn't realized he was treading on his CO's territory. He'd backed off deferentially enough. Monty turned toward Opal. "I hope you had fun." The words were meant to be polite, but they sounded like an accusation.

She stared at him, saying nothing.

Monty tried again. "I'm sorry. I didn't mean that the way it sounded."

She shrugged. "That's fine. I'm just glad you rescued me." She backed toward his cabana. "Mind if I change so I don't have to walk home like this?"

The clothes she'd worn to the party were apparently in the little shower house. "Of course not. Go ahead."

She firmed her lips and disappeared from sight.

Mulling her words over, Monty dismissed the idea of inviting her inside—he was too confused by his feelings to want to talk about them. He went and fetched her coat, hanging on the hall tree by his front door. By the time he brought it out to her, he only had to wait a minute before she emerged, wearing the pretty blue dress she had worn to his party.

He was dying to know, "Did you want to be rescued?"

"Hah. Very much," she said with feeling. "That man is like a..."

"Shark?"

She cocked her head. "Yes, sharks are misunderstood creatures, as well."

Monty's sour mood returned. She sounded sorry for Amos. "I hear he hates women. You shouldn't see him again." He hadn't meant to tell her what to do, but the words slipped out.

"Oh?" Opal's eyebrows shot up. "I didn't take you for the kind to judge people out of hand, Monty. What if there's a perfectly good reason for him to mistrust women?"

"Sounds like you know him pretty well now." He couldn't help the petty comment.

She sent him a tight smile as she plucked her coat from his grasp. "I see how it is. To you I'm just the girl next door, but I can't be friends with anyone else, is that right?"

Her accusation annoyed him. "That's ridiculous!"

"Good night, Monty." Upset, she turned and marched off his deck, following the same path the senior chief had taken.

Monty stewed in her wake. How dare Opal imply he was being possessive. She'd said so herself—she'd needed to be rescued! Of course, he was willing to share her with other people, but Amos McLeod wasn't one of them. He would have trampled Opal's gentle spirit. He imagined her being McLeod's confidant and his temples throbbed.

Monty heaved a sigh of defeat. This was all his fault. He never should have kissed her the other night, putting romantic ideas in her head. There wasn't any excuse for that kind of misleading behavior—even though he still savored the memory of their surprising chemistry.

Monty clapped a hand to his forehead. "I'm a mess." Opal was right. He had no business interfering in her love life. He would apologize to her as soon as possible. Meanwhile, he would reap the consequences of his actions and clean up after his scattered guests, all by himself.

From the door of her home, Opal signaled to the police at the curb that she was locking up for the night. She couldn't believe Monty had wrenched her away from Amos, citing no other reason than that Amos hated women. Then when she'd accused Monty of being proprietary, he'd utterly denied it. "That's ridiculous," he'd said, like feeling jealous of her was the last emotion he would ever feel. The words still seared Opal's heart. This night couldn't have ended on a worse note!

Intent on rushing up to her room to shed tears of humiliation, she threw the deadbolt, hung up her coat, then hurried to the family room to turn off the lights there. The sight of Ruby on her couch, still in the dress she'd intended to wear to the party, drew Opal up short. Tears were streaming down her sister's cheeks.

"Ruby!" Opal rushed over and sat next to her. "You never came to the party. What's wrong? Why are you crying?"

Ruby's jewel-like eyes were bloodshot. "I'm such a terrible person," she lamented. She lifted a book from the arm of the couch and showed it to her.

"What's that?"

"It's a book Tony gave me to read. He came by to tell me he was leaving on a mission." Her voice wobbled. "I didn't realize until now that... he's really important to me, you know? I thought he was just a kid. He's only twenty-one years old, but now that I'm reading this book, I've realized *I'm* the kid. I'm like a twelve-year-old, maturity-wise, and he's the adult. I'm so ashamed of myself!" A fresh wave of tears crested in her eyes and dripped off her lower lashes.

"Oh, honey." Opal couldn't bring herself to lie and tell Ruby she was wrong. It came as a relief to hear of her sister's growing pains. "It's okay to realize that we're flawed. How else are we going to improve? Here." She reached for the box of tissues on the coffee table and offered it to her sister.

Ruby dabbed at her cheeks and blew her nose. "What if something happens to him? Everyone I love dies."

Foreboding tightened Opal's scalp. "Don't say that, honey. I'm still here. You love me, don't you?"

"Very much."

Ruby's immediate reply surprised Opal. "Aww."

"I'm so sorry. I've caused you so much grief over the years."

Opal tsked her tongue to signify that it was nothing. "You're my sister." She stroked Ruby's lovely ringlets, wishing she'd inherited them as well.

Ruby thought for a moment. "I just wish I'd been nicer to Tony. I'll never forgive myself if something happens to him."

At the anxious look in Ruby's eyes, Opal put an arm around her shoulders. "Honey, SEALs train day in and day out for what they do. They're prepared for just about anything."

"But accidents happen. Like the one Monty was in."

Opal leaned away to look at Ruby. "You haven't told anyone about that, have you?"

"No!" Ruby seemed offended that Opal would even suggest it. "Has he ever talked to you about it?"

Opal nodded. "Several times." Hurt pricked her anew as she recalled her mortification that evening. Now Monty had to know she was smitten with him. "Let's talk about you and Tony." She handed Ruby the book that had slipped to the floor. "I suggest that while he's gone, you read this book he gave you, and you focus on your career. That way, you'll dazzle him with your maturity when he returns."

Ruby sent Opal a tremulous smile. "I was going to do that." Her smile faded as she searched her sister's face. "How was the party?"

Opal lifted a shoulder in a shrug. She wasn't about to tell Ruby about Amos's attempt to flirt with her or of Monty's possessive response. "It ended rather suddenly. I think Monty was tired or something."

"You're not helping him clean up?"

"Not tonight." Opal stood abruptly. She was proud of herself for walking away and not staying to help like she'd offered to, earlier. If Monty had no intention of dating her himself, then he had no right telling her who she should or shouldn't talk to—not that she would ever date Amos McLeod. But she wasn't Monty's girl Friday either, there to help and comfort him, getting nothing in return. "I need to wash this chlorine from my hair. You going to be okay?"

Ruby sent her a feeble smile. "Yeah. I think I'll stay up and read for a while."

Opal had never heard her sister say those words before. "Good for you. Goodnight, honey."

"G'night."

Slipping into bed thirty minutes later, Opal couldn't help but notice Monty's lights were still on. No doubt he was still wiping up sticky stains and taking out the trash. Ignoring her twinge of guilt, she rolled away from the glow in her windows and willed herself to sleep.

CHAPTER 15

"*H*ey, it's Charlotte," said the woman on the other end of Fitz's office phone.

The question in her tone was clear. She wanted to know why he'd left a message on her phone earlier, requesting that she call him back. After all, they'd seen each other at Monty's change-of-command ceremony just the other day.

Fitz sat back in his desk chair, happy to hear from her. "Thanks for returning my call, Charlotte. I'm sure you're very busy."

"I've got ten minutes."

In other words, get to the point. He loved that about Charlotte. She didn't beat around the bush. "I've got a question for you." He couldn't wait for her to finish filling in her "coloring book," as the saying in the Bureau went. Every young agent was required to take on a number of different jobs before becoming an investigative special agent. "I'm not sure if you're aware, but there've been four high-ranking military leaders who have died under mysterious circumstances in the past eighteen months. I managed to arrange for all four bodies to be exhumed, and it turns out every one of them was poisoned by ricin." He backtracked, explaining the case he was working on for Opal and

Ruby Bonheur. "Seems to me, whoever stole the ricin has been busy using it."

"What do all four victims have in common apart from their military service?" she wanted to know.

"Too much, actually. They all served for the last three decades. They've all worked as military consultants in the D.C. area. They all tend to lean to the left, politically. I need to narrow down their commonalities. I was hoping you could suggest a way for me to do that."

"Hmm." She fell silent. "I don't know any of them well enough to connect the dots. What if you were to leak your theory of ricin poisoning to the press?"

Fitz balked at the suggestion. The FBI and the press were not on the best of terms. "And I would do that because...?"

"Number one, so that high-ranking officers know to be vigilant. The killer might be plotting to kill someone else in the same manner. Two, there's a chance that someone out there knows exactly who runs in all of the victims' circles."

Fitz scratched his clean-shaven chin. "I'll think about that," he promised. "Everything good on your end?"

"Could be better. Lucas is heading overseas right after Thanksgiving. You're still coming over to celebrate with us, right?"

"Wouldn't miss it for the world."

"Great. See you then, my friend. Gotta run."

Fitz put the phone down, remembering a time when Charlotte mistrusted him. Their friendship had come a long way. He sat back in his chair, considering her advice. After a minute of weighing the odds, he shrugged and sat forward. "What the heck." Toggling his mouse, he roused his computer to look up the best way to contact WAVY Television's newsroom.

～

Within his office at the Team building on Dam Neck Naval Annex, Monty rounded his desk to gently close his office door. It took all of his self-control not to slam it shut. As the noises that had been distracting him all afternoon dimmed, he heaved a sigh of relief.

Maintaining an open-door policy was an intentional leadership decision, but it was giving him a headache. The buzz of voices, punctuated by laughter in the break room or Senior Chief McLeod's bark, was making Monty as edgy as a Gerber blade.

He returned to his desk and thumped down into his wheeled chair. He found where he'd left off in the manual he was perusing, but after reading the same line three times, he accepted that he'd lost focus.

Monty slapped the book shut. He dropped his face into his hands and rubbed his closed eyelids. A vision of Opal standing there with accusation in her eyes taunted him. *"I see how it is. To you I'm just the girl next door, but I can't be friends with anyone else, is that right?"*

Her words betrayed feelings for him and the wish that he would think of her as more than the girl next door. Who could blame her? Their kiss by the fire had been lovely—so lovely that it made him think of her in ways that weren't exactly platonic. And now, apparently, she wanted something more between them than just friendship —which he did not. Or did he? Now that she had gone radio silent on him, a hole gaped in his chest where previously he'd felt nothing but warmth and satisfaction.

He missed their friendship. For days, he'd been wanting to pick up the phone to tell her how his first few days in the office were going. He was itching to know if there were any updates on her end, especially with regards to the FBI investigation. He had noticed on his way into work that the police weren't standing guard outside her home anymore. What was the deal with that?

Monty consulted his wristwatch. Normally Opal was just getting home around now. What would she do if he called her? He couldn't picture her hanging up on him. Longing just to hear her voice, he scrounged up his courage and punched an outside line. As he tapped out the number he had memorized, butterflies swarmed his stomach.

Why am I nervous? he asked himself as he listened to her cell phone ring. Once he reestablished their easy rapport, he would be content again.

On the fourth ring, she picked up. "Hello?"

Affectionate feelings ambushed him. "Hey, it's Monty."

"Oh." She sounded startled, like she hadn't been expecting to hear from him. "Hi."

"I'm calling from my office to check up on you. Are you home from work already?"

"No, I'm still at the hospital doing paperwork. It's been like this since Sparks went on maternity leave."

Her willingness to talk to him warmed him. Surely things would go back to normal between them. "How much longer until she comes back?"

"Two more weeks. So, how's the new job going? Do you like it?"

Pleased to hear her interest, he examined his sizeable office, content with his new digs. "It's good. My XO's been a real asset. He's been running the Team for a year, so there's nothing he doesn't know."

"That's great. What's the atmosphere like?"

Was that her way of asking how he was getting on with his senior chief? "It's surprisingly relaxed, considering we're responsible for the safety of the entire southern hemisphere."

She hummed thoughtfully. "How's Senior Chief McLeod?"

She'd come right to the point this time but with no rancor in her voice. "He's fine." He kept his own tone neutral.

"There's no tension between you two?"

She sounded concerned that she might have caused problems for them. "No, we're professionals. We don't let personal stuff drive our working relationship."

"I'm glad to hear that."

Monty was glad he'd called. In just a few words, they had brushed the incident under the carpet. He remembered the purpose of his call. "Hey, I noticed your watchdog wasn't out front this morning. What's going on with the case?"

"Well," her tone turned disapproving, "Skags scrubbed our security because he needed his men for another job. Fitz is working on replacing them, but that takes time, apparently. At least we haven't been harassed since Eric's death. Maybe his killer's not a threat to us."

Monty didn't want to make any assumptions. "Did you see the article about ricin poisoning in Sunday's paper?"

"Yes, Ruby reported on it earlier today. So far, four murders by ricin are confirmed. Fitz says a fifth body is going to be exhumed soon."

"Unbelievable. Is there a way to know if the ricin used to kill them was the same that Novak sold?"

"I don't know. And now that Eric's dead, it's up to Fitz to determine what ties the victims together—or, rather, who."

Monty pictured the savvy special agent. "I wouldn't underestimate Fitz. I wish he were protecting you and Ruby, though, now that I'm at the office twelve hours a day."

"Don't worry about us. We'll be okay."

Her firm and slightly distant tone took Monty aback. Maybe they hadn't whisked the incident under the rug completely. Maybe an apology was in order.

"Listen, I'm sorry for being a jerk at my party. It's just that you're a really good person, Opal." He pitched his voice lower so he wouldn't be overheard. "And Amos McLeod isn't worthy of you. I didn't want to see you used by him, that's all." He hoped she hear his underlying message: *In other words, I'm not jealous. You can be friends with whomever you want.*

Opal met his apology with silence. Finally, on an even cooler note, she said, "I appreciate your keeping an eye on me, Monty. But I can decide for myself whether a man is worthy of me. Thanks for calling. I need to finish this work now."

She hung up on him abruptly. Monty stared at the receiver in his hand, stunned. The contentment he'd been feeling seconds earlier gave way to a knot of discontent.

Opal had rebuffed his attempt to reconcile. Wow. Plainly, their friendship didn't mean as much to her as it did to him. That rankled. "Fine." He put down the receiver with a huff of frustration. He'd never wanted Opal in the first place.

With a scowl of determination, Monty opened the manual in front of him and continued reading.

~

Tony was shaking the vending machine in the TV lounge on the *USS Gerald R. Ford* aircraft carrier, trying to get his can of much-needed caffeine to un-lodge itself and tumble down to the dispensing trough. At the sound of a familiar voice, he whirled toward the sofa, where two of his teammates flipped through channels looking for something to watch.

"Hey, go back to the news station," Tony demanded, forgetting his stuck beverage.

Theo, his roommate, cast him a funny look but complied all the same.

Tony gasped. There was Ruby Bonheur standing in front of a building with the sun shining in her eyes, giving a report recorded earlier that day. It had found its way onto a national news station and then, via satellite, onto the aircraft carrier where the SEALs had been plotting their extraction of four CIA operatives who'd landed in a Venezuelan prison.

"Hey, that's the girl who came to our house." Theo turned up the volume so they could hear her better.

"Man, she is hot!" the third SEAL exclaimed.

Hot was right. Wearing a snug yellow sweater, her copper hair billowing in the breeze, Ruby took Tony's breath away.

"—from this laboratory at BioTech two years ago," she said as she gestured to the building behind her. "Ricin, which is a deadly toxin derived from castor beans, has been identified by Homeland Security as a potential bioweapon for terrorists, as just the tiniest bit is deadly if inhaled, ingested, or injected into the bloodstream. A recent investigation into the deaths of *four* high-ranking military officers suggests a disturbing chain of events. Master Sergeant Ernest Aimes, U.S. Marine Corp; Colonel Luis Sauers of the U.S. Army; Navy Commander Jonathan Pruitt; and most recently General Mason Blinn of the U.S. Joint Chiefs of Staff were all injected with ricin and died within eighteen months of each other. Law enforcement believes the four men were killed with the very same ricin that disappeared from BioTech the summer before last."

The three SEALs remained silent, glued to the words coming out of Ruby's mouth.

"Whoever murdered these four officers is also believed to have killed two of BioTech's technicians—first, Danny Bonheur, who died in a hit-and-run five months after the ricin disappeared."

The man's photograph made Tony's nape prickle. Ruby looked just like her father.

"And, most recently, Eric Novak, the man suspected to have sold the ricin in a desperate bid to pay off his ailing wife's medical bills, was left dead on the side of the road. The FBI has issued the following warning to top military officials: Remain vigilant. The Ricin Killer is still at large. Anyone with insight as to the killer's motive should contact the FBI at the number on the screen. This is Ruby Bonheur for WAVY TV News at Noon, reporting from Norfolk, Virginia."

Tony scraped his palm over his stubbled jaw as he suffered the sudden conviction that Ruby was in danger now. And here he was, almost two thousand miles away, unable to protect her.

Theo turned the volume back down while he twisted in his seat to look back at Tony. "Bet you wish you weren't here right now."

"Hey, I've got a motive for the FBI," drawled the third SEAL suddenly.

They both looked over at Wooly, thus named for his blond afro and the fact that his real name was Woloszynowski, which no one could pronounce, let alone spell.

"What?" Tony and Theo asked simultaneously.

"All of the victims are passivists. They got old and lost their taste for war."

Theo rounded on him. "How do you know that?"

"I watch a lot of news. All of those old guys wanted to end the war in Afghanistan."

"So? That's no reason for someone to kill them," Theo stated.

Wooly shrugged. "If you can't take the heat, get out of the kitchen—that's what I say. I should call that number now." He nodded at the screen where the number for the FBI was still displayed.

Calling was impossible, of course, as all three SEALs' cell phones were secured in their lockers back at the Team building. Wooly jumped up and started for the costly pay phone installed next to the vending machines.

Just then, their squad leader, Xavier, poked his dark head into the portal. "Let's go, Blue. Helo's waiting."

The three SEALs shared a look of frustration as they headed for their packs. There were rare occasions when Tony wished he weren't in SEAL Team Six's most elite platoon, Blue Squadron, and this was one of them. But the sooner they rescued the imprisoned CIA operatives, the sooner he could get back to the Beach to protect Ruby from an unknown threat.

Lyle Ritter had expected his phone to ring ever since the news story aired at noon that day. Not ten minutes after the second airing at 6:00 p.m., he got the call he was expecting. He answered, putting his phone on speaker so he could talk and cook dinner at the same time. "Hello."

"Did you watch the news this evening?"

Lyle would have recognized the creaky voice anywhere. "Yes. I told you it was only a matter of time before someone connected the victims."

"I don't care if they know about the ricin. I only care if they can trace it back to me. The news just stated Eric Novak was left dead. I thought you made it look like a suicide."

Lyle winced. "Apparently, I'm not that good at suicides." But he excelled at homicides.

"What did Novak say to you? How did this whole thing get leaked to the press, anyway?"

"Novak told me Danny had a journal, and his daughters found it. He must have put his suspicions of Novak in the journal. I doubt there's anything in there about us."

"You don't know that for sure, Ritter. I want you to find this journal. If the cops already have it, question the younger Bonheur sister, and find out what they know."

Lyle snorted with disgust. "None of this would've happened if we'd taken Novak out of the picture earlier."

A pregnant pause followed his statement. Finally, "That's the difference between you and me, Ritter. You kill because you like it. I kill as a matter of justice."

Lyle bared his teeth. "Dead is dead," he pointed out.

"I don't want you hurting the girl. And don't leave any clues that can be traced back to you."

Lyle leaned a hand on the countertop. "I wasn't hired for this kind of thing. I want 10K wired to me. Now."

The caller sputtered on the other end. "I don't owe you a dime, Ritter. If not for me, you would have been dishonorably discharged and never been hired at BioTech in the first place."

Lyle shrugged. "Find the journal or question the girl yourself, then, if you're so worried."

"You know I can't." Frustration frayed the caller's voice. He growled into the phone. "Fine. I'll wire the money now."

The phone clicked in Lyle's ear. Mollified, he stabbed a finger at his phone, ending the call. Stepping closer to the stove, he stirred the bubbling sauce for his stroganoff.

～

Lyle noted the white Oldsmobile backed into the driveway with relief. Only the younger Bonheur sister was home from work, and she'd left the garage door wide open for him. Finding out how much Danny's daughters knew ought to be easy, provided he could get that much out of Ruby before Opal came home.

It was already dark. Lyle parked at the curb and killed his engine. He donned a ski mask, hiding his face, then darted across the lawn into the unlit garage. Sure enough, Ruby had left the entry from the garage to the house unlocked. He slipped through it, finding himself in a laundry room. Creeping toward the brightly lit foyer, he could hear Ruby upstairs playing loud music. She might as well have rolled out the red carpet for him.

He was just about to climb the staircase and confront her when the headlights of a car strafed the glass insert at the front door. Drat! The elder sister was arriving home already. Lyle's heart raced as he reviewed his options. He reached inside his jacket for his gun. Managing two women at once was more than he had bargained for. He would wait to grab just one of them later.

As the garage door rumbled closed, Lyle darted for the front door, unbolting it, and letting himself out. Half a second later, Opal Bonheur let herself in through the laundry room.

"Hello!" Opal called up to the second story, but Ruby couldn't hear her over the music she was playing.

Heaving a sigh of frustration that Ruby had left the house wide open, Opal shook off her coat and hung it in the hallway closet. Thank goodness Fitz had found a SOG to keep an eye on them—that had to be who the sleek black Dodge across the street belonged to. She would go out and introduce herself to him later. Maybe she would cook for all three of them—anything to keep from dwelling on Monty, who didn't like the thought of her dating Amos but didn't want her for himself.

Closing the closet door, Opal found Ruby coming down the stairs with a huge, unwieldy box in her arms.

"What's going on? Why did you leave the garage door open?"

Ruby peeked around her load. "Oh, hi. I didn't know you were home."

"What are you doing?"

"Moving back to my apartment. The friends I was subletting it to found a place of their own."

"What?" Opal blocked Ruby's path as she came off the stairs. She reached out to steady the box. "No, you can't move out now. We don't know that it's safe yet."

"I'll be fine. If the Feds aren't worried, then I'm not worried. But, just in case, I bought a weapon."

"A weapon! Stop. Give me that." Opal wrested the box from Ruby's grasp only to discover that it weighed a ton. She put it down before she dropped it. "Who taught you to pack this way? Honey, please, just slow down and explain why you're moving out now, of all times."

Ruby heaved a loud sigh and put a hand on the newel post. "I miss my stuff and having my own space. That book Tony gave me—it's changed the way I think. All I have to do to have an awesome life is to trust in God to look out for me. Every morning, I say, 'All things are possible, through Christ who gives me strength,' and then get up and go. It works. It's amazing!"

Opal stared at Ruby in astonishment. To her surprise, she did look different. Her face was flushed with purpose. She was dressed in practical jeans and a pretty peach sweater that covered her midriff. She looked capable and determined. "You bought a weapon?"

"Not really. It's a self-defense siren that can be heard for a mile. Criminals run when they hear it. Besides, you've met my neighbor. Who's going to get past her?"

A vision of Ruby's self-appointed watchdog came to mind. "But..." She caught herself from revealing how reluctant she was to live alone.

"And you have Monty keeping an eye on you."

Opal looked down at the box. She couldn't bring herself to tell her sister that her friendship with Monty had cooled off substantially—not that it was ever very hot in the first place.

"Well..." She smiled up at Ruby, fighting to keep her dismay from showing. Far be it from her to undermine her sister's growing independence. "If you've made up your mind, I can't stop you. But I want you to keep your cell phone charged and on your person at all times."

"Don't worry. I keep my cell on me for work anyway. You'll always be able to reach me. Listen, Opal..."

Hearing something new in her sister's voice, Opal waited.

"I just want to say thanks." Ruby sent her a tremulous smile. "And not just for taking me in recently but for everything you've done for me in the past two years—even before that. If not for you, I'd probably be living on the streets and unemployed."

Opal clicked her tongue at the exaggeration.

"No, seriously. The reason I fell apart and you didn't was because you had faith in God, and I didn't. It's a huge thing, isn't it? But I get it now. You've been such a good role model to me."

Opal's throat clogged with emotion. Closing the distance between them, she hugged her sister hard, happy for her but sad for herself. "That's what sisters are for," she murmured.

They clung to each other for a long moment, then both stepped back at the same time. Ruby bent down to pick up the box.

"Let me help with that." Opal got the other side, and, between the two of them, they carried it to the front door. "Why isn't this bolted?" Over the top of the box, she sent her sister an exasperated look.

"I didn't unlock it."

Thinking it more likely that Ruby had just forgotten, Opal let it go. They descended from her porch with the box and headed for Ruby's car.

"Who is that?" She strained to see around the box.

The Dodge across the street was still there, its engine idling. Its tinted windows kept them from seeing inside. "I think that's one of Fitz's surveillance guys. I'll tell him to keep an eye on your place tonight."

"Thanks." Ruby frowned at the vehicle. "I'm surprised I didn't notice him earlier."

As they set the box in Ruby's trunk, Monty's Jeep appeared around the corner of their block, headed for his home. Opal quelled the leaping of her pulse. Ruby waved at him as he turned into his driveway, but Opal averted her gaze.

"I assume you have more boxes in your room?" She didn't want to have to look at him.

"About four more, plus my suitcase."

"Let's go get them." She turned toward the house, determined to forget about Monty.

Wordlessly, Ruby followed Opal inside.

Ten minutes later, Ruby's trunk was packed with everything she'd brought with her. The sisters hugged one more time, then Ruby got into her car and drove off, clearly excited to be moving onward and upward. With a sigh of loss, Opal started toward the surveillance specialist to ask him to keep an eye on Ruby and not on her. Before she got anywhere close to him, the dark Dodge pulled a U-turn and roared after Ruby's Oldsmobile.

Opal stepped back and shrugged. "Okay, I guess you read my mind." Doing an about-face, she plodded toward her door. A solitary cricket gave a lonely trill from within the mulch of her flowerbeds. No doubt his companions had all perished in the recent frost. With that bleak thought, Opal climbed her stoop and went inside, bolting the door behind her.

CHAPTER 16

*L*yle Ritter glared at the intruder through his night-vision goggles. *Who the devil is that?*

Wedged between a pair of overgrown holly bushes, Lyle had waited hours to catch Ruby Bonheur alone. When she'd moved out of her sister's place, he'd had thought nabbing and questioning her would be a piece of cake. He could not have been more wrong.

Upon arriving at a nearby apartment complex, Ruby had been greeted by an older woman who'd helped her unload her vehicle, then Ruby invited her neighbor to her own apartment and fed her dinner. Lyle had gone in search of his own meal. When he came back, he'd hidden himself in his current hiding place, where he'd determined Ruby was alone in her apartment. He'd watched her lights go out, then waited for a quiet moment in which to approach her door. Alas, every soul living at Fair Oaks had to walk by Ruby's door to get to their own apartment.

It was ten minutes to ten when a young man strode from the parking lot, straight up to Apartment 101. Watching from within the bushes, the leaves of which pricked Lyle even through his coat, Lyle scrutinized the interloper. The young man was dressed like he'd come straight from one of the local military bases. He knocked on Ruby's door and waited. Great. Now Ruby would have a boyfriend staying the night. At this rate, Lyle would never get to question her.

With a mutter of frustration, he deliberated his next move. There was more than one way to skin a cat. His boss had said to leave the elder Bonheur be, but she was easier prey, living in a big house all alone. For that matter, she worked just down the road from BioTech, where Lyle worked security.

He'd already gotten his money, so what did it matter where his information came from?

Something roused Ruby from a light slumber. She lifted her head from the pillow, then looked and listened. The diffuser had run out of water, as indicated by the solid red light. Ruby pried a wax plug from one ear and strained to hear over her white noise machine. Her bedroom doorknob gave a rattle.

With a stab of fear, she groped under the pillow for the self-defense siren she'd stowed there. Jerking to a sitting position, heart jumping in her chest, she pointed it at the door as it swung inward. *I should have stayed with Opal.* She thumbed off the siren's safety.

A man's silhouette filled the doorframe. Ruby leaped to her feet, squeezed her eyes shut, and depressed the siren's button.

The result was a deafening blare that sent the stranger diving for the floor. What? He was supposed to turn tail and flee! With the siren still shrieking, she snapped on her lamp and braved a peek over the edge of her bed. At the same time, Tony looked up with an incredulous expression.

"Turn that thing off!" he shouted, coming to his feet.

She depressed the button again, and the blaring stopped.

They stood there staring at each other. Then Ruby tossed aside the noisemaker and threw herself at him. "You're back!"

"Whoa, whoa." He pried her off him. "I'm filthy. You don't want to get too close. What the heck was that thing? I think I'm deaf!"

"Isn't it great? It's even better than pepper spray."

"Argh." Tony stuck a finger in his ear and wiggled it. "You could've just answered your door instead of blasting me."

"I didn't hear you. How'd you get in?"

He shot her a grin. "You know how. I went to your sister's house first and woke her up. She told me you were back in your apartment and that no one's been arrested yet for all these murders." He crossed his arms, biceps swelling beneath the rolled-up sleeves of his uniform. "Why would you move out? You're putting your life at risk."

Ruby raised her chin. "Because I'm my own woman now. I don't need to impose on my sister anymore."

Tony took in her defiant stance, his gaze appreciative. "You look like your own woman," he volunteered.

"The book you gave me," she continued, eager to update him, "it's really helped. I'm living in a positive frame of mind every day. Good things are happening at work. It's changed my life!"

"You actually read the book?" He sounded dubious.

"Yes!"

"Well, good for you." He rewarded her with a grin.

"So, how was the mission? I've missed you so much!"

"Op," he corrected. "It's called an op, short for operation."

"Well, how was it?"

"Good, but I can't give you any specifics, except to say I think I tracked mud into your apartment. I'm sorry. When you didn't answer the door, I freaked out and let myself in. I was afraid I would find your body."

"Don't even think that."

"I know, but I saw you on the news, *Bella*. And I realized you're caught up in this ricin thing. I've been worrying about you ever since. Now that I'm here, I can protect you."

The macho assertion would have offended her if anyone else had said it. "Thank you. I really want to hug you." It was all she could do to keep her distance.

"Not until I've had a shower. I'd like to use yours. Then I'll sleep on your couch, if you'll let me."

"Sure." She would rather he slept in her bed, but Tony, she suspected, was the old-fashioned sort. "Wait," she added as he started for her bathroom. "There's something I've been wanting to say."

As he faced her again, she had second thoughts. What if Tony had changed his mind about her?

"Go ahead and say it. Be brave."

"I think I'd like to date you now."

His slow grin let her know he was happy to hear it. "Well, guess what?"

"What?"

"You're going to want to marry me next."

Ruby gulped.

A pounding at the door interrupted their conversation.

"Ruby!" came Mrs. Vater's voice. "Are you okeey? Shall I call the police?"

"That would be my watchdog, Mrs. Vater."

Tony chuckled and gestured for the door. "Yeah, we've met. Better go and tell her that you're okeey." He imitated Mrs. Vater's accent. "I'm going to go scrub the filth off."

At six in the evening, Opal slapped shut the file in her hands. She was done reviewing treatment on her long-time patients, including Admiral Jenkins whose knees were resistant to therapy and would soon require surgery. After placing the folder in the surgery tray for Dr. Huxley to review, she snatched up her coat and purse. On her way out of Orthopedics, she bid goodnight to the petty officer still at the reception desk, before heading for the elevator. The Portsmouth Medical Center stood quiet, with only the ER open past regular hours.

At the exit to the flyover, Opal donned her jacket. The open-air walkway led from the hospital to a three-story parking garage for patients and employees. Her footsteps blended with the sound of traffic from the nearby interstate as she crossed it. All at once, the lights in the parking garage blinked off. Opal's step faltered. No thanks to the early dusk, the garage, which was usually well illuminated, stood in utter darkness. She fetched her cell phone from her purse, thinking she would use the flashlight feature.

But then a figure bearing an actual flashlight appeared at the threshold up ahead. "Sorry, ma'am. We've got a breaker problem. Can I help you find your car?"

He wore the uniform of a security officer. Happy to take him up on his offer, Opal continued forward. "Sure." Behind the glare of his light, she could make out a large frame and a square face.

"Watch that step, ma'am." He pointed his light at the floor.

"Thank you. I parked along the left inner wall, this way."

Following her cue, he struck out with an efficient stride that had her hurrying to keep up. Their footsteps echoed in the quiet, virtually empty deck.

With her phone still curled in her hand, Opal started to call Monty. The rift between them had become unbearable. If all he wanted from her was friendship, then so be it. It wasn't his fault that he didn't see her as his potential wife. Their attraction was undoubtedly one-sided. But now that her humiliation had faded, she realized she would rather remain neighborly than become estranged just because of her pride. Perhaps tonight, he would join her for dinner. They could do take-out since she hadn't found time to pick up groceries lately.

Thumbing through her contacts, she found the number he had called her from the other day—his office number. Chances were, he was still at work, as both of them had been coming home late these days. She would place the call as soon as she got into her car. Lifting her gaze, she discovered they were nearing it.

"Here I am. The blue one." Whoever had parked right next to her was still at work, evidently.

Opal kept her phone in her left hand and unlocked her car with the right. The security guard had come up behind her to shine the light on her door. "Thank you." She flashed a smile to send him on his way.

His light turned off. "You're welcome."

The door she was pulling open slammed abruptly shut. A massive hand clamped over Opal's mouth and hauled her back against his larger frame. Her cell phone clattered to the concrete floor, followed by her purse. Through the sleeve of her trench coat came a searing prick. As she struggled to free herself, Opal kicked her phone with her heel.

Confusion turned into horrifying clarity as she realized she'd been injected with a foreign substance. *Ricin?* No, she decided. Ricin took up to twenty-four hours to poison someone, yet she could already feel the effects of whatever was in her bloodstream. His thick hand over her mouth muffled her scream for help. How could this be happening here, at this high-security hospital?

Don't give in. Don't give in. But the substance was turning her thoughts fuzzy, making her muscles useless. As her knees gave out, her attacker caught her from crumpling. She managed a moan of protest now that his hand was gone from her face. The sound was too feeble for anyone to overhear. That was her last conscious thought.

Annoyed by the interruption, Monty snatched up his ringing office phone and rapped out, "Commander Monteague." The proposal he was wading through required concentration. "Hello," he said when the caller failed to speak.

Strange noises captured his attention. He leaned over the phone to see who was calling him. His pulse jumped as he recognized Opal's number. "Hello," he said again.

He was thinking their connection was bad when the sound of heavy breathing reached his ears, accompanied by a virulent curse—in a man's voice. Then the line crackled as if someone had grabbed the phone and dragged it closer. The call abruptly ended.

Monty gently lowered the receiver. Instinct told him not to ignore what he'd just heard. Why would a man be speaking into Opal's phone? He waited three seconds, picked up the receiver, and called her back.

The phone rang and rang. When Opal's voice mail picked up, goosebumps sprouted on Monty's forearms. "This isn't good." The number he needed was on his cellphone, which was out in his car. He buzzed the duty desk.

"Xavier, put me through to the physical therapy clinic at Portsmouth Naval Medical Center, ASAP. I'll wait."

"Yes, sir."

Monty counted the beats of his heart as he waited.

"Putting you through now, sir."

"Good." At last, a phone rang on the other end.

"Petty Officer Davis."

It was the corpsman who put moist heat packs on his back. "Davis, Commander Monteague here. Can you tell me if Lieutenant Bonheur has left the hospital yet?"

"Uh, yes, sir. She left about ten minutes ago."

Oh no. That wasn't what Monty wanted to hear. "How far away does she park?"

"In the parking deck, sir. Third level."

"Send someone to check the garage for her, STAT." He didn't want to waste time explaining. Setting the proposal aside, he snatched up his car keys and left the office.

Xavier regarded him inquiringly as he hurried toward the exit. "I have a personal emergency," Monty tossed over his shoulder.

Once in his car, he took his cell phone from his glove box and accessed Fitz's number, glad he'd put it in his contacts. Starting up his Jeep, he put the call through on Bluetooth and took off driving.

⌒

Still in his office long past the usual time he went home, Fitz leaned toward his monitor, sensing he was on to something. The momentum in this ricin case was building. He couldn't produce any evidence yet, but he knew he was close to naming the killer. Whether that man posed a threat to the Bonheur sisters was still open for debate. With the local police department's resources stretched thin, Fitz was working to assign experts from the FBI's Special Operations Group to keep an eye on them. Normally, SOGs did surveillance, not security, but Fitz couldn't get U.S. Marshals to watch the sisters, so the SOGs would have to do.

His first break in the case had come shortly after WAVY TV aired the story of the four murdered officers. Someone had left the message on the tip line that all four victims had argued for an end to the Twenty-Year War in Afghanistan. Fitz had jumped on that information and run with it, requisitioning transcripts of the panels that had taken place all up and down the East Coast prior to the president's decision to pull out troops.

At least eight officers total had taken the position that the war had dragged on for too long. They'd argued it was draining U.S. resources that were better spent counteracting the threat imposed by both Russia and China. The majority of top brass opposed pulling out, however, citing the inevitable collapse of the coalition-supported government and the threat of a Taliban takeover. As he waded through the transcripts, the certainty grew in Fitz that the Ricin Killer had also attended these panels, at least some of them.

His suspicion had driven him to compile a complete list of attendees. He'd created the list just that afternoon. His first step was to divide it into two groups, those who approved the pull-out and those who dissented. That task took him well beyond the time at which he usually left the office.

Fitz glanced at his watch. It was nearly six-thirty, and he was starving. Putting off his intent to research each attendee, Fitz shut down his computer resolutely. He wouldn't get that done tonight. He was putting on his jacket when his office phone shrilled. He heaved a sigh, deliberating whether or not to answer it.

His allegiance to duty got the better of him. "Fitzpatrick."

"Thank God," said a familiar voice. "This is James Monteague, Opal's neighbor. Something happened to her as she was leaving work. She tried to call me, but then she dropped her phone, and I thought I heard a struggle. Then a man cursed in the background, picked up the phone, and hung up. I called back right away, and my call went straight to voice mail."

Fitz didn't like the sound of that. "Where are you now?"

"On my way to where she works, the Portsmouth Naval Medical Center. Opal parks on the third level and crosses the flyover."

"I'll meet you in the parking garage."

"Thanks."

Fitz hung up with a cold feeling in the pit of his stomach. Something told him his SOGs ought to have been guarding the sisters sooner.

Opal awoke in a room as cold as a tomb and scarcely more comfortable. The musty scent reminded her of a basement, but she couldn't tell for sure, as a blindfold covered her eyes. She lurched upright, hearing the squeak of a metal bed, feeling a thin mattress beneath her. The cotton-dry taste in her mouth brought back the memory of being drugged.

The blindfold, knotted at the back of her head, blocked out even a suggestion of sunlight. A vinyl zip tie bound her wrists, eliciting waves of panic as she struggled to free herself.

She had to pee. Opal mastered the urge, crossed her legs, and forced herself to calm down.

What's going to happen to me? The terrifying question overrode her self-imposed calm. She curled into a ball and shivered with bone-deep vulnerability.

At last, the sound she dreaded hearing reached her ears: the slow, calculating step of a heavyset man, likely the same man who'd drugged her.

A key scraped into a lock, which gave with a click. The door groaned open. Through the blindfold, Opal detected a beam of light. Her captor shut the door and relocked it.

For a nerve-fraying moment, he regarded her wordlessly. "Opal Bonheur." His deep voice was the same as the man's in the parking garage. Devoid of emotion, it filled her with fear.

"Yes." She didn't bother to deny who she was. The man would have her purse. Her driver's license and credit cards identified her. Perhaps if she were cooperative, uncomplaining, he would let her live. But then she remembered the fate of her father and Eric Novak, and fear spiked anew.

At his approach, she shrank against the wall. She could sense him standing in front of her, close enough to kill her with his bare hands. "What do you know about the ricin taken from BioTech in December two years ago?"

Was that all he wanted, information? "Eric Novak sold it to pay his sick wife's medical bills." That was common information at this point.

"Sold it to whom? What did Danny's journal say?"

So, he knew about the journal. "Nothing," she said truthfully. "My father never found out who the buyer was."

The blow came out of nowhere. She landed facedown on the mattress with her left ear ringing. To her utter chagrin, she felt a wet warmth dampen the mattress under her hip. *Oh, God.*

"Don't lie to me."

She could tell by the cold quality of his voice that he suffered no compunction about hurting her.

Don't cry. Don't! Pleading with him would gain her nothing. "I'm not." Gathering her pride and her resistance, she pushed back into a seated position. "I'm telling the truth. We don't know who bought the ricin."

"What does the FBI know?"

Opal swallowed against her parched throat. "If they knew anything, they wouldn't be asking the public for help, would they?"

"What about Novak?"

She licked her dry lips. "What about him?"

"What did he tell you when he entered your home?"

Her captor knew about that? "All he said was that he hadn't killed my father."

"Who did then?"

His mocking tone made the answer clear. "You did." A sharp-pronged rage rose in her suddenly. Opal lurched to her knees. Encountering a thick arm, she opened her mouth and bit her assailant's forearm as hard as she could.

Yelping in surprise, he gripped her hair at the scalp and yanked her head back. Calling her a name, he flung her off him.

Opal's head struck a cement wall. Stars exploded before her eyes. She fell back onto the bed from which she'd risen, playing possum in the hopes that he would leave her alone. Holding perfectly still, she quieted her ragged breathing.

He flung a horrible word at her as he wheeled away, presumably to staunch the blood she'd drawn and now tasted in her mouth. Before he was out the door, there came a buzzing noise.

It took Opal a second to realize that the man's cell phone was ringing. "What do you want?" he snarled.

The faintest thread of a man's voice reached Opal's ears.

"I told you, I've got it in hand."

The caller made some type of request.

"What do you care?" the abductor demanded. "It's the older sister," he added, startling Opal by mentioning her name. "Opal Bonheur."

The caller's incredulity was obvious, though Opal couldn't hear his words. Whatever he said caused her abductor to return to the bed. She continued to feign unconsciousness.

"So what if she is?" her captor retorted.

"—me, Ritter." The caller's voice was suddenly audible. "I told you to question the other one!"

Opal had a name now—Ritter. More than that, she recognized the caller's voice!

"—make the connection," raged the voice coming from Ritter's phone. "You need to let her go right now before this hits the news."

Opal melted with relief. They were going to let her go. But then—

"I don't think so," Ritter refused. "She could identify me."

"That's not my problem. Let her go, Ritter, or, by God, you won't get another cent out of me."

Ritter snickered, an ugly sound devoid of humor. "You think you're in a position to tell me what to do? We both know that's not true. Stop fretting. Nothing will trace her death back to you."

Opal swallowed her gasp of horror as Ritter headed for the door. It slammed shut. The lock turned again, leaving her lying on her side, quivering in terror. Ritter intended to kill her, even though his boss had told him not to. She knew that man's voice. Who was he?

In her terrorized state, she couldn't put a name to it.

CHAPTER 17

$\mathcal{F}$itz leaned over Monty as he sat at Opal's kitchen table. "Would you like more coffee?"

"No, thanks." Monty had already consumed two cups while he and Fitz waited for the Navy to release the footage from security cameras in the parking garage. Since tracing Opal's cell phone to a garbage can in downtown Portsmouth, Monty felt like he was slowly coming unraveled.

Ruby, surprisingly, had kept herself composed while pacing nonstop from the kitchen to the front door, through the dining area, and back to the kitchen. It wasn't until Tony Caruso joined them that she started crying. Monty listened to the couple's conversation in the foyer.

"It's my fault," Ruby sobbed. "Everyone I love dies. She's going to be killed. I know it."

The words congealed Monty's heart into a block of ice. He suffered the same sense of guilt Ruby did. Was this his fault? He'd been aloof from Opal, trying to send her the message that his kiss before the fire hadn't meant anything. But if that was true, why would he give anything in the world to sit before her fire and kiss her again for the rest of their lives?

The thought of Opal in harm's way sickened him. She, who brimmed with optimism, who'd risked his ire to patch him up, who'd assured him of God's forgiveness did not deserve this. If something happened to her, he would lose faith in all goodness.

Tony's soothing voice reached his ears. "Don't say that, *Bella*. Remember God loves you both. Let's pray for her."

At the sound of them praying in the foyer, Monty closed his eyes and silently joined in, offering up his own petition: *Protect Opal from all evil. Bring her safely home.*

But they'd heard nothing reassuring since that prayer. Time seemed to stand still. Monty rubbed his burning eyes and checked his watch. It was just past midnight.

"Finally!"

Fitz's exclamation of relief had him looking up. The agent had resumed his seat next to Monty and was opening an attachment in his email. The Navy had forwarded the requested footage from the parking garage.

Monty shifted closer to the agent's laptop. Ruby and Tony hurried from the foyer to stand behind them. On Fitz's screen was a view of the third-story parking deck where they'd been just hours earlier. It looked just like it had then, with the lights blazing. Opal's car was visible, one of two cars parked side by side with only a handful of other cars in sight. The time stamp at the corner read 18:12. Fitz tapped a button to advance the time. All at once, the screen went dark.

"Here's when the lights went out," Fitz murmured. Authorities at the hospital had advised them of the outage, having discovered the fuse box tampered with.

As the screen remained dark, Fitz advanced the feed, taking them closer to the time Opal had called Monty's office. He stopped forwarding when a flashlight broke the darkness. Monty, Fitz, Ruby, and Tony all drew a collective breath as two figures emerged from the darkness, one much larger than the other.

"That's Opal!" Ruby gripped the back of Monty's chair.

He had recognized her in the same instant. "She's holding her cell phone. See the light in her hand?" His gaze darted to the time stamp. "This is right before she called me."

His pulse seemed to bounce off his eardrums as the couple approached Opal's car. Opal behaved no differently than she would if she were by herself. She reached for her door handle, turning her head at the same time to speak to the man. He stepped up behind her, blocking their view of her with his much larger frame.

"He just grabbed her."

Fitz stated aloud what Monty's brain was telling him. He himself couldn't speak. In helpless disbelief, he watched as the silhouette of the man wrestled briefly to subdue Opal. Had he suffocated her? Killed her? A minute later, with the flashlight held between his teeth, he trundled her limp body into the back seat of the car next to hers.

Ruby grabbed Fitz's shoulder. "Did he just kill her?"

Fitz paused the video, then turned his head to meet Ruby's panicked gaze. "No. I think he jabbed her with something."

"What if it was ricin?"

Ruby's question, spoken on a sob, froze the blood in Monty's veins.

Fitz shook his head while zooming in on the license plate of the second car. "No. Ricin doesn't cause an immediate reaction."

"The license plate is covered up." Monty saw nothing but black where the plate ought to be.

By the time Fitz zoomed out, the abductor was down on his knees between the two cars.

"He's looking for Opal's phone," Monty guessed.

Sure enough, when the man stood again, he was holding a cell phone in his hands. It lit up his face briefly.

Fitz froze the screen, then backed up the feed to where the attacker's features were clearest. A chill skittered down Monty's spine as Fitz magnified the hard, square features of Opal's kidnapper—likely Eric Novak's killer, too.

"Gotcha." Fitz took a screenshot. "We should be able to ID him with this."

~

The creaking of the door jarred Opal from a shallow sleep. Adrenaline spurted through her bloodstream, making it impossible to play possum a second time. She wriggled away from Ritter, cringing into the corner between the bed and the wall. *Help me, God!*

Ritter said nothing. In the awful silence, she wondered what time it was. Not a trace of light penetrated Opal's blindfold, suggesting it was still night. She'd lost all sense of time.

As his heavy tread approached, she braced herself for the worst. He fisted her hair, yanking her head closer. The tug on her scalp caused the blindfold to rise slightly. Opal glimpsed a window. The faintest suggestion of sunlight framed the lowered blind, telling her that dawn was near. He would want to kill her before the sun came up.

The blow came out of nowhere, smashing into the side of her skull with such force that she lost consciousness.

~

Monty lifted his head off the table and wiped drool surreptitiously from the corner of his mouth. He'd fallen asleep while Fitz sat beside him, typing away on his laptop.

"It's morning," Fitz said without looking at him.

A glance toward the French door revealed that it was dawn. The sky was a dark pewter. Tiny flakes of snow pattered the windowpane.

Chagrined, Monty checked his watch. SEALs weren't supposed to sleep while civilians did the work. He noted the silence in the house. "Where's Ruby?"

"She and Tony just left for Portsmouth. She's arranging for Opal's disappearance to get broadcasted on the morning news."

Monty stood and stretched his tight back. "Any developments?"

"Yes. We have a positive ID on the kidnapper."

Monty let his arms fall. "Who is he?" And why didn't Fitz sound more pleased?

"He's a security guard at BioTech. A former Marine master sergeant. Apparently, while stationed in Afghanistan, he shot an unarmed woman and her child while performing a house raid. The Marines let him go with an other-than-honorable discharge."

Monty, suddenly weak in the knees, sank back into his seat. "That's it? Other-than-honorable for a crime like that? He must have friends in high places."

Fitz gave a thoughtful hum.

"You think he'll kill Opal." It wasn't a question because Monty already knew the answer. He could feel it twisting his gut into knots. "Ruby will fall off the deep end." He scrubbed his face with his hands. "Heck, I might, too."

He would never have said as much to anyone but Opal. But Fitz's attentive gaze made him confess, "When I came home from my last mission, I was a wreck. I wanted to crawl into the bottom of a bottle and stay there." He shook his head. "Opal—I don't know how she did it, but she dragged me out of that hole. She doesn't deserve... " His voice cracked, rendering him silent.

Fitz's face turned into marble. "We're not going to let that happen. We have an all-points alert out for Ritter. Who knows what Ruby's broadcast might turn up?"

Monty headed for the half-bath under the stairs. After splashing water on his face, he stared at the red-eyed stranger in the mirror. He hadn't known Opal all that long. Yet, in that short amount of time, she'd become his lifeline, his closest confidant. How had he not realized before now that he wanted her in his life forever—as his better half?

A sob of remorse escaped him. He closed his eyes in utter misery. Now, if the worst thing were to happen to her, Opal would never find out she wasn't alone in her feelings.

Movement roused Opal to consciousness. She came to, realizing she was hanging upside down. Ritter was carrying her up and out of what had to be a basement. *This is it! He's going to kill me now.* She reared up, only to grow limp again as pain clashed in her head.

"Hold still!" Steps creaked beneath Ritter's feet. They reached the building's first floor, crossing through a room bright enough to penetrate Opal's blindfold. A doorknob jiggled and cold air swept over her as Ritter carried her outside. He went down three steps, gouging her belly with his shoulder and driving the air from her lungs. Moisture penetrated the fabric of her uniform, making her realize her military-issue trench coat had been left behind.

"Help!" she screamed out the word, hoping to be heard.

Ritter's grip on her thighs became brutal. "Shut up. No one's around to hear you." He crunched across frost-stiffened leaves, then stopped, bending to set her on her feet as he opened his car door.

Run! Opal ordered herself, but the shock of ice on her bare soles kept her frozen. He'd removed her shoes as well as her jacket.

"Get in." He flung her across his car's back seat.

She vaguely recollected being transported this way before. At least he hadn't drugged her, this time. Why was that? Did he want her conscious when he killed her?

Shivering with cold, Opal drew her knees to her chest, thinking. She heard Ritter get behind the wheel. Why would he have taken her shoes? To slow her down if she tried to run from him?

He started the car and commenced to drive. To where? Some secluded spot where no one would hear her screams, no doubt.

Stop it. You're not dead yet. You're not defenseless. Think!

The voice in her head seemed to belong to Monty. Monty! He would take her death personally. And Ruby... Ruby would be devastated. Opal couldn't leave them. She *wouldn't* leave them, not like this.

The squeaking of the windshield wipers inspired an idea. It was snowing. The roads were slick. If Ritter lost control of the vehicle, he might never get her to his remote destination.

With her heart hammering, Opal slunk lower in the seat. She spared a second to pray the prayer Ruby said really worked. *All things are possible, through Christ who gives me strength.*

Then, slowly, stealthily, she moved her feet up the back of the driver's seat. Her legs responded sluggishly. If only she could see what she was doing. Relying on her other senses, she listened for the sound of Ritter breathing, felt the headrest with her toes and paused.

She would only have one chance to do this right. If she messed up, Ritter would secure her feet, and then she'd be truly helpless.

On the count of three, she told herself.

One.

Two.

Three! Pulling her right foot to her chest she extended her leg in an explosive move that connected her heel with Ritter's head. But he was built like a bull.

Roaring out an expletive, he seemed unfazed. Opal's hopes crumbled. Her prayer hadn't worked. But then the car was swerving, spilling her all over the back seat. Ritter grappled with the steering wheel, fighting to bring it under control.

Tires skidded over the slick pavement, prompting a steady stream of curses. They were going fast, too fast to elude the laws of physics. The left tires dropped onto the shoulder. Ritter pulled a hard right and sent them into a spin. Opal braced herself.

Crash! They hit something unyielding. She was flung against the door, hard enough to knock the wind from her lungs. The vehicle came to a sudden, shuddering halt. Glass shattered. But then the whole car started to slide forward. It slammed against something solid then slowly tipped, nosedown, groaning as if in agony. Still blind, Opal braced herself with her feet.

Whoosh! The car flipped end over end, bouncing as it landed on its hood. Opal found herself sprawled in a puddle of broken glass on the car's ceiling.

Have to get out! her brain commanded, but she was too stunned to move. She listened, hearing nothing but a ticking and a hammering as the engine still tried to run.

Realizing she could see out of one eye, Opal scraped the blindfold off her head using the top of the headrest close to her. Lit by gloomy light, the mangled interior of the vehicle pulled a whimper of fright from her. She looked down at herself. Her arms, still bound at the wrist behind her back, were cut by bits of glass. She didn't appear hurt, otherwise.

Daring a peek over the seat, she got her first good look at Ritter. Still strapped in his seat, his head lolled, dripping blood onto the airbag that pressed against his chin and chest. The dashboard, crumpled inward, appeared to be trapping his legs.

She, on the other hand, could move. *Hallelujah!* Apparently, all things were possible through Christ. But she still had to get out, to get help.

With her bare feet, she kicked out the sagging, shattered pane of the rear window. It fell in on her in one thick piece. She threw it off her, then pushed her head through the opening, rejoicing in the cold, fresh air that hit her face.

With her hands bound, Opal squirmed out of the car like a worm. She fell off the top of the trunk and rolled in a ditch that left her clothing sodden and cold. At last, she got to her feet to stagger up out of the ditch. Her legs, weak with the dizzying realization that she was still alive, were slow to cooperate.

When she reached level ground, she found herself on the edge of an empty rural road. Withered cornstalks and trees were all she could see in any direction. Surely a car would come along. But all was quiet, save for the pattering of snowflakes and the sounds of Ritter's vehicle clanking and hissing behind her.

She walked away from the wreck, hopeful of coming across a house or dwelling of some kind, aware that her bare feet were turning numb and might soon be frostbitten. The snow was starting to accumulate. Her damp uniform was stiffening with frost. If only she still had her cell phone, not that she could use it with her wrists bound.

When a low purring carried over the unearthly quiet, Opal stopped and listened, her heart in her throat. *Help me, please!*

The running lights of an eighteen-wheeler emerged out of the vale of snow behind her. The truck was moving at a clip that made her heart accelerate. "Hey!" Unable to flag the driver, she jumped up and down, fighting the urge to step off the road as he barreled toward her.

The truck veered suddenly into the oncoming lane to avoid hitting her. With a cry of denial, Opal watched as the vehicle rumbled past her. Her hopes plummeted toward despair, only to rise back up again as the brake lights flared. With a roar of downshifting gears, the truck decelerated. Hydraulic brakes hissed as it slowed to a careful stop many yards down the road.

Opal started to run.

A bearded stranger leaped from the cab. She slowed her approach, suddenly cautious.

"Ma'am?" The concern in the trucker's voice was reassuring. "Are you all right?"

"I need help!" Her voice cracked as the effect of the last twelve hours caught up with her.

His weather-beaten face was a picture of consternation. He bore down on her with his hand out. "Good gravy," he exclaimed in a thick local accent, "you're the Bonheur woman, ain't ya?"

"How'd you know?"

"Saw it on the news; heard it on the radio. Whatcha doin' way out in here in Pungo?"

"Trying to get home."

"Don't worry, ma'am. I'll get you home."

Opal's eyes brimmed with grateful tears. *Thank You, Father!*

～

Monty was the first to step through the door of the Pungo County Sheriff's Office, a small brick building in the middle of nowhere. In his eagerness to set eyes on Opal, he left Fitz to catch the closing door. Apparently, they had beat Ruby and Tony, who were coming all the way from the news station.

Monty spotted Opal sitting in an empty foyer, wrapped in an old woolen blanket and staring at the paper cup she was holding. "Opal!"

Her aqua-blue gaze tore into him as she looked up. Her hair was disheveled, one cheek swollen and bruised. "Monty!"

He reached her in less than a second, dropping into the chair next to her and pulling her into his embrace.

She squirmed to free herself. "I'm filthy. I smell bad."

"No, you don't." He craved her in his arms but let her go as Fitz joined them.

"Where's Ruby?" She peered past Fitz, longing for her sister.

"On her way. She's coming from the news station, where she's been trying to help you."

Opal seemed dazed. "The man who found me heard about me on the radio."

"Yes, that was Ruby's doing." Fitz regarded Opal with a look of self-recrimination. "I'm so sorry." His voice was even more gruff than usual. "What happened is my fault. You should have had a SOG watching you twenty-four/seven."

"I thought we had one." Opal's voice sounded like it was coming from a great distance. "There was a man out front. He followed Ruby before I could ask him to."

Fitz frowned and glanced at Monty. "What kind of car did he drive?"

"A black Challenger or Charger. I can never tell the difference."

Feeling agitated, Monty pushed to his feet. Opal kept her eyes on Fitz, who cleared his throat. "Did Ritter tell you why he took you?"

"Yes," came the faint reply. "He wanted to know what was in Daddy's journal, whether it mentioned who the buyer was. And he wanted to know if Eric told me anything."

Monty turned toward Fitz. "Do we have to do this now? She needs a doctor. She needs to rest."

"I'm fine."

The thin voice sounded nothing like the confident Opal Monty had come to know.

"Just one more question." Fitz shot a wary glance at Monty. "How did you get away, Opal?"

Opal wet her chapped lips. "He'd been keeping me in a basement. But this morning, he carried me outside and put me in his car. I knew he was taking me somewhere to kill me. So, I... I kicked him in the head while he was driving. He lost control of the vehicle."

The horror reflected in Opal's eye made Monty want to pull her into his arms, but she didn't want that. He dropped back into the seat next to her and placed a gentle hand on her back. "It's okay. You're safe now."

Opal didn't seem to hear him. "I think he's dead. The car went upside down into a ditch, and Ritter was trapped in there."

Fitz stepped closer. "He told you his name?"

"No. I heard him talking on the phone while he thought I was unconscious. The man who bought the ricin had called him and was yelling at him for taking me. He was supposed to grab Ruby, for some reason." She drew a shaky breath. "I recognized the buyer's voice, the man on the phone with Ritter. I've heard it somewhere; I just can't remember." She shuddered. "I'm so sorry."

"That's okay," Fitz rushed to reassure her. "Don't think about that now. You're safe. It's over."

Monty curled his hands into helpless fists. If only he could do something to comfort Opal!

"I climbed out of the window and started walking." She glanced toward her feet which were hidden in the blanket. "Finally, an eighteen-wheeler came along, and the driver brought me here. He said he'd heard about me on the news."

The door behind them flew open suddenly. In came Ruby, who threw herself into the empty chair on the other side of Opal and embraced her like she never intended to let go. Tony caught the closing door and entered more sedately.

"Oh, my God. You're safe. Thank God, you're safe." She began to sob, all the while hugging Opal, who hadn't let Monty hug her.

A horrible thought occurred to him. *Had Ritter forced himself on her?*

A sheriff approached them tentatively. Fitz turned away to have a word with him. Monty got up and joined them in time to hear Fitz introduce himself.

The sheriff read Fitz's card and nodded. "I just got word from one of my deputies that a Dodge Charger was found in a ditch off Old Barnes Road. The driver was dead on the scene. License number identifies him as Lyle Ritter."

Better him than Opal, Monty wanted to say.

"Thank you, Sheriff." Fitz glanced back at Opal. "Ritter is an accomplice to several other murders that are part of an ongoing federal investigation. If you plan to search his home, you'll need to talk to me first."

"Yes, sir." The sheriff's face lit up with curiosity.

Monty interrupted. "Opal needs medical attention. Now."

Fitz stood a little taller. "Agreed. Let's get her out of here."

As they turned back toward Opal, Ruby lifted a wet face at them and declared, "I'm taking her. She's coming with me."

Monty went to protest that Ruby had been up all night, but then so had he. Besides, Tony would be driving, and the young SEAL still looked fresh-faced while Monty was running on fumes. He sought Opal's gaze to determine her preference.

"I'll go with Ruby." Her tone was emotionless. She barely even glanced at him.

Worry simmered in Monty. If Ritter *had* violated her, would Opal ever look at Monty the way she used to?

They all watched Opal shrug off the blanket and slide her feet out from under it. Monty was appalled to find her barefooted. She went to stand with Ruby's help, only to wince and fall back in her seat. And no wonder. Her toes were bright red and swollen.

"Let me carry you," he offered.

"No." Her answer was immediate. It did nothing to reassure him.

"I've got a wheelchair in the storage closet," offered the sheriff. "I'll go get it."

Minutes later, Monty watched Ruby and Tony help Opal into the passenger seat of Tony's Honda. To his relief, Opal finally looked out the window and raised a hand goodbye to him. When her door was shut, Fitz shared a quiet word with Tony, then patted him on the back and sent him on his way. He rejoined Monty on the curb, where they watched the Honda speed off in the direction of Princess Anne Sentara Hospital.

Monty felt sick to his stomach. When he'd been emotionally and physically wounded, Opal had risked his ire to tend to him. Now she was the one in need of healing, and she could scarcely bring herself to acknowledge him. He'd taken a bullet in the thigh once, and it hadn't hurt this bad.

Fitz cast him a sidelong glance. "She just needs time."

Monty nodded, hoping it was really that simple. He, more than anybody, knew that rising out of horror took more than time. It took unwavering love and grace—the kind Opal had displayed when taking care of him. *God give me the opportunity to do the same for her,* he prayed.

Opal sat on her sofa, while Ruby worked to start a fire with instruction from her older sister. Night had fallen while they'd napped, both of them in Opal's bed, holding onto each other. It filled the windows and French door with darkness, provoking memories of being blindfolded.

A thought occurred to Opal, turning her anxious. "The press isn't going to show up at my doorstep demanding interviews, is it?"

Ruby straightened from the hearth where flames now flickered and dusted off her hands. "Nope. I made phone calls to all three rival stations and claimed exclusive rights to the story. Out of respect for your ordeal, they're going to keep their distance."

Opal sighed her relief, then admired the fire Ruby had managed to strike. Memories of the night Monty had kissed her flickered like flames, warming her from the inside out. She could still taste his kiss, still feel its power stealing over her. Yet so much had happened since then, causing a grim, empty feeling to replace the belief that they might end up together forever. She could tell her withdrawn state that morning had confused him. It had confused her even more.

Ruby plopped down beside her. "Feels like it should be morning."

Opal hummed her agreement. At least her thoughts were sharper following their long afternoon nap. That morning she'd been in shock, which in itself could have explained her cold attitude toward Monty. If not that, then the fact that she'd sustained a concussion. All excuses aside, however, she worried she might never be herself again.

"Are you hungry yet?"

Before Opal could answer, a knock sounded on the door. Her senses sharpened. "It's Monty." She knew by the low-key yet commanding tenor of the knock. Her heart started to thump with dread and anticipation mixed.

"I'll get it."

As Ruby hurried off to let him in, Opal ran fingers through her clean but unbrushed hair, chagrined by the state he'd seen her in that morning. She trusted she looked and smelled better now, having scrubbed herself in the bath while keeping her feet above the water.

With the back of the couch facing the hallway, she listened for his approach, then managed a smile for him as he rounded the couch to regard her.

"Well, you look a thousand times better." He sounded immensely relieved.

To her surprise, he dropped a gentle kiss on her cheek before he helped himself to the recliner across from her. Ruby, uncharacteristically astute, busied herself in the kitchen.

"I feel better." The fragrant soap she'd used in the bath had erased all the smells associated with her nightmare experience.

"What did the doctor say?" Monty seemed to brace himself.

"Um, well, I have mild frostbite; no surprise there." She regarded her bare feet, shiny from the mint-and-lavender balm the doctor had given her to alleviate the pain. "I had some glass taken out of my skin." She showed him the cuts on her forearms. "The bruise on my cheek will get worse before it gets better, and I have a mild concussion."

"That's it?"

She regarded him a moment, wondering what he was thinking, then guessing what his biggest fear might be. "That's it," she said firmly.

Monty clasped his hands together and studied them while exhaling deeply. "I've never prayed harder in my life," he admitted, looking up.

The words touched her. "You prayed for me?"

Ruby chimed in from the kitchen, "We all did."

The memory of her ordeal bubbled up suddenly. Opal squashed it down. "Well, your prayers worked. I'm home safe."

Monty shifted suddenly from the recliner to the couch, where he took one of her hands, cradling it like it was made of the finest china.

Opal was pleased to discover that his touch still thrilled her. It was just her heart that remained unmoved.

Sympathy shone from his golden-brown eyes. "From what you've told us, Opal, you did most of the work."

The memories surfaced again. She gripped his hand to beat them back. "It was horrible," she admitted hoarsely.

He caught her eye. "Believe me, Opal. I know *exactly* how you feel."

He did, she realized, somewhat heartened, but that didn't eradicate the awful feeling inside her.

He cleared his throat, and she could tell what he was about to ask before he said it. "Any luck remembering whose voice you heard talking to Ritter?"

"No." Opal shook her head, beyond frustrated with herself.

"It's okay. Hey." He lifted a hand to stroke the hair on the top of her head.

His caress, like the kiss earlier, surprised Opal. After all, he'd made it clear at his party that they were only friends.

"Cut yourself a break, huh? You've been through hell. Nobody expects you to remember anything."

Opal expected it of herself. She managed a smile for him and nodded.

"By the way," he lowered his arm, "Fitz is sending two special operators your way right now. They're going to rotate watch, one of them outside and one inside. You'll need to give up your couch soon."

Ruby came toward them bearing two steaming mugs. "They can have the guestroom if you don't mind, Opal. I'd rather sleep with you for a while."

Opal, who knew the only way she would sleep at all was for Ruby to be with her, nodded. "Yes, there are clean sheets on the guest bed. Thank you." She took the mug Ruby held out to her.

Monty thanked her for the second mug. As Ruby returned to the kitchen for her own, he sniffed it. "Chamomile tea." Through its steam, he sent Opal a warm smile. "Perfect."

The memory of their kiss before the fire warmed her briefly, only to give way to the memory of striking Ritter's head with her heel. She could still feel the tires slipping on asphalt, still hear the glass shattering. More and more details were coming back to her. She stared into her mug, stricken by the inescapable realization.

She had killed a man.

The truth robbed her of breath. It took her a moment to realize Monty was rubbing her back.

"You should talk about it," he murmured quietly.

She shook her head to signify she wasn't ready yet, then buried her nose in her mug, taking a cautious sip. The steaming liquid coursed a warm path down her throat to her stomach. Monty pulled his hand back.

"Opal, will you look at me?"

The softly spoken appeal made her turn her head to regard him.

"I know what just happened to you was the worst thing you've ever experienced. I know it'll take time to wrestle with the memories and to be at peace with what happened. You take all the time you need," he assured her. "I just want you to know that I'm here for you, the way you were for me."

The words melted a portion of the frost encasing her heart, but not all of it.

"What happened was a nightmare for me, too, and a wake-up call," he added. "You mean so much to me. I wish I'd realized that before."

So much? Opal's breath caught as she waited for him to say the words that had the potential to thaw her frozen heart completely.

"I'm here for you. Anything that you need," he repeated.

What she needed couldn't be asked for. It had to be given. But even if it were given, she couldn't accept it in this state.

"Thank you." She couldn't manage any more than to acknowledge him. Something inside of her was knocked off-center. She didn't feel like the same person.

Monty sipped his tea in reflective silence. Ruby joined them with her own mug, occupying the recliner Monty had vacated. He must have felt like a third wheel, for he checked his watch and stood. "Thank you for the tea, Ruby. The SOGs will be here any minute. Fitz said 9:00 p.m. I'm going to go wait outside for them, and then I'll head home." He laid a gentle hand on Opal's head. "If you need anything, you just call me, okay?"

She tipped her head back, smiling wanly up at him. "Okay."

"Remember, you're safe now." With that, he carried his mug to the kitchen. Seconds later, Opal heard their front door closing. She met Ruby's contemplative gaze as the fire crackled softly in the hearth.

"Did you hear what he said, Opal? He said he didn't realize how much you meant to him. I think he's finally falling in love with you."

While a part of Opal thrilled at the possibility, another part hoped he was not. She couldn't even think about the future right now. Her thoughts were stuck in one gut-wrenching place. It didn't seem to matter to her conscience that Ritter would have killed her if she hadn't gone on the offensive. She had killed *him*. And then she'd felt relieved about it. Did that make her as evil a person as he had been?

CHAPTER 18

"We're almost done with this puzzle." Monty smiled across the table as he reached for one of the last pieces still missing. "What's next?"

By all outward appearances, Opal had healed from her ordeal with Ritter four days earlier. The bruise on her cheek was scarcely visible in the chandelier's glow. She hadn't gone back to work yet, but she'd admitted that her patients were clamoring for her return.

But her answering smile still struck him as forced as she replied, "Another puzzle?"

That hadn't been what he was aiming at, but he didn't push. After all, he'd told her to take all the time she needed, and he could tell she needed more. Besides, he privately enjoyed her recuperation period as it gave them more opportunity to hang out together. Every night after work he dropped in for a visit. Once she had dinner waiting for him. Usually, though, he'd called ahead of time to ask Ruby and her what sounded good for takeout.

Just yesterday, Ruby had moved back to her apartment. Monty had stayed with Opal while her SOG remained upstairs in the guestroom. Hoping to create a romantic atmosphere, he'd lit a fire and even kissed her. The spark was there, but he'd sensed Opal's heart wasn't in it, so he'd backed off.

Where are you, Opal? He wanted to ask her, but he didn't. She would come back to him when she was ready.

The issue of not remembering the voice of Ritter's accomplice was one source of her preoccupation. Last night, together, they had made a list of everyone Opal knew, yet none of them, she was certain, matched the voice she'd heard.

"I heard from Fitz today." She snapped the next-to-last puzzle piece in place.

Monty's hopes rose. "Oh?" Maybe once the buyer was apprehended, Opal would relax and become herself again.

"He told me the calls Ritter got from the mastermind were all made on a burner phone, so they're impossible to trace."

That wasn't the kind of news Monty wanted.

"He also found out that it was Ritter who'd traveled by car, as far as Mississippi, to prick their victims with ricin. That kept the buyer from seeming to be involved. Fitz is now questioning both the officers Ritter hadn't yet killed who'd advised an end to the war, as well as those who opposed it. He believes he'll end up talking with the buyer himself at some point, and hopefully the man's behavior will betray him."

Monty grunted. That sounded like a long and tedious process. Wanting to give Opal something else to think about, he asked her while pressing the very last piece into place, "Do you have any plans for Thanksgiving?"

She looked up at him, seeming confused by the question. "Thanksgiving?"

"You know, that holiday where we stuff a turkey and then ourselves while giving thanks for all our blessings?"

His joke teased a wry smile from her. She averted her gaze and shook her head. "Nothing firm yet. Why?"

"Well." His pulse ticked upward. "Since my parents will be visiting, I was hoping to introduce you to them."

That got her attention. Her beautiful eyes grew watchful. "As your friend next door?"

This was his big chance. Something wasn't exactly right about it, but he pressed on anyway. Opal needed to hear about his revelation. "As my girlfriend." There, he'd said it. He ought to be relieved and then joyful, but Opal just sat there with her mouth slightly parted. He stretched an arm across the table and seized her hand. "When you were taken, Opal, I had an epiphany. I want you to be more than my best friend. I want you to be my other half."

She blinked, visibly astonished by his confession. To his relief, she turned her hand over and squeezed it tightly—a little too tightly.

"Monty," she said, then paused to swallow. "I can't tell you how much that means to me, but the time just isn't right. I'm not right. Something is off its tracks inside of me, and until I can center myself again, I can't think about a relationship."

He ought to have expected her response because, deep down, he'd already realized as much, but it still came as a blow. No woman in his entire life had ever rejected him. "Of course." He rushed to reassure her. "I understand. Have Thanksgiving with us anyway. I'll introduce you as my best friend."

"I'm so sorry. I can't give you an answer—" her face crumpled unexpectedly—"until I'm better."

Her private torment obliterated his dismay. Pushing back his chair, Monty rounded the table to hug her from behind. He nuzzled his cheek against hers. "It's going to be okay," he promised her. "I don't need an answer right now."

"Thank you," she whispered.

As he held her, he was struck with a thought. "Maybe you should talk to your pastor or priest or whatever you call him at your church."

"Pastor Tom." She was quiet for a moment. "That's a good idea. I think I will."

Relieved, Monty gave her cheek a parting kiss then straightened, only to realize his back had not appreciated the position he'd been in. A spasm dragged a groan out of him.

She looked up at him sharply. "You just hurt your back, didn't you?"

He didn't bother to deny it. Opal came resolutely to her feet. "This is what's next." She pointed toward her family room. "Go lie down on my couch. Let's see if I can make it better."

He had no doubts about that. Indeed, she could make his whole life better if she could just get past this depression she was in. *Stop that.* It had taken weeks for his own mental state to right itself—matter of fact, he wasn't there yet. Nightmares were still common. Sleep was fitful. Who was he to rush Opal into thinking of the future when she was still coping with the past? He, more than anyone, ought to understand the process she was going through.

Opal coursed the carpeted corridor in the basement of her church in search of Pastor Tom's office. She had never heard the building as quiet as it was on this Thursday morning. The sound of keys clicking on a keyboard played descant to her muffled footsteps as she neared his office. She found the door wide open. The pastor looked up from his computer. Surprise and then pleasure registered on his broad face. "Opal!"

It amazed her that he knew her name. She'd attended church with intermittent regularity and joined only one group—Coastal Christian Singles—in the hopes of finding a husband with similar values. That had obviously not worked out.

"Hi." She clasped her hands together, suddenly nervous about being alone in yet another basement in the presence of a man. "Do you have a moment? I could use your advice."

He was already out of his seat, heading toward her with outstretched arms. "Are you kidding?" The instant he clasped Opal's shoulders, her uncertainty fled. Love and compassion seemed to flow out of him into her broken heart.

"Great." She sent Tom a tremulous smile. In the back of her mind, she thought, *Thank you, Monty. This will be good for me.*

∼

The next day, Opal sat across from Ruby at a restaurant next to the Elizabeth River. It had been Ruby's suggestion that they meet for lunch since Opal was due back at work on Monday and the opportunity would be gone.

"I'm glad we got to do this," Opal declared as they occupied a table for two. Their bodyguards had gone off to perch at the restaurant's bar. "What a place!" Opal took the time to admire the view beyond the wall of windows. Moored sailboats rocked in their berths beneath a cold gray sky. Seagulls hunkered miserably on the harbor pilings. She focused back on Ruby. "Do you always get an hour off for lunch?"

"As long as my story gets written, I can take all the time I want."

"Well, you look great." Wearing a lime-green sweater and winter-white slacks, Ruby looked every inch the professional journalist she was becoming.

Ruby did not repay the compliment as she took in Opal's lumpy sweater, her face without makeup. "What about you? Are you feeling any better yet?

Opal's smile faded. She busied herself with freeing her silverware from the napkin rolled around it. "A little. Once Fitz finds the buyer, I'll feel better still." Even if he didn't, Opal had a plan to make life better. The seed of her plan had been planted by Pastor Tom, and she hoped it would work. After all, Monty had asked her to be his other half—that was practically a proposal! She had every reason to want to regain what she'd lost.

"Are you sure you're ready to go back?"

The question wrested Opal from her thoughts. "Well, my patients have been asking for me. Besides," she glanced toward the bar, "it's not like I'm going anywhere unprotected."

Ruby followed her gaze to Dobson and Dawes, the two SOGs protecting them. Even with their pistols tucked out of sight, they seemed like men who could handle themselves in a fight.

Ruby turned a grin at Opal. "I think we should call them the Double D's."

The suggestion brought a choked laugh out of Opal.

"It's good to see you smile."

Opal's smile abruptly faded. She looked pointedly at the menus.

"You still haven't remembered whose voice you heard on Ritter's phone," Ruby guessed.

Opal heaved a silent sigh. "Nope."

The waitress appeared by their table, saving her from having to talk about a subject she was heartily sick of. Once they'd placed their drink orders, Ruby laid her hand on the table.

"I wanted to show you something." With her eyes, she drew Opal's attention to the pretty ruby ring on her fourth finger.

"Oh, my goodness." The sensibly sized ruby had been cut in the shape of a heart.

"It's a promise ring."

The words eased Opal's worry that her sister and Tony were moving too fast.

"It's so pretty. When did he give it to you?"

As Ruby launched into a detailed story of an evening cruise on the *Norfolk Star,* Opal struggled to keep her spirits up. Here Ruby was, six years her junior, promising her future to a wonderful man, while Opal had put off the man she'd loved for years just because she didn't feel like herself inside.

But hearing Ruby recount how Tony had shown her the best night ever, topping it all off by presenting her the ring, Opal couldn't help but be happy for her. Her sister really was a new woman, she marveled.

"So, here's the deal." Ruby sent her an apologetic look. "I won't be here for Thanksgiving."

"Oh." The confession secretly relieved Opal, as Pastor Tom's suggestion meant that she would be doing something quite different from the usual over the entire holiday season. "Thank you."

The waitress delivered their drinks and said she would be right back to take their food orders.

"I'm going with Tony to Philadelphia to meet his mother and sister," Ruby added as the waitress walked away.

"Oh, wow." Opal could tell her sister was apprehensive about the meeting.

"What if his mother hates me?" Ruby's smooth forehead furrowed. "You know how mothers are with their sons."

"Honey, you have nothing to worry about." Opal used her most assuring voice while crossing her fingers in her lap. With Tony as young as he was, his mother might be shocked and horrified to meet "the older woman."

"You think?" Ruby didn't appear convinced. "Tony says she's really nice and that she'll love me the minute she sees me."

"It might take her a little longer than that." Opal chose to be more practical.

"Right." Ruby studied her for a moment. "What about you? Any chance you'll celebrate Thanksgiving with Monty? He's sure spending a lot of time at your place."

The question distressed Opal. If only her ordeal with Ritter hadn't rattled her so badly, she would be meeting Monty's parents, basking in his attention, and looking forward to the future. "He asked me to," she admitted, withholding for a little longer that she hadn't given him an answer.

"Oh, good." Ruby assumed she'd accepted and that the matter was settled.

The waitress's reappearance kept Opal from explaining right away that she'd made other plans. She would tell Ruby toward the end of their lunch so her sister had less opportunity to talk Opal out of her intentions. Leaving Monty for more than a month was daunting enough. Every day she had second thoughts. What if he tired of waiting for her and went in search of someone else to share his life with? Yet, he'd told Opal she could take all the time she needed to recover from her ordeal. Would that still be true when he found out what her plan was?

Let God handle it, she counseled herself, then smiled at the waitress and ordered the clam chowder.

~

"Good morning, Admiral." On her first day back at work, Opal had worked steadily throughout her day. She greeted her next-to-last patient while anticipating her last one—Monty.

Admiral Jenkins was seated on the examination table, with his cane close at hand. "Where have you been?" His watery blue eyes impaled her in a way that struck her as threatening.

"I took some personal leave." She moved closer while skimming his file. "I see you canceled your last appointment. Is that because I wasn't here? Commander Sparks is just as capable as I am, you know. Perhaps even more so."

"Nah." Jenkins waved away her assertion. "She's too rough."

His gruff reply stirred an unpleasant feeling in Opal. She attributed it to the news she had to tell him. "Well, I wish my contribution could be greater, sir, but I'm afraid I have some tough news for you. Doctor Huxley has reviewed my notes and confirmed my recommendation that you have a double knee replacement. We've made all the headway we can with manipulation techniques."

When her words got no visible reaction, Opal tried again. "Do you understand what I'm saying, sir? You'll never walk normally again, climb stairs, tie your shoes, unless you have surgery."

"Of course I understand it," he snapped, scowling at her.

All at once the hairs at Opal's nape stood on end. Alarm shot up her spine. *That voice.* No, it couldn't be. She went stock still, staring in horror at him. But it was. Her thoughts flashed back to their last session together when he'd displayed an edge to his character she'd never seen before. *His* was the voice she'd heard on the phone with

Ritter! Heavens, had he been talking to Ritter during their last session together?

Her shocked expression betrayed her. With a look of determination, Jenkins pushed off the table and came to his feet. "I knew you'd put it together."

Opal backed toward the door, her alarm spiking.

He hobbled closer. "You need to realize that pulling out of Afghanistan meant my son died for nothing."

"I understand." Perhaps if she placated him, he would let her go. Surely, he wouldn't hurt her here.

"My colleagues—men like me who'd served their entire life—they *betrayed* me by supporting the withdrawal." He reached a hand toward her. "They took Norman's sacrifice and turned it into dust." He opened his fist as if to let ash sprinkle to the floor. "My son's life into *dust!*"

Her heart broke for his loss. "I'm so sorry." But that didn't give him the right to kill his colleagues.

He must have heard the judgment in her tone, for his expression darkened. "Who else have you told?"

Opal groped behind her for the doorknob. Her heart pounded. "No one. I didn't realize until just now. I won't tell anyone. I swear."

"Hah."

Without warning, he snared her wrist, jerking her away from the door.

Opal resisted. His grip was astonishingly strong. The soles of her new pumps slipped on the smooth vinyl flooring. She drew in a gasp, about to cry out for help, when he whipped her around, her back to his front, and clapped a beefy hand over her mouth. Her thoughts flashed to the stories he had told her about his imprisonment in a POW camp. Violence was nothing new to him.

She tried to fill her lungs, but his hand covered her nose, as well. She thrashed her head, squirming to break free. *He's going to suffocate me.* Panic had her kicking him with the heels of her shoes, but he seemed impervious. *Oh, God, help me!*

Stars burst in front of Opal's eyes as he growled into her ear, "I'm sorry. I'm sorry Ritter was a brute and an idiot. But I can't have you telling anyone else. I'm so sorry."

In his sixth hour at the office, Fitz did the usual research with the next name on his list of top-brass officials who'd attended the Afghanistan panels. Fitz wanted to know all about the man before calling him. Lucky for him, every man on his list had been around long enough that they all had Wikipedia pages.

Admiral Leslie Jenkins was no exception. His experience as a POW in the Vietnam war made Fitz's eyebrows rise with respect. The final paragraph was a tribute to his son, Norman Wade Jenkins, a Marine who'd died in Operation Enduring Freedom, a decade ago. The hair on Fitz's forearms prickled as he reread the closing paragraph. If anyone had a right to be angry about the pullout of Afghanistan, it was Norman's father. Next question was, did Opal know him? Because if she did, chances were high that Fitz had stumbled onto the mastermind behind the ricin killings.

He snatched up his phone and dialed the number Opal had given him so he could reach her at work—not that he would interrupt her on her first day back at the hospital.

"Orthopedics, Petty Officer Davis speaking. Can I help you, sir or ma'am?"

"Davis, this is Special Agent Fitzpatrick from the Federal Bureau of Investigation. I need you to ask Opal Bonheur if she knows Admiral Leslie Jenkins."

"Uh." The request startled Davis into silence for a second. "Well, Jenkins is a patient of hers, if that helps. She's actually seeing him right now."

"Oh?" Alarm made Fitz's extremities tingle. "That's not good. Where's the man who's supposed to be watching her?"

Davis peered past a patient waiting at the window in order to see into the waiting room. "He was here a minute ago. He must have stepped out."

"Find him ASAP, and tell him to detain Jenkins for me. I'm on my way."

"Yes, sir." Davis's bemused tone was not encouraging. With no choice but to trust him, Fitz jumped to his feet, took his gun and credentials out of his desk drawer, and ran out of his office.

~

Monty waited for Davis to hang up before greeting him. He had come for a final appointment with Opal—not that he needed it—for his back. He might have canceled if he didn't want to see how she was doing on her first day back at work.

"Hey, Davis."

The man hung up, looking anxious. "Hang on, sir. I'm trying to find Lieutenant Bonheur's bodyguard. I don't know his name."

"Dawes. Why?" Monty followed Davis's gaze into the waiting room.

"Um, the FBI just called me. They want the bodyguard to detain Admiral Jenkins until they can get here."

The FBI! Jenkins? Monty envisioned the aged veteran with the sad story that, all at once, took on a sinister aspect. Jenkins had every reason to loathe those who'd voted for an end to the Twenty-Year War. Moreover, Opal would have recognized his voice since she treated him.

Monty turned back to Davis. "Is she with him right now?"

Davis couldn't answer. He was busy making an intercom request for Mr. Dawes to return to Orthopedics STAT. Monty's concern got the better of him. Without permission, he swiveled toward the door to the consult rooms and let himself in.

"Sir, you can't be back here." Davis had just gotten off the intercom. He followed Monty, who held up a finger enjoining him to be quiet while moving quietly and listening.

"What room are they in?" he demanded. Before Davis could answer, he heard a muffled cry and headed straight toward the source of the sound.

"Sir, you can't—"

Without so much as a knock, Monty thrust his way into the room, drawing up short at the sight of Opal struggling in the admiral's death grip, while that man's beefy hand cut off her airways.

Instinct took over. Monty flew at them. Wresting Opal free, he sent the man flying against the back wall. Opal staggered into Davis's arms.

Jenkins, stunned by the force with which he'd struck the wall, slid down it, his pale eyes wide, his mouth agape.

"Were you going to kill her, too?" Fury roared through Monty's veins. He grabbed the man's shirtfront with both hands to keep from smashing in the admiral's nose. "It's not going to bring your son back!" He drew a shuddering breath. "He's dead! Just like all of my brothers are dead. Nothing is going to change that. Killing your peers doesn't change that. And this woman," he pointed at Opal, who regarded him from Davis's arms, "is an innocent therapist! You've let hate turn you into a monster, Jenkins. I won't let that happen to me." He released the man to slide the rest of the way to the floor, then whirled toward Opal, who watched him with a stricken expression from the circle of Davis's arms.

Opal's bodyguard careened through the open door. He took one look at what was happening and drew his gun.

Davis stammered out the message that Fitz wanted Dawes to detain the admiral until Fitz got there.

Relinquishing Jenkins to the competent SOG, Monty drew Opal from Davis's arms and escorted her out of the small room to her even smaller office down the hall, where he shut the door behind them.

"Opal." He held her firmly against him. Even though the pounding of her heart had subsided, he could still feel her trembling. Drawing a deep breath, he put her at arm's length and nudged her chin up so she would look at him. "You're safe now. Did he hurt you?"

She shook her head no. "I couldn't breathe. I almost passed out."

"But you're okay now." His scalp tingled at the realization that God had looked out for her yet *again*. What an incredible blessing.

"Violence begets violence."

Her words brought him back to the present. What was she thinking? "But it's over now. We know who was behind the ricin killings and why. Did Jenkins tell you about his son?"

"I know he was killed in Afghanistan."

"Right. He had good reason to be angry over his son's sacrifice. But that's no excuse for killing his peers."

"I want to go home," she said in a small voice. "But I was supposed to see you next."

"I can miss my appointment. Come on, I'll take you home myself. Dawes can follow us in your car."

"Okay. Let me get my purse."

As she stepped away to collect her purse, a knock sounded at the door. Fitz stuck his head in, spearing Opal with a look of regret as she turned back with her purse.

He stepped inside, leaving the door open. "I heard what happened. Are you okay?"

"Yes, thanks to Monty." Her words warmed Monty, especially when she slipped her hand into his. "If he hadn't barged in when he did, I would be dead right now."

Fitz frowned up at him. "How'd you know to barge in?"

Monty thought back. "God's timing, I guess. Davis had just gotten off the phone with you. He was searching for Dawes at your request. Davis told me why, then I put two and two together."

"You knew Jenkins' history?"

"Yes. We talked out in the lobby once. In hindsight, it's almost obvious that he was the culprit." Monty wanted to kick himself.

"It's not that obvious." Opal gripped his arm. "He's a sweet old man until he's backed into a corner. I never would have thought him capable of murder."

Fitz sighed with lament. "I'm sorry you had to go through that, Opal—again. If I'd worked faster, I could have spared you."

She stepped toward Fitz to lay a hand on his shoulder. "It's not your fault. But I am pretty shaken up, so Monty is going to take me home." She pulled her car keys from her purse. "Would you give these to Dawes for me and tell him to meet me at the house?"

"Of course." Fitz stepped back, allowing Monty to sweep Opal out of her office.

They were crossing the flyover when Opal added, "I have to tell you something on our way home."

"Okay." Her words made Monty's stomach tense with worry. Had she given more thought to his indirect proposal the other evening as they were finishing up the puzzle? He hoped she wasn't going to tell him that she couldn't have Thanksgiving with him. The more he'd imagined her being in his life, the more excited about his future he became. They belonged together! If he hadn't been so blind to her true beauty, he'd have realized it earlier.

Minutes later, they were taking the exit to the highway that would take them to their neighborhood. Monty couldn't wait any longer. "So, what did you need to tell me?" Glancing over, he found her sitting with her hands gripped in her lap, looking anxious.

She swallowed. "Remember when you suggested I go talk to my pastor?"

"Yes." Oh, gosh, what had that man said to her?

"He suggested that the surest way for me to heal was to do something completely selfless."

Her words summoned a vision of Christ in agony on the cross. "Like what?" He hoped it wouldn't be anything that selfless.

Opal drew in a breath and then said quickly, "For the holidays, I'm swapping places with a PT who hasn't seen her family in a year. The Navy allows officers with the same training and pay grade to do that."

"For the holidays? You mean for Thanksgiving."

"Thanksgiving and Christmas."

Her decision both astounded and disappointed him. "Where is she stationed, exactly?"

"Bahrain."

"Bahrain?" He failed to hide his dismay. "What the heck, Opal?" Even to his own ears, his protest sounded like a whine.

"The woman I'm replacing hasn't seen her family in a year. She has two young children."

The extra information made him feel petty. "Oh." Then he considered how SEALs left their wives all the time for extended periods, and the women were expected to be stoic about it.

"Listen." Opal put a hand on his forearm, gripping him through the canvas material of his sleeve. "I need to do this, Monty. Violence begets violence." She repeated the same ominous words she'd spoken in her office. "But if I do something completely selfless, then I break the cycle. And I really believe if I do this, I'll get back the part of me I've lost." Her exquisite blue eyes pleaded for his understanding.

The look utterly melted him. "I understand." Catching hold of her hand, he brought it to his lips and kissed her knuckles. "Just so you know, Opal," he declared, meaning every word, "I'll be right here when you get back. How long will you be gone?"

"Until the day after New Year's."

"More than a *month?*" He could already feel the void that was coming.

"Yes, but imagine Lieutenant Moreno's joy at getting to spend time with her kids."

He had to admit, picturing their reunion took the edge off his desolation. "You know who you're swapping jobs with?"

"Yes. She's a physical therapist like me, based out of Norfolk Naval Station."

"Have you told Ruby yet?"

Opal nodded. "I told her last week. She and Tony are going to visit his family over Thanksgiving. Then, for Christmas, they're going to drive down to Florida to visit our grandmothers."

Monty kept quiet. He felt like he'd drawn the short stick in this new arrangement, and that was a first for him. Maybe he should just let go and trust that God knew what was best for Opal. So long as she was whole again after her selfless service, he was willing to let her go.

"If you think this is what you need, Opal, then I support your decision."

"Thank you, Monty." Her voice was scarcely more than a whisper and imbued with both regret and resolve.

"We'll use WhatsApp, and we'll text each other every day."

She cast him a grateful smile. "I would like that."

Monty kissed her knuckles a second time. A feeling of impending loss swept through him. He thrust it aside with the reminder that a month was nothing, really, so long as he and Opal got to spend the rest of their lives together.

CHAPTER 19

Opal eyed the line at the security checkpoint in Norfolk International Airport and groaned. "I can't believe the Navy put me on a civilian flight."

Monty made a sympathetic sound. "Well, at least your flight's on time."

"True." She'd secretly hoped it wouldn't be if only to enjoy a few more minutes with Monty, whom she was loathed to leave. One month seemed like such a long time to be gone until she recalled that the woman whose job she was filling would only have one month off to spend with her children, whom she hadn't seen in a year. This wasn't just the right thing to do; she was confident it would fix something inside of her that felt broken.

Monty sighed as he checked his watch. "Well, I guess you'd better get in that line."

"I guess I should." Facing him, Opal wondered if he would tell her that he loved her. While he'd hinted at them marrying one day, he'd never said the words. Then again, had she? No, she hadn't, not to his face, anyway, but surely he knew, given the way she'd reacted on the night of his party. "I'm going to miss you, Monty."

259

His golden-brown eyes reminded her of a sad puppy's. "I'll miss you, too, more than you know." To her delight, he bent down and kissed her soundly, right there in front of everyone.

Swayed by his kiss, Opal clung to his broad shoulders, unwilling to let go. Regret that she had to walk away seared her. She forced herself to step back. "I love you." The confession was spoken before she could call it back.

"I love you, too."

The calm and certain way he said those words flooded Opal with euphoria. She felt herself grinning as she turned away. She hadn't gone five feet when he caught up to her, seized her arm, and pulled her back into his embrace.

"One more time." His lips, warm and fervent, stole a second kiss.

As giddy as a teenager in love, Opal nearly forgot she was leaving until he set her regretfully away from him and gave her a push in the right direction. "Go, before I abduct you myself."

His words were a joke, of course, but they reminded Opal why exactly she was walking away from the man she loved. Monty deserved a woman who was whole and happy, and she'd been neither of those since Ritter grabbed her in the parking garage.

"Don't forget to message me on WhatsApp," he called after her.

As Tony parallel parked before a line of clapboard row houses on the south side of Philadelphia, Ruby wiped her moist palms on her pant legs. Nothing looked familiar. The buildings crowded each other. Trash fluttered in the gutters, thanks to a cold, wet wind. "Which house is it?" she inquired.

Tony pointed to a butter-yellow home with flaking paint and a sagging front porch. "That one there."

Ruby swallowed hard. She and Tony came from different worlds.

He cut his engine, catching her look of uncertainty. Leaning toward her, he touched his forehead to hers. "Don't be nervous. I'm right here."

"Okay." She would brave the unknown for his sake.

They'd barely stepped out of his Honda when the front door of his home flew open. A teenage girl who was all hair and coltish legs ran off the porch. Squealing with delight, the girl threw herself into Tony's arms. Ruby recognized Corinna from the photos on Tony's cell phone.

Crushing his sister into a bear hug, Tony then set her on her feet and turned her toward Ruby. "Corinna, this is my girlfriend, Ruby. She's gonna marry me one day."

Cherry-brown eyes took critical stock of Ruby. "Hi."

"Hello." Ruby forced a smile. She could have hoped for a warmer look. "I brought you something," she added. "It's in my suitcase."

"Okay." Corinna sounded like she couldn't care less.

"Let's go inside," Tony suggested. "I'll get our luggage later."

At this rate, why bother even bringing it in? She caught the negative thought before it manifested. *All things are possible through Christ.* She pinned a brave smile on her face, accepted Tony's hand, and trailed his sister onto the listing porch to the door.

The aroma of basil and garlic hit them along with a wall of warm air as they stepped into a dark, narrow hall.

"Mama's in the kitchen, of course." Corinna led the way.

Positioned at the back of the home, the kitchen touted fresh wallpaper and several curtained windows. It overlooked a tiny yard that, given the makeshift greenhouses, was used to grow vegetables and herbs. A plump woman with the same cloud of hair as her daughter turned from the stove while wiping her hands on her apron. She didn't so much as glance at Ruby, who watched as Tony's mother lit up to see him.

He rushed into her outspread arms, embracing her with love that would have been evident to a blind man. Ruby thought of her own mother, and a wave of longing brought tears to her eyes.

After ten seconds of clasping his mother close, Tony released her and stepped back. He held out a hand to Ruby, who shuffled forward, suddenly terrified. *All things are possible.*

"Ma, this is the woman I told you about. Ruby, this is Mama."

The shy but welcoming smile his mother sent her was all the reassurance Ruby needed. "Call me Anna." The woman offered her hand.

"So nice to meet you, Anna." The woman's hand was soft and warm. Ruby felt moved to hold onto it. "Tony talks about you all the time. Both of you." Ruby turned her head to catch Corinna's eyes. She finally let Anna go.

"You must be hungry after your long trip." Anna gestured to the collection of pots steaming on the stove. "I made food."

"We can eat in a little while." Tony backed toward the hallway. "I'm gonna fetch our bags. Corinna, why don't you show Ruby where she's going to sleep?"

Uncomfortable with Tony gone, Ruby waited for Corinna to respond. The girl looked at her mother. "Does she have to sleep in my room?" Her sullen tone filled Ruby with dismay.

"Oh." Ruby spoke up. "I'm fine on the couch. I don't want to impose."

Anna scowled at her daughter. "Nonsense, show Ruby up to your room. Corinna will sleep with me," she said to Ruby. "It's no imposition."

Great. Tony's sister hated her. *Think positive. Think positive.* Praying for Tony to join them quickly, Ruby followed a silent Corinna down the hall and up the creaking stairs to the second story.

"How old is this house?" Ruby could hear Tony outside. He wouldn't be too long.

Corinna didn't look back at her. "I don't know—like a hundred years." She turned at the top of the stairs and stomped past a couple of doors including one to a bathroom, to a small room at the front of the house. Like the kitchen, it was covered in fresh wallpaper—a soft purple and white pattern that complemented the quilt on the single bed. Large posters of Broadway musicals hung in white frames on every wall.

Ruby stopped at the door. "Wow. I love what you've done in here!"

"Thanks." Slightly more warmth colored Corinna's tone.

Ruby stopped to examine the poster nearest to her. "*Phantom of the Opera.* I love that show! Did you go to this performance?"

"Tony took me for my fifteenth birthday, just the two of us. We took the train to New York and stayed overnight."

"Wow. He's a good brother, isn't he? I have a sister who's amazing, too. Sometimes it's hard to follow in her footsteps."

Turning back to Corinna, she found the girl studying her less critically. "Yeah. Anyway, you can sleep here." She gestured to her bed.

Ruby grimaced. "Thank you. I'm sorry you have to give up your bed."

"Eh." Corinna's shrug reminded Ruby of Tony's. "It's no big deal."

Hearing Tony on the stairs laboring to carry up their suitcases, Ruby went to help him and found his mother had beat her to it. She backed into Corinna's room as Tony and his mother joined them.

"Here you go." Tony set her suitcase at the foot of Corinna's bed.

Ruby went to unzip it. "I bought you both some gifts." She handed a small, wrapped box to his mother first.

Anna tsked her tongue. "You didn't have to." All the same, she tore into it with gusto. "Seeds for my garden. Oh, this is wonderful—cucumber, arugula, carrots, and watermelon. I've never tried watermelon. Thank you."

"Tony raves about your homegrown vegetables," Ruby explained. She then passed Corinna a large gift bag. "He also raves about your beautiful voice. I hope I get to hear you sing soon."

Corinna took the gift bag, lifted out a crush of tissue, and blinked at what she saw. "It's a microphone and a speaker."

"You can sync them with your phone using Bluetooth," Tony inserted. "This way you can sing at parties and start becoming famous."

The interest shining in Corinna's brown eyes encouraged Ruby.

"Thank you," the girl said, pulling the microphone and then the speaker out and examining them both. She glanced up at Ruby. "I hear you're on TV."

Ruby nodded. "I report the news. Just don't ask me to sing. I definitely don't have that gift."

Corinna tried to tear apart the packaging. "Can I try it now, Mama?"

"After we eat," Anna insisted.

Corinna rolled her eyes, and Ruby smiled. Just like that, she felt at home. *Thanks, God. I knew You could do it.*

Monty felt like Old Man Scrooge himself climbing the steps to Jonah Mills's beach house. The sound of merriment that escaped the lofty contemporary almost made him turn around. He wasn't in the mood for merriment. While Opal's "I love you" had kept him in decent spirits during his parents' visit, when he'd told them all about her, he had since sunk into the doldrums as her absence stretched on. Certainly, he understood her reason for leaving and he'd told her to take all the time she needed. He just hadn't realized how much he would miss her when she was gone.

At least they'd been able to communicate via WhatsApp. He'd learned many new details about her past while also learning about her experience overseas. She seemed happy in Bahrain, and that worried him, as well. What if she decided not to return, after all?

He'd taken advantage of her absence to make himself truly worthy of her. He was seeing a private counselor twice a week. He'd tossed out the contents of his liquor cabinet to keep from being tempted. When Opal came home, completely whole, he wanted to be whole for her, also.

His crisp knock was answered by Jonah Mills's stepdaughter, Miriam, and her golden retriever.

"Hi." The teen then praised the dog who wagged her tail but didn't jump on him—this time. When they'd invited him to dinner a few weeks back, Sabrina had been all over him. "We're training her. Glad you made it. Everyone's been taking bets on whether you would show up."

Monty had first met Miriam at his swearing-in ceremony, then again two weeks ago at the dinner. Her candidness reminded him of Ruby, whom he actually missed since she'd been scarce since Opal's departure. "Oh?" So, others had noticed his surliness. That was humbling.

"Come on in. I'll take your coat."

Jonah walked up as Monty was shaking off his coat. "Sir, you made it." He sounded both surprised and relieved.

"Of course." Monty handed him the gift he'd brought, the last full bottle from his stash.

Jonah admired the label. "Jamaican Rum. Thanks. We can spike our eggnog now."

Monty trailed him into the open-concept living area he had admired upon his first visit. The spacious, brightly lit space was filled with the scent of the live Christmas tree twinkling by the vintage, cone-shaped fireplace. A gathering of familiar faces stood around the breakfast bar in the kitchen. Monty mustered a smile as everyone looked over at him. "Hello."

"Monty!" Jonah's wife, Eden, came forward to embrace him. "So good to see you."

Her protruding belly was impossible not to notice. "Two weeks left?" He'd been keeping track—not difficult to do since Jonah had asked for time off, right after Monty himself planned to take a few days of leave.

"That's right." Eden patted her belly. "And not a day longer," she said to her stomach.

Monty pictured Opal carrying his child, and his heart clutched with longing. "Any idea of the gender?" he asked the proud parents.

"Miriam wants a brother, but we'll take what we get," his XO replied. "Can I fix you a drink, sir?"

"A Diet Coke would be great." Monty ignored the speculative

glances his answer provoked. Looking around, he greeted Charlotte Strong, whose auburn hair made her look amazing in a green velvet Christmas dress. "Good to see you again, Charlotte. Lucas and his squad are on their way back from their assignment."

"I know. I can't wait. All I want for Christmas is my husband to come home."

Monty knew the feeling. "How's the job going?" He'd learned recently that she worked with Fitz, who'd persuaded her last year to turn down the CIA and apply to the FBI instead. Lucas had likely contributed to her decision.

"It's great, but I'm looking forward to taking some days off this week. Lucas and I have all of our Christmas shopping yet to do."

His gaze went to the unfamiliar couple standing nearby.

"Oh, I'm sorry." Charlotte turned to introduce them. "You haven't met Santiago Rivera and his wife Nina yet, have you?"

"Ah." Monty encountered the dark eyes of the legendary former master chief and smiled. The woman next to him was a slender brunette holding an infant. Monty acknowledged her first. "And who's this?" The baby, he thought, looked just like a doll.

"This is Esme." She nodded with pride toward Senior Chief McLeod, who was down on his hands and knees in the living room. "And that's her twin brother over there, Rodrigo."

"Twins," Monty marveled. A vision of Opal holding their own baby filled him with yearning. "You're doubly blessed," he said to the handsome couple. *Just eight more days until Opal comes home.* He jutted out a hand to Rivera. "It's good to meet you, Master Chief." The man was retired, but the title still seemed to fit him. "From the stories I've heard of you, I wasn't sure if you were real. The men revere you."

Rivera's dark eyes shone with pleasure at the compliment. "I could say the same for you, sir." The sympathy in his tone told Monty he had heard of his part in the Mother Eagle disaster.

Charlotte peered around. "Do you know everyone else here?"

Monty swept the faces of those around him, all senior members of his Team, minus Lucas Strong, who headed up the squad coming back from Thailand. "Yes, thank you." The sound of a baby squealing with laughter drew his gaze back to Amos, who was blowing raspberries on the baby's belly. The sight transfixed him. Who'd have guessed the surly senior chief had a soft spot for babies?

"Sir, I have a favor to ask." Jonah captured his attention as he brought Monty his drink. "Have a cookie first." He held a tray of colorful cookies in his other hand.

Monty helped himself to a frosted Christmas tree. "Is this bribery?"

"Sort of. Let's talk over here."

Bemused, Monty followed Jonah to the far corner of the room where no one could hear them. Biting into the cookie, he found himself thinking Opal's pumpkin bread was better.

"I'm sure you recognize the name Saul Wade," Jonah began.

"Of course, he's our top sniper, the best in the world." Although, disappointingly, Wade had failed in his objective to kill the drug lord, Emilio Díaz, the previous summer. "He just took out the leader of the Golden Triangle," Monty added under his breath.

"Yes, sir. Lucas sent word to me right after that happened. He also told me Saul has hit a wall. He says he can't do his job anymore. Killing Somchai was the last straw for him."

"Hmm." The news was not expected. "Any idea why?"

Jonah's catlike light-green eyes were pinned on Monty's face, "Actually, yes, I do. According to Lucas, Saul's heart isn't in his work anymore. He's got a ranch in Oklahoma and the woman he loves lives there with her son. The boy's father was Blake LeMere, a former team-mate who died in a parachuting accident."

Monty had heard about that tragedy, ultimately linked to Dwyer's corruption. "What do you want me to do?" Plainly, Jonah was asking him for something, and Saul Wade wasn't of much use to him if his heart wasn't in his work.

Jonah didn't break eye contact. "There's a base about an hour from his ranch, Camp Gruber. I found the perfect job for him there, training National Guardsmen how to shoot."

Monty considered the idea of a highly decorated sniper turning into an instructor. "If I sent him to Gruber, who would take his slot?" No sooner was the question out of his mouth than a vision of Ben Harmony, the chief he'd replaced in Afghanistan, came to mind. "Actually, let me think about it. I'll get back to you tomorrow."

"Yes, sir. I appreciate it."

As they rejoined the party, Monty found himself pondering Jonah's request. Why not do something nice for the sniper who had distinguished himself with twenty kills? Opal would approve of any effort to return Saul to his home and to the woman who'd suffered the loss of one husband already.

Looking around at the lively group, Monty found himself thinking she would fit in perfectly. With her gracious, caring spirit, it would be an honor to call her his wife. His heart clutched with the love that had grown steadily in him, nearly from the day they'd met.

A sudden thought entered his head. He could end up thoroughly humiliated not to mention devastated if it didn't work. But from their correspondence, he knew Opal considered herself fully recovered from the chain of events that had driven her to leave in search of healing. What's more, she'd said she loved him. And if he did this favor for Jonah, then Jonah owed him one. Before he left the party that night, he would pull aside his XO and make the necessary arrangements.

Stiff-limbed from her trans-Atlantic flight, Opal shuffled behind the military personnel thronging toward the exit of the C-141 Starlifter. Most of them were returning from months-long deployments. She could sense their anticipation as they waited their turn to disembark. Over the hum of the jet's dying engines, Opal discerned the cheers of family and friends welcoming their servicemen and women home on this second day of January.

The sound filled her with anticipation but also with worry. It felt like she'd been gone for ages. In that time, she and Monty had messaged each other quite a bit, but not once had he written that he loved her. What if she'd just imagined him at the airport saying those words? Had she let the opportunity for a future with James Monteague slip away? What if he had only thought he loved her but had since found some other beauty to chase? After all, that had been his modus operandi before the disaster.

As she stepped from the plane, blinking against a bright winter sun, she caught herself looking for him as she descended three steps to the tarmac. Of course, he wasn't here. She'd told him on WhatsApp that she would be home today, but she hadn't told him when or where. Monty was a busy man, after all, commanding an entire SEAL Team. Opal was relying on Ruby to pick her up.

A sizeable crowd had gathered at the military airfield. They stood behind a metal barricade, waving banners and crying out names. With her heart in her throat, Opal watched as young husbands rushed ahead of her toward tearful women. Mothers waved down sons and daughters. Young fathers snatched up their children and whirled them in the air. At the back of the crowd, the words MARRY ME had been painted across a sheet that billowed in the breeze.

Praise God, it was good to be home! Moreover, Opal's service to humanity had done exactly as she'd hoped. The darkness that had lingered in her after her ordeal was gone, replaced by the peace that came from committing a completely selfless act. The cloudless sky seemed to represent a brand-new start to life, and to a new year.

Her uniform trench coat whipped at her calves as she pulled her suitcase through the crowd, heading for the terminal. Ruby's last text had stated she would be waiting out in front of the building to pick her up.

A hand came out of nowhere, stopping Opal in her tracks. "Can I help you with your bag, ma'am?"

Pivoting, Opal gasped to find Monty dressed in digital print camouflage, which had rendered him invisible in a crowd full of military personnel.

"Monty! What are you doing here?"

"Picking you up, of course." He grinned at her as if waiting for something.

"But how did you know this was my flight?"

"Ruby told me." His expression became admonishing. "You could have asked, you know."

"But you're so busy."

"You come first, Opal."

She didn't waste another second talking. With a muffled sob, she threw herself into his arms, laughing when he banded them around her and lifted her off her feet.

His low rasp tickled her ear. "I've missed you so much."

"I've missed you, too." Joy made her eyes water. He lowered her gently to her feet, then put her at arm's distance. Again, he seemed to be waiting for her to say something. "You haven't seen my sign yet, have you?"

"Sign?" She turned her head scanning the many signs right in front of her: WELCOME HOME, HENRY. DADDY IS MY HERO. WE LOVE OUR E-3. Behind them was the sheet, which she could now see was strung between two poles being held aloft by two stone-faced men with military caps pulled way down over their eyes. As the sheet stopped billowing, the last word became readable. MARRY ME, OPAL?

Astonishment welled in her as she looked to Monty for corroboration. "Me?"

"I don't know any other Opal." His forehead had furrowed, like he was afraid she would turn him down. "You said you loved me when you left. I hope you haven't changed your mind."

His uncertainty endeared him to her even more. "Oh, Monty." She clapped a hand to her jumping heart. Not even in her wildest dreams had she envisioned a reunion like this! All at once, she realized Ruby was standing at the edge of the crowd watching them with a big smile on her face. The man behind her was holding an enormous camera on his shoulder. Wait, was he filming Monty and her?

Looking back at Monty, she found him sinking to one knee with a velvet box in one hand. Opal gulped as people in the crowd hushed others and pointed in their direction. The top of Opal's head tingled. *I have to be dreaming.* But Monty's words, solemnly spoken, assured her she wasn't.

"I love you, precious Opal." He pitched his voice lower, keeping the rest of his message personal. "You took a broken man and showed me the way to wholeness. You brought me back to the faith I'd forgotten." As he spoke, he opened the box, withdrew the solitaire glittering inside of it, and slipped the box back into his pocket.

Opal shifted her focus from the glittering solitaire to Monty's damp gaze. Tears of unbridled joy rushed into her eyes and clogged her throat, keeping her from speaking.

"I don't know when I fell in love with you," he continued on a low, fervent note. "I'm just sorry it took me so long to realize how much I need you in my life. The weeks that you were gone felt endless. And I don't want to lose another day. I need you in my life, now and forever, Opal. Please say you'll marry me."

Opal sensed the crowd leaning in to hear her answer. Recovering her poise, she basked in the beauty of the moment as she wiped a tear from her cheek. "Of course," she finally replied. "You've had me all along, Monty."

"What'd she say?" asked an older woman in the crowd.

People in the crowd broke into applause at Opal's response. Others chorused, "Aww," as Monty stood and slid the ring onto Opal's left hand. Drawn into his embrace, Opal felt the promise he communicated in a warm and thorough kiss. He would love her for the rest of his life.

From a distance, Opal heard Ruby say, "And that, ladies and gentlemen, is what we call a memorable welcome home."

Peeking over at her sister, Opal realized Ruby had positioned herself between them and her cameraman.

"This is Ruby Bonheur reporting to you from Oceana Naval Air Station. WAVY TV News at Noon wishes you and yours a very happy New Year!"

Looking back at Monty, Opal realized her prayers for a husband had been answered after all. God's faithfulness astonished her. She lifted her hands to his broad shoulders, stood on tiptoe, and whispered, "Happy New Year, darling."

Something told her it would be the best yet, for both of them.

BRAVING THE VALLEY

ACTS OF VALOR, BOOK 5

VENEZUELA, PRESENT DAY

The classroom door burst open, startling Grace Griffiths as she stood at the chalkboard instructing ten local first graders how to read words with double vowels in them. Manuel, the four-year-old she was working to adopt, sat at his own desk drawing.

In the doorway, sounding out of breath, stood Peter Anderson, the Irish missionary, her host both last summer and this one. His towering stature, blue eyes, and beaked nose reminded her of Liam Neeson. He even had the same charming accent. "Sorry to interrupt, but I need to talk to you."

Grace glanced toward her waiting pupils. "Right now?"

"It's urgent."

"Okay. Maite?" She summoned the youngest but brightest student to the front of the room, handed her the chalk, and told her to play teacher for a few minutes.

"*Sí,* señora." As Maite bellied up to the chalkboard, Grace joined Peter in the hallway.

"What's up?"

Peter fixed his troubled gaze on her upturned face. "I've got unpleasant news. You know how both the Venezuelan Army and Navy have bases here in Puerto Ayacucho. Well, I've just received word from a friend in the British Embassy that they have orders to arrest any and all Americans. This is happening all over Venezuela, not just here."

The words chilled Grace, though it wasn't unexpected. Ever since a handful of English-speaking mercenaries—aka CIA agents—had tried to assassinate President Maduro, then escaped from prison with the help of American Special Operators, the Venezuelan dictator had been bent on revenge, putting every American in his country behind bars. "All Americans? Even someone doing mission work."

"Yes, all." Peter's tone was nothing short of grim.

Grace thought back to the local airport, where she'd supplied Customs with the address where she would be staying. "They know where to find me." She flashed a hand to the wall in the hall as the floor seemed to tilt.

"Yes, but don't worry. I'm going to the port now to find a fisherman who'll take us across the river to Colombia."

"Us?"

"You, Amanda, and I," he said, including his wife. "I doubt the soldiers will be any friendlier to Irish nationals harboring an American."

"I won't leave Manuel," she warned him. "He's coming, too."

Peter's countenance softened at the panic in her voice. "Of course. I'm going now to prepare for our exodus. Be ready to leave at any moment."

"But...who'll care for the orphans with us gone?"

"Padre Tomás will watch over them. He did it once before when we made a trip back to Ireland."

Grace nodded, stunned and worried. Could she legally take Manuel from his native country when the paperwork wasn't yet complete? "I'm so sorry, Peter, for causing you all this trouble."

The words fell woefully short. Not only had the Andersons given her room and board two summers in a row, but now they were risking their very lives for her.

"It's not your fault, Grace. Best advise your sister, but no more phone calls. There's only one wireless provider in this country. It's easy enough to discover who's placing calls to the United States. Send her a WhatsApp message. That should be secure."

She nodded, relieved. "Okay."

Her thin voice must have betrayed her fear, for he stopped and caught her eye. "It'll be all right, Grace. God will protect us."

She nodded, wanting very much for that to be true. But where was God when her marriage was falling apart and when her pregnancy ended in a miscarriage? She would certainly never have ended up in Venezuela, in danger of imprisonment.

After gulping down her uncertainty, Grace went back to the classroom where Maite had added four more words on the board, similar to the first.

"Very good, darling," Grace said to her in Spanish, though Wayuu, an indigenous language, was her first tongue, Spanish her second. "You're a natural-born teacher."

Taking back the chalk from the shyly smiling Maite, Grace glanced protectively toward Manuel, who had stopped coloring when she left the room. His dark, worried gaze tugged at her heartstrings.

Don't fret, my darling. I won't go anywhere without you.

SUFFOLK, VIRGINIA, UNITED STATES

Through the windshield of his silver Lexus, FBI Special Agent Casey Fitzpatrick studied the freshly painted sign erected at the head of a gravel driveway as he slowed to turn down it. There was nothing in this part of Suffolk, Virginia, but fields of cotton and forests of deciduous trees. The sign read, BACK-IN-THE-SADDLE HIPPOTHERAPY RANCH.

Horse therapy, Fitz realized, not *for* horses, but referring to the benefits of riding them. He'd read an article about it, once. People with all kinds of challenges—physical mental, even emotional—benefited from having to balance and to adjust to the horse's movements. Interesting.

With a stab of his finger, Casey curtailed the haunting aria from the opera *Carmen* and continued down the graveled driveway. He was here to interview Faith Saunders, a woman who had called him at the FBI field office no less than six times between yesterday and this morning asking for his help in finding her sister. Her increasingly desperate messages had told him where to find her. She stated that she was just too busy to drive to the Norfolk Field Office, and could he please come out and see her?

Clearly, she knew who Casey was, since she'd called him by his nickname, Fitz. Since her voice *did* sound familiar and since her sister's situation sounded dire, Casey's curiosity got the better of him. He'd slipped into his car over the lunch hour and driven thirty minutes to the address Faith Saunders had supplied. All the while, he racked his brain trying to remember who she was. She wasn't in his lengthy list of contacts. He didn't know of anyone who offered hippotherapy.

He figured he would remember as soon as he saw her. The trees on either side of the driveway gave way to open land. Straight ahead of him stood a butter-yellow farmhouse in need of a fresh coat of paint. A newer barn stood off to his right with a fenced-in riding ring behind it. Casey parked before the farmhouse, cut the engine, and reached for his iPad.

As he rose from his car, he was struck by the peaceful quiet of Suffolk. Over the ruffling of leaves and the birdsong came the nicker of a horse. He started for the farmhouse, his glossy dress shoes crunching gravel. Bushes, shrubs, and weeds overran the walkway. The planks of the porch groaned beneath his weight, though he was not a large man at 190 pounds. Curtains covering the glass insert kept him from seeing inside as he raised a hand and knocked. The door immediately popped open.

"Yeah?" A boy perhaps thirteen years old confronted him. His brown hair was in need of a trim. His scowl and hard gray eyes were meant to chase Casey off.

"Hello." He tried to soften the rasp of his injured vocal cords. All the same, the boy's gaze dropped immediately to Casey's throat, where his scar was visible above his crisp white collar. "I'm Special Agent Fitzpatrick with the FBI. Is Faith Saunders home?"

The hostility in the boy's expression evaporated. "She's in the barn." He eyed Fitz more closely, as if looking for his sidearm.

A blonde head poked out from under the boy's arm. "You want to come in first? We made cupcakes."

Casey couldn't help but smile back at the friendly, freckle-faced girl of about seven.

Her brother tugged her back from the door. "We don't let strangers into the house."

"He's not a stranger. Mommy knows him."

The words lit a fire under Casey's feet. He'd better remember who Faith Saunders was, and soon. He backed away. "I shouldn't keep your mother waiting."

As Casey hastened toward the barn, the siblings' bickering grew indistinct, at least until the girl shouted, "You can't tell me what to do!"

The words strummed poignant memories. How long had it been since he'd heard his own children squabble? They'd been dead eight years now, long enough that his bottomless grief had turned into an ache that never went away.

He focused his attention on the barn as he approached it. In contrast to the house, it appeared brand new, touting a ruddy red stain and a fence so recently erected that the tempered wood still looked green. Fitz slipped through the slightly opened double doors, then slowed his step to let his eyes adjust to the shadows.

Dust motes floated in the rays of sunlight slipping through the sturdy boards of the walls. He started forward, breathing in the faint odor of horse manure mingled with the scent of fresh lumber, straw, and feed. Passing one empty stall after another, he was starting to think there weren't any horses here until he heard a nicker. Then a large head poked out over the last stall's divider as a bay eyed his approach.

A woman's voice came from the same place. "What's the matter, Otis?"

Fitz went around the bay's head and encountered the wide eyes of the woman grooming the animal. She gasped, stilling her brushing. "Fitz!"

"Hello." He knew her chestnut ponytail and heart-shaped face at once, but the reason eluded him until she yanked off her gloves, prompting a memory of her doing something similar in a hospital.

"Fitz, thank God." She tossed aside the gloves and went to let herself out of the stall.

How could he have forgotten her? Faith had been the first one to greet him when he'd been swept into the ER with a laceration to the neck. She'd kept him calm, assured him he'd be fine, even as he choked on the blood pouring down his throat. Then later, after surgery, when he'd been moved upstairs to a hospital room, she'd dropped by to cheer him up.

As she eased out of the stall, it was impossible not to notice she was pregnant. Apart from that, she looked exactly as he remembered with a wide smile, brown eyes, and a dusting of freckles across her piquant nose.

"Oh, my." She embraced him briefly, her baby bump brushing his belt buckle.

The smells of leather and hay and bodywash teased his nostrils.

"I wasn't sure you would actually show up."

"Of course. How could I not?" No way would he admit he'd forgotten who she was.

"I know. I didn't give you much choice, did I?" She gave his person a quick inspection, which ended at his neck. "Your voice is almost normal."

"Hah. You're too kind." He knew he sounded like a gargoyle when he spoke. "So, this is where you live?" He gestured to encompass the country estate. "Did you change careers or something?"

"Yes, actually. I gave up nursing to do hippotherapy." Her smile grew strained. "But that's not why I called you. Let's go back into my office and talk."

She led him through a nearby door into a large room, bright with windows. It was filled with sofas and mismatched chairs, all positioned to look out of the windows at the horse ring.

"Have a seat." She crossed to the nearest sofa and sank down on it, gesturing to the armchair across from her.

"You're expecting." He stated the obvious as he eased into a worn armchair.

She propped her feet on a scarred coffee table, relieved to be off them. "Yes, eight weeks to go."

Casey heard only exhaustion in her answer "Congratulations. And your husband? Is he still with the state police?"

She shook her head. "No, no he's not. But that's not why I need to talk to you."

Clearly the matter was urgent. Casey set his iPad on one knee and roused it. "You said in your message that your sister has disappeared while doing mission work in Venezuela."

"Yes."

"What on earth made her go there?" A level-four travel advisory warned Americans not to set foot in that tumultuous country. Ruled by a tyrannous dictator, Venezuela's economy had crumbled, resulting in rampant crime, civil unrest, poor health infrastructure, hunger, and kidnapping.

"Well, last summer, Grace went on a church-sponsored mission trip to an orphanage in Puerto Ayacucho. She's is a first-grade teacher, and she also speaks fluent Spanish, so it sounded like something right up her alley, but the truth was she went to get over her divorce." Faith shrugged. "Anyway, last summer she came across a little orphan boy and fell in love with him. She started the adoption process right away, but, of course, it takes so much time, as U.S. authorities also have to agree. She had to leave him there last summer and it nearly broke her heart. This summer, she intended to bring him back with her." Faith paused to catch her breath. "But ever since the assassination attempt on Maduro by those American mercenaries," she used air quotes around the last word, "every U.S. citizen in Venezuela is being rounded up and arrested."

"Right." Casey had read about that in a report two weeks ago.

Faith rubbed her stomach as she spoke. "Grace stopped calling me because there's only one cellular provider in Venezuela, and she didn't want to advertise her location. Her last message to me was on WhatsApp three days ago. She said Maduro's soldiers were looking for her. Her British host had found them a boat so they could cross the Orinoco River into Colombia, but the weather wasn't cooperating. That's the last news I've heard from her." Faith's anxious gaze held his.

"You don't think she's safely in Colombia but has no internet connection?"

"No. I don't know if you give credence to this kind of thing, but Grace and I are mirror twins. We've always known when something is wrong with the other. I started to feel like something was wrong yesterday."

"I see."

"You probably think I'm panicking for nothing."

"Not at all. I'm a big believer in intuition. It has saved my saved his life more than once. He opened the app in which he took his notes. "Spell the name of the town she's in."

"I can do better than that." Grace rolled onto one hip and pulled an index card out of the rear pocket of her shorts. "Here's her exact address in Puerto Ayacucho. She's been staying with an Irish missionary and his wife who live there year-round."

Casey copied the address into his software program. "Care of Peter and Amanda Anderson," he read as he entered their names in his form. "What's your sister's full name?"

"Grace Elizabeth Griffiths. She reverted to using her maiden name."

"Do you know her social?"

"Yes." Faith relayed it to him, then heaved an audible sigh as he finished entering it into his form. "I'd be so grateful if you could find her and bring her home."

Looking up from his iPad, Casey caught a careworn expression on Faith's pretty face as well as a sheen of tears in her bottomless eyes. For the first time, he noticed the dark circles under them and the stress firming her lush lips. His nurturing instincts prompted him to ask, "When was the last time you slept?"

She managed a wan smile for him. "I look that bad, huh?"

"You look beautiful but exhausted."

"Hmph." Her eyes twinkled briefly with the liveliness he remembered her for.

"Hey." He surprised himself by moving out of the armchair to sit beside her.

She regarded his offered hand for a split second, then lay her slim, warm hand over his. Awareness swirled in him, catching him off guard. "Try not to worry. That's my job now, okay?" He used the very words she had spoken to him when he'd been wheeled into the ER drowning in his own blood.

"Okay."

She'd completely forgotten what she'd said to him then. Her thoughts were too preoccupied with her sister's welfare. Letting go of her hand, he saved his document on his iPad, then closed it. "Let me get to work on this. I'll notify you the instant I discover anything."

"That would be great." She dropped her feet to the floor and they both stood. "Can I feed you lunch in return for your kindness?"

He wouldn't have minded sticking around, but her husband might not appreciate her entertaining a special agent while he was away at work. A healthy competitiveness existed between the state and federal lawmen. "I appreciate the offer, but I have an urgent mission." He started for the door. "I'll see myself out."

She followed him. "I'm going that way, too. I have to feed my kids lunch."

"I just met them." He pushed the door open for her.

"Oh? I hope they weren't rude."

They crossed through the quiet barn, watched by the giant bay as he munched on hay.

"Not at all." Fitz wasn't going to rat out her son, who was just being protective of his home and his sister. "How old are they?"

"Grayson is twelve and Olivia is seven."

"Ah." His heart gave a pang as he pictured Rory and Rosy, his older two. Thirteen and four at the time they went to heaven, they'd been farther apart in age than Faith's two. But she would soon welcome a third child. Fitz pictured his youngest's gummy grin with a stab of pain.

As they stepped into the blinding sunshine, he shaded his eyes to take in her home. Viewed from the side, it looked immense. "Have you always lived here?"

"Oh, no, but I grew up here. I just bought the place from my parents, who wanted something more manageable."

From what he could tell, her parents hadn't been able to manage the property for some time. Then it registered. She'd said I, not we.

Casey's heart skipped a beat. Had she divorced her state-police husband? Not wanting to get into that now, and, sensing Grayson's eyes watching them from within the house, Casey slowed and touched Faith's arm. "I'll be in contact."

Her brown eyes softened. "I can't thank you enough, Fitz. Please call me soon. You have my number?"

"Oh yes."

A divorce would explain the weariness that hung over her like a shroud. Casey was tempted to hug her, but that might put thoughts in her head. He had no romantic notions whatsoever, not for a mother of nearly three.

"Bye." He sent her a nod, instead, then crunched across the gravel to his car.

～

Watching Fitz slip into his silver Lexus, Faith caught herself thinking he moved just like an Irish boxer—with the name to match. She had only once seen him dressed in something other than a hospital gown: a salmon-pink button-up covered in blood. Still, remembering the pink shirt, it didn't surprise her that Casey should wear a light-green blazer over white slacks and a pink-and-green-striped tie. The colors suited his auburn hair and freckled complexion perfectly.

As he smiled at her through his driver's window, a weight seemed to lift from her heavy heart, easing the anxiety that held it in a vise. How pleasant to see him again, in person, a human being she had bonded with immediately, only to lose touch, as with most of her patients.

But as Fitz backed up, then pulled away, her anxiety returned.

In her rush to give him all her sister's information, she hadn't had the chance to tell him she was widowed. Every morning she awoke to the panicky realization that her family's welfare rested on her narrow shoulders. Her baby, Jerry's surprise legacy, would be born in eight short weeks, and she had so much left to do before she could give a baby the attention he or she deserved. Compounding all of that was this feeling that Grace's very life was in danger.

Wiping perspiration from her brow, Faith turned and plodded to the house to feed her hungry children. She must've been crazy to think she could tackle her and Jerry's dream alone. But now that she'd started, she had no choice but to see it through.

Available in Paperback and eBook from Your Favorite Bookstore or Online Retailer

ABOUT THE AUTHOR

Rebecca Hartt is the *nom de plume* for an award-winning, best-selling author who, in a different era of her life, wrote strictly romantic suspense. Now Rebecca chooses to showcase the role that faith plays in the lives of Navy SEALs, penning military romantic suspense that is both realistic and heartwarming.

As a child, Rebecca lived all over the world. She has been a military dependent for most of her life, first as a daughter, then as a wife, and knows first-hand the dedication and sacrifice required by those who serve. Living near the military community of Virginia Beach, Rebecca is constantly reminded of the peril and uncertainty faced by US Navy SEALs, many of whom testify to a personal and profound connection with their Creator. Their loved ones, too, rely on God for strength and comfort. These men of courage and women of faith are the subjects of Rebecca Hartt's enthusiastically received *Acts of Valor* series.

RebeccaHartt.com

Sign up for the Rebecca Hartt Newsletter Here

https://rebeccahartt.com/contact

www.ingramcontent.com/pod-product-compliance
Lightning Source LLC
Chambersburg PA
CBHW070443030726
47503CB00004B/879